COMPANY OF THIEVES

BOOK YOUR PLACE ON OUR WEBSITE AND MAKE THE READING CONNECTION!

We've created a customized website just for our very special readers, where you can get the inside scoop on everything that's going on with Zebra, Pinnacle and Kensington books.

When you come online, you'll have the exciting opportunity to:

- View covers of upcoming books
- Read sample chapters
- Learn about our future publishing schedule (listed by publication month *and author*)
- Find out when your favorite authors will be visiting a city near you
- Search for and order backlist books from our online catalog
- Check out author bios and background information
- Send e-mail to your favorite authors
- Meet the Kensington staff online
- Join us in weekly chats with authors, readers and other guests
- Get writing guidelines
- AND MUCH MORE!

Visit our website at
http://www.kensingtonbooks.com

COMPANY OF THIEVES

Gil Roscoe

KENSINGTON BOOKS
KENSINGTON PUBLISHING CORP.

http://www.kensingtonbooks.com

Chapter One

I have heard people say that we waste a third of our lives sleeping. I say, if you want to begin to treasure that supposedly wasted time, just stop doing it for a while. I swear that, for the rest of my life, I will look upon a good night's sleep as a gift from human history.

There is a line from Shakespeare, I forget which play, where a sleepless character bemoans his lack of rest. He describes sleep as "knitting up the raveled sleeve of care." What a wonderful description. Believe me, I am not a great reader of literature. But I had heard that line somewhere and it would run through my head all night as I stood at my machine. I would come home after work and lie on my bed. My body would be dying for sleep, but my brain kept telling me it was time to get up. One day it occurred to me that I was fighting evolution and that such a course was bound to have consequences.

I took to drinking wine. Dark red wine at nine o'clock in the morning while I read the editorial pages of the *Los Angeles Times*. Slowly I would drift away and usually wake up about two in the afternoon, looking as if I had wrestled with the newspaper. Sometimes I would sleep again for a couple of hours, but on many days I lived on five.

I was trying to reform myself. Get my life in order. I had fallen in love with slipping into neutral. Fallen in love with that blessed state of not caring about other people. It made everything so much easier. I had earned a living based on trickery and deceit for a long time and, like my present lack of sleep, it had yielded unpleasant consequences. Unfortunately, the time I chose to reform myself was also a time of recession. I had to take what I could get, and what I got was the good old graveyard shift. I had left Omaha in a hurry and didn't know anyone here. However, I was determined to build up some cash so I could go to college. I had finally found something honest that I was interested in and was going to do my best to pursue it. I guess I was really just another person looking to be reborn in California.

Living in the world of the graveyard shift is not without its comical moments. There was a lot of sleepy humor in the phone calls I would get during my wine-induced visits to the sleeve factory. There were calls where I carried on a decent conversation for more than a few minutes and later had little or no memory of them. Sometimes they would come back to me days later. They'd return in pieces, like a remembered dream. A silver ring arrived in the mail once and the bill referred to my having bought it over the phone. I paid for it and still wear it. It's the right size and everything. Some hidden part of me must have wanted that ring. I began to wonder if maybe I wasn't more alert when I talked in my sleep.

One morning, while I was in a deep sleep, the phone next to my bed rang. I lay there for a couple of rings, trying to clear my head, and then picked it up and said a groggy hello.

"Hello, Doctor Allison?" said what sounded like an Australian accent. "Doctor Warren Allison?"

"Yeah."

"This is Peter Blackmund, calling from Sydney, Australia."

"Wait a minute, did you say Doctor Warren Allison?" I asked slowly.

"That's right, Doctor Allison. We're looking for your granddaughter."

"My granddaughter?"

"Yes."

"Well, I don't have a daughter, let alone a granddaughter. I don't have any children and I'm not a doctor. I work at night and sleep during the day. Right now I'm not fully convinced that this isn't a dream."

"Oh, this is not a dream. This is very serious business," the voice warned.

"You know my granddaughter?" I asked sarcastically.

"Ah, well, no, but my client does. I've seen her picture."

"Your client? Who the hell is that?"

"I'm not at liberty to reveal that at this time."

"This is a dream," I muttered.

"Sir, your granddaughter has some serious charges to face up to."

"You say you've seen her picture?" I asked.

"That's right."

"How old does she look to be?"

"Oh, mid-twenties, I'd say."

"I'm thirty-one, you idiot. How do you suppose a thirty-one-year-old man could manage to have a granddaughter in her mid-twenties? That is, unless I started having sex when I was two? Is that when they start doing it down Australia way?"

"Are you sure?"

"About what?"

"About being thirty-one."

"I'm hanging up now," I said as I did just that.

Later that night as I stood at my machine, I remembered the call. The woman at the machine next to mine said some-

thing about her daughter and the whole sleepy conversation
came back. I couldn't make any sense of it. I told the story
to a few people and they found it curious, but nobody seemed
to think that I should do anything about it. What could I
have done anyway? Besides being a bizarre experience,
the whole thing felt slightly unreal. I probably would have
completely forgotten it, but two weeks later it happened
again. It was another Australian, but this guy's name was
Roger something or other. The conversation was virtually
the same, and again I was half asleep. The only difference
was that this guy was a bit more talkative. He said he was
from a detective agency in Sydney and he'd been hired to
find this woman. One of the few things he knew about her
was that she had a grandfather with my name living in Los
Angeles. I once again did my best to convince him that I
was not his man.

The week after that, my roommate decided to marry some
old girlfriend of his back in Texas. He packed up and was
gone in ten days. I couldn't afford the place by myself and
hated the idea of bringing in some stranger to live with me.
I got an offer from a friend at work to share his apartment,
so I went and looked at it and decided to move in. It was
a nice, big, airy place just below The Hollywood Hills and
the price suited me just fine. I got my own phone and when
I was asked by the phone people if I wanted my number
listed, I said yes. Three weeks later, one Saturday afternoon,
I was sitting on the couch with a woman named Martha. I
was getting the feeling that some serious kissing was about
to begin, when my phone rang. I went down the hall to my
room and soon found myself talking to another one of those
Australian accents.

"Doctor Allison?" he asked.

"I'm Warren Allison, but I'm not a doctor. Who is this?"

"My name is Willem Block."

"Let me guess, another guy calling from Australia."

"No, actually I'm calling from the Los Angeles airport."

"You're here?"

"Yes. I'm here to see you."

"What? You flew all that way to see me?"

"Yes. I must talk to you."

"About my granddaughter?" I asked.

"Exactly."

"Look, I told those other guys, I don't have a grand-daughter."

"I know, that's what they told me. Could I meet with you? I have a picture I want to show you."

"I'm not going to know who she is," I said.

"Look, I'll buy you dinner somewhere. All you have to do is look at the picture and tell me if it's anyone you know."

"Why should I?"

"Because this woman is a criminal. She's a thief and she needs to be stopped. I've flown all the way from Australia with the hope of talking to you about her. Meet me at a restaurant. I'll show you the picture and buy you a meal. Bring someone along if you don't want to meet with me alone."

"I guess I can do that," I said with a sigh.

I told him the name and address of a very expensive Italian place down on Melrose Avenue. We agreed to meet there at eight o'clock that night. I went back to the living room, told Martha the entire story, and invited her to come along. I could tell that she loved the mystery of the thing. It made the kissing even better. When Martha left I told her that I would come by her apartment at seven-thirty. I also told her where we were going and to dress like a queen. I got out my blue suit and even fussed with several different pairs of socks. At seven I left to pick up Martha.

On the way to her apartment I tried to think through this strange situation. I was sure I wouldn't know who had ripped off this guy. It was true that in my life prior to California I had been involved with a lot of shady characters. Some

of them were capable of doing just about anything to get
their hands on a few dollars. However, as reluctant as I was
to admit it, they were all small-time criminals. Some of the
frauds and cons we pulled were actually more like hobbies
than anything else. I was always having to find real jobs to
tide me over. That in itself tells you what kind of crook I
was. Nobody I ever knew was into the big time. It was a
long way from selling stolen watches in Omaha to international crime in Australia. Besides that, none of my old buddies from Omaha even knew I was in California. I just had
to make sure that this thing wasn't some kind of setup. That
someone wasn't trying to do a con on *me*. Other than that,
this looked to be a free meal and an interesting story to tell
my friends. I also knew it was a turn-on for Martha. That
alone might make the whole thing worthwhile.

At eight o'clock Martha and I were sitting at a table
sipping red wine. At eight-fifteen the waiter signaled for me
to join him by the entrance. After I excused myself and
walked over, he led me to a tall, pale man in blue jeans and
a sweater.

"I'm Willem," he said. "I'm sorry, I didn't realize this
was going to be such a fancy place. Now they won't let me
in."

"Great," I said. Martha was going to love this.

"I noticed a place a few blocks away that seemed quite
nice," he said. "Rosa's, I think it was called."

"You like Mexican?" I asked.

"I'd like to try it," he said with a shrug.

I went back and explained the situation to Martha. She
pouted for thirty seconds and then I paid for the wine. The
three of us walked down Melrose Avenue to Rosa's Cafe.

"What was your name again?" I asked.

"Willem Block. You've received some other calls about
this, haven't you?"

"Yeah, you were the third. This is more than a little
weird, so I wish you'd tell me exactly what's going on."

"Well, I've been a terrible fool and you seem to be my only clue to set things right."

"I'm not so sure I want to be a clue," I said as I looked over at Martha.

"I'm afraid you are. If you're able to help me, I'll find a way to reward you."

"Reward me?"

"You must forgive my clothing and rather haggard look. I've been through a lot these past few months. I don't look it right now, but actually, I'm a man of some means."

Just then we got to Rosa's and he held the door for us. We got a table right away and were soon staring into very large strawberry margaritas After the waiter took our food order, Willem looked over at me. He may have been chalk white and his clothes did just hang on him, but there was definitely a fire in his eyes.

"This particular embarrassment of mine involves a lot of money. Money in the form of jewels. If the jewels are recovered, I'll give you a very nice reward."

"What does he have to do?" Martha asked when I didn't respond.

"He has to help me find someone. It might be quite easy."

"I take it you're talking about my nonexistent grand-daughter," I said.

"That's right."

"Do you have the picture?"

"Yes."

"Well, let's see it."

He leaned forward and reached into his back pocket. He pulled out his wallet without taking his eyes off my face. From inside the wallet he withdrew a picture of a man and a woman standing in front of a palm tree. He was the man, and the woman was my old girlfriend from Iowa.

I had completely convinced myself that I wouldn't know this woman. I hadn't even thought about what to do if I did. I caught myself squinting at the picture in disbelief. I tried to mask over my shock, but it was too late. He had seen my expression.

"So you know her," he said.

"She looks a little familiar," I said weakly.

"I think she looks more than a little familiar. I think you know her," he said with a nasty tone in his voice.

"Do you?" Martha asked excitedly.

"I need to know what this is all about," I said as I gave Martha a look meant to shut her up.

"What do you need to know?" Willem asked.

"For starters, tell me exactly what she is supposed to have done."

Willem leaned back in his seat and stared at me for a second. Then he smiled and reached for a sip of his margarita. After he swallowed, he put the drink down and looked at me again.

"Supposed to have done?" Willem said slowly. "You do know her, don't you?"

"Tell me why you want to find her," I said, a little louder than necessary.

"We were engaged."

"What?"

"Three weeks before our wedding, she got her hands on a whole shipment of black opals that belonged to me. I haven't seen her since."

"How awful," Martha said.

"You're sure she took them?" I asked.

"She disappeared the same day as the opals. She missed her own bridal shower. Everyone stood around waiting while she was getting on a plane for Tokyo."

"Tokyo?"

"That's right. I'm assuming that she flew home to America from there."

"Assuming?" I asked doubtfully.

"Yes, assuming," he said with a flare of temper. "She was an American, after all. The only thing I know for sure is that she got on the plane to Japan. That's the one thing those idiot detectives were able to find out. After I realized what she'd done, I tried to recall all the things she had told me about herself. There were only a few of them, and the only one that turned out to be something was Doctor Warren Allison. Her grandfather who lived in Los Angeles.''

"Only I'm not a doctor and you can see for yourself that it would be pretty difficult for me to be a grandfather."

"True. But one night, in a conversation with my parents, she had to come up with a name for a grandfather and she came up with yours. She even picked your city to put him in. She was lying all the time she was with me, but it's hard to make up a name on the spot. You must have popped into her mind."

"Do you have any proof of this? A police report or something like that?''

"Back at the hotel. We can go there after dinner."

"We've got plans for after dinner," I said as I looked at Martha.

"It won't even take an hour," he said quickly.

"Look, we're going to be late as it is," I said calmly. "If you show me a police report that tells me exactly what you've just said, I will tell you who I think she is. You know my number. Call me tomorrow and we'll arrange a place to meet.''

"How do I know you won't contact her? Try to warn her," Willem said angrily.

"Hold it a minute," I said as I held up my hand. "You piss me off and you've got nothing."

Willem gave me his icy stare once again. He leaned back in the booth and let out a long, deep breath.

"If you contact her, she'll disappear again," he said slowly.

"Willem, I have no idea where she is. If I decide to tell you who I think she is, you've still got to find her."

"You know for sure who she is, don't you?"

"Bring me the police report and we'll talk."

"She robbed and humiliated me. People like her deserve to be punished," Willem said fiercely.

Just then the food came and we fell silent as the waiter placed the plates in front of us. Willem stared at me for a few more seconds. When the waiter left, Willem started to open his mouth to speak, but I raised my hand again.

"No more," I said. "Call me tomorrow."

Everything was quiet as we ate. Martha tried to make some small talk with Willem, but he wasn't in a chatty mood. He eyed me several times, as if he might figure out some new way to make me tell him right then and there. I looked away each time and one time shook my head before I did. After the meal was done, he paid the bill and then we walked out of the restaurant. He got a cab back to his hotel and Martha and I walked up the street to my car.

"Well, who is she?" Martha asked.

"An old girlfriend."

"Really?"

"Yes, really. From the bad old days."

"I didn't know you had bad old days."

"Now you do."

"Were the days bad or were you?"

"Both."

"Oh," Martha said quietly. "Do you think she did it?"

"I suppose it's possible. If she did, she's really jacked up the stakes. I knew her more as a small-time prankster. She must really be feeling her oats these days."

"Do you know where she is?"

"No, but I know where she's from. I could probably find her if I wanted to."

"Are you going to try?"

"I don't know," I said as I unlocked the car.

"In a way I hope he finds her," Martha said as she got in. "That was a rotten thing to do."

"If she did it."

"Yeah, but if she did, she deserves to be punished."

"Maybe," I said. "But I get the feeling that this guy may want to do the punishing."

"I see what you mean."

"He looks like he needs to vent a little rage."

"What are you going to do?" Martha asked.

"Maybe I will try to find her. I'll call around. When I get her on the phone, I'll see what I can figure out."

"Good luck."

"God, this is unreal," I said as I started the car.

Chapter Two

I met Margaret, or Maggie as she liked to be called, at a rock concert. It was a Kenny Loggins concert and we both got caught trying to sneak in. We ended up going before a judge the next day. Her case was right after mine. She paid her fifty bucks just like I did, and then she and I got to talking. We ended up going out to lunch and making a date for the following weekend. We had our date and were soon seeing a lot of each other. I was living in Omaha at the time and she was living in western Iowa. That summer it seemed that I was always heading off into Iowa for a weekend with Maggie.

She and I became little scamming twins. It made the romance very exciting, and before too long I was completely hooked on her. We used to sneak into everything. We'd also do these little deals that she and I would think up. One Saturday, we drove down to Lincoln with these catalogs for blue jeans. We took orders and collected checks from students from all over the campus at the University of Nebraska. They never got their blue jeans, but we sure had a good time with their money. Maggie loved to think of new ways to separate people from their money. I liked doing it, but for her it was an obsession. Once she and I were joyriding along a country road in Iowa and we came across a group of abandoned brick buildings. Maggie demanded that we stop and investigate, so we got out of the car and started poking around. We could tell it was an old clothing factory of some kind. In one of the rooms we found twenty boxes of old wooden thread spools. Maggie insisted that we take all the boxes back to my place in Omaha. We spent the rest of the day calling every knickknack shop and craft store in Omaha. We told them that we were looking for old-fashioned wooden thread spools. Not a one of them had them. The next weekend we called again and this time left a phony number for them to call if they came across any. A few days later, Maggie and I drove around to each of them asking if they wanted to buy any wooden thread spools. We sold every box and made over four hundred dollars. It was small-time stuff, but it was fun and the money helped pay the rent.

I knew that Maggie also had something going in Des Moines. I asked her about it, but she would never tell me. All I knew was that I could count on not seeing her on Tuesdays and Wednesdays. It bothered me a lot that she wouldn't tell me, but not enough to risk losing her because of it. She was beautiful and fun and I felt like one very lucky scammer.

If we had had a big argument and broken up, that summer would still be a pleasant memory. Unfortunately, it didn't end that way. I got a call from her one day telling me that she had fallen in love with somebody else and that I wasn't to come by anymore. So naturally I drove out there the next day. Her apartment was empty. Her mother lived thirty miles away, so I went over to see if Maggie was there. Her mother told me that Maggie had called and said she was going away for a while. She hadn't even come over to say good-bye to her. The funny part was that Maggie's mother didn't seem surprised at all.

"She'll be back," she said. "This is where she rests."

That was all she would say. I left there a mess. I moped around for several weeks. I drove back to her place once more and someone else was living in her apartment. A month later I met a woman at a softball game, and I was soon recovered from Maggie.

Her sudden disappearance was strange, and I know Maggie liked other people's money, but that didn't mean that she had stiffed this Willem guy. I had no reason to believe that she was capable of doing something that huge. Sure, the end of our relationship was unusual, but it was filled with unknowns. Maybe she had to go off on some emergency. Who knows? Maggie liked small-time hustle, but I had no reason to believe she was a big-time crook.

I drove Martha home and we parked in front of her place. She didn't want me to come in because her roommate was home. We talked for a bit and then got back to some serious kissing. I was right about Martha being turned on by our little adventure. I managed to get her out of her fancy dress and she did a pretty good job of undressing me. We were both pretty hot, but she thought that doing it in the car was undignified. I shared no such worries, but took it like a good sport. She also gave me a look that suggested a bright future for my sex life. That would be a welcome change and served to cheer me up quite a lot. After we got ourselves dressed again, I walked her to her door and kissed her good night.

I could have gone home and called information for Weaver, Iowa and asked for Maggie's phone number. But if I went to where I worked, I could get her phone number, her address, and a free call to Iowa. It wasn't that far from where I lived, so I swung onto the Golden State Freeway and drove up to Glendale.

The machine that I stayed up all night running had the glorious name of MailStar. What it did was fold people's phone bills, stick them into an envelope, wet the glue, fold the flap over, and then run the whole thing through a postage meter. It wasn't a job that was good for much more than a steady paycheck and a break on my phone bills. One thing it did offer was access to a computer that had an amazing amount of information on people's phone numbers and addresses. A person just had to know one little password. As a mere machine operator, I was not supposed to know the password. My boss wasn't even supposed to know it. However, my boss wasn't as nosy as I was. He also didn't know that the manager from day shift was very careless about putting away his computer instructions.

The security guard at the door knew me. All I had to do was sign in and write where I was going. I told the guard that I had forgotten something on Friday. He didn't seem to think anything of it. I walked through the deserted building and slipped into my boss's office. I turned on the computer, went through a few menus, and then typed in this month's password. I soon found my way to the directory for Weaver, Iowa. I typed in Margaret Willis and one second later the information came up on the screen. The address next to the phone number was not the apartment I had visited when we were snuggling up that summer. I picked up my boss's phone and dialed the number. A sleepy voice came on after the fifth ring and said hello. I let her say hello again and then hung up.

There could be no doubt. It was Maggie's voice. I wrote the number and the address on a piece of paper and then turned the computer off.

"Find what you were looking for?" the security guard asked.

"Right at my station," I said as I signed out.

I drove home thinking about what I should do. I also

spent a lot of time thinking about Maggie's beautiful legs. I decided to sleep in on Sunday and call her again as soon as I woke up. That plan didn't work out too well, though. My phone rang at eight the next morning, and of course it was Willem.

"Where can we meet so I can show you the police report?" he asked me.

"Listen, I have a lot to do today and I have to work tonight," I said. "I get off work at eight o'clock tomorrow morning. Why don't we meet then and you can buy me breakfast."

That suggestion did not please him at all. He tried very hard to get me to see him right away, but I shot down every proposal he made. After he was convinced that it had to be Monday, I told him where I worked and we arranged to meet at the restaurant down the street. When he hung up, I stared at the phone for a moment before I replaced the receiver. I knew this guy was going to show up with a legitimate police report and he was going to want me to tell him what I knew. I figured he would get very nasty if I didn't come up with some information. But I couldn't just hand Maggie to him. I had to get her on the phone and see if I couldn't figure this thing out. I got out the piece of paper with her phone number on it and dialed her again. This time her line was busy. I went out and got the Sunday paper, and after reading the sports section I tried her again. She picked up the phone on the fifth ring.

"Hello," she said in that sweet voice of hers.

"Hi, Maggie," I said.

"Who is this?" she asked cautiously.

"It's Warren Allison. We were a summer fling a couple of years back."

"Oh my God, Warren! How are you?"

"I'm all right."

"Are you in Omaha?"

"No, I'm calling from Los Angeles. I live out here now."

"Oh," was all she said.

Neither of us said anything for a few seconds.

"So," I said at last. "What happened to you? One day we were hot stuff and the next day you were gone without a trace."

"Hot stuff?" she asked.

"We were lovers, wouldn't you say? Wouldn't you say our relationship would have qualified for that term?"

"Yes."

"So, I was shocked. It's not the kind of thing I like to have hanging over me. I kept wondering what I had done wrong."

"You didn't do anything wrong. I just met somebody else."

A funny thing was happening to me. The truth was, I hadn't thought about Maggie very much during the past year. Yesterday I would have said that all the hurt and frustration were gone. But now that I was talking to her, I was getting mad all over again.

"Don't you think it was a bit rude to just vanish?" I asked.

"Warren, why did you call me?" she demanded. "All this was a long time ago. Why all of a sudden do you need to talk to me?"

"Well, my little vanishing lady, there's a hound on your tail and right now he's sniffing around me."

"What are you talking about?"

"I think you may have pulled your disappearing act on him, too. Only he doesn't want to say good-bye just yet. As a matter of fact, I'd say he's really looking forward to seeing you again."

"Are you crazy?"

"Look, Maggie, I assure you that you would never have

heard from me again, but someone is asking about you and he's not a happy man."

"Who is he?"

"Maggie, tell me you don't know what I'm talking about and I'll tell him to go to hell. If you do know what I'm talking about, you better come clean with me. He's going to keep looking and he's going to find you. I can only help you if you tell me the truth."

"Tell me how he found you. How did he get your name?"

"You gave it to him. You said I was your grandfather. Do you remember saying that to anyone?"

"Shit," Maggie muttered.

"You did pretty good, I think. You pulled my name out of your head and then thought quickly enough to put me in another city. You had a lot of cities to pick from. You just got unlucky, Maggie, because here I am."

"Shit," she said again.

"So, tell me the story of you and Willem. Did you vanish on someone again and this time manage to take a few things with you?"

"Warren, it's a very long story."

"I bet it is," I said with a laugh. "The trouble is, the story is not over."

"That man is obsessed and maybe a little crazy," Maggie replied quickly. "You would do me a great favor if you told him you didn't know anything about me."

"It's too late for that. He showed me your picture and my eyes involuntarily gave you away. The game was over before I even opened my mouth."

"Where is he now?"

"At a hotel somewhere. We're supposed to meet tomorrow for breakfast. He shows me an official report and then I spill my guts. He's promised me some sort of reward."

"So, you decided to call me and see if maybe I would raise his bid. Is that it?"

"Not exactly, though that isn't a bad idea."

"I thought so," she said sarcastically.

"The main reason I called was to find out if it was true. I must say that I now believe him."

"What do I have to bid to keep you quiet?"

"I don't know. He promised me a reward. He hasn't been very specific about what that means. He says he's rich. Is he?"

"Oh, he's rich, all right. He's also cheap, if you know what I mean. Why don't you squeeze him for some big bucks and then tell him a bunch of lies. That way everybody but Willem is happy."

"Because he would come looking for me. I get the feeling he's got a real mean streak."

"That he does. It was a pleasure taking his opals."

"Ah, the truth at last."

"So, I'm not a good girl. That shouldn't be news to you."

"No, but your bad is bigger. You and I were nickel-and-dime, not bags of opals."

"He had them, so I took them. Don't worry about Willem—he's got plenty more. His father owns a sheep ranch that's bigger than Rhode Island. Last year they discovered a huge vein of black opal underneath it. Willem's been put in charge of the mine. I got the first shipment."

"I'd love to hear that story sometime."

"Warren, what are you up to these days?"

"I work for Pacific Bell. I run a machine that stuffs phone bills into envelopes."

"Why on earth are you doing that?"

"I'm earning a living, Maggie. Plus, I'm establishing residency out here. I'm planning to go to Cal State Northridge next year. Going to get a B.S. degree."

"That's appropriate."

"Bachelor of Science, wiseass."

"So, how much do you make stuffing envelopes?" she asked while she laughed.

"I'm not going to tell you how much I make," I said angrily.

"Must not be very much if it makes you that mad," she said as she laughed again.

"This is not exactly a good time to piss me off, Maggie!" I shouted into the phone.

"All right, don't blow your cork. Look, Warren, I like you. I always have. I need you to not tell this man where I am. Willem is chasing me because I hurt his pride. Made him look bad in front of his daddy. All he needs is to have a few obstacles thrown in his way and he'll go home. Believe me, in the long run he'll never miss the money."

"He wants me to be a clue and you want me to be an obstacle. I want to thank you for this wonderful position you've put me in."

"Listen, get on a plane and come back here. I'll give you enough money for your first year of school. You come here, stay for a month, and I'll give you ten thousand dollars."

"Jesus, how much did you take from this guy?"

"Hey, you don't want to tell me how much you make. So why should I tell you how much I make?"

"Somehow, I don't think it's the same thing."

"That's my offer. Come back here, stay for a month, and earn an easy ten thousand."

"How do I know you'll pay me?"

"I'll give you two thousand a week. You'll get the first two thousand tomorrow. Of course, you have to come here to get it."

"You're crazy."

"Warren, it's worth it to me. I made one very unlucky mistake, but other than that, it was perfect. You are the only possible link. Without you he will have nothing. Get on a plane, we'll have a fun month."

"Maggie, I have a job."

"Yeah, and how long would it take you to save ten thousand dollars in the envelope-stuffing business?"

"A long time," I said quietly.

"You can call them from here. Tell them you had a family emergency and had to fly home. They may even hold your job for you. Mail in your rent. Come on, Warren, California can get along without you for a month."

"Just like that, huh?" I said. "I pack my bags and get on a plane and fly away?"

"Sure. I do it all the time. Warren, picking up and going on a moment's notice is one of life's greatest pleasures. It cleans your slate."

"Sort of a hobby with you, isn't it?"

"You might say that. Sometimes it's part of the job."

"Jobs like Willem?"

"Willem was more like a project."

"That isn't over," I added.

"Are you coming?" she asked impatiently.

"Are you working now?" I asked.

"No, I'm resting."

"How long do you rest for?"

"Months at a time. Don't worry, you'll be the first to know if something comes up."

"Was that what our breakup was all about? Something came up?"

"If you must know, yes. However, I don't think of it as a breakup. We just stopped for a while."

"What the hell does that mean?" I asked.

"You figure it out."

"So we'll un-stop if I come flying back?"

"Maybe. You may have changed. Come back and we'll find out. You still get the ten thousand."

"So, does that make you a kind of bonus?" I asked sarcastically.

"Now you're being rude," she said. "Are you coming or not? When you get here you can do as you like. If you're going to play bitter, you'll have your own room for sure."

"I can't just instantly decide something like this. I have to think about it."

"No longer going with the gut? Too bad. Okay Warren, you go for a walk, take a bath, listen to some music, whatever it takes for you to make up your mind. Then you call me in exactly one hour. If I don't hear from you in one hour, I will have to make some other plans."

"Like what?"

"Well, maybe this rest will be shorter than I thought. One hour, I'll be here."

She hung up the phone. I put mine back down slowly and sat there for a few moments. I rolled the whole thing through my mind once to make sure I had it right. Every last part of it was crazy—except for the idea of how much easier my life would be if I added ten thousand dollars to my savings account. I had been working for six months and had barely saved two thousand dollars. I was living like a hermit in order to save even that small amount. I was planning to start college in a year. At the rate I was going, I wouldn't have enough money to live on, let alone pay the college fees.

I got up, put on my baseball cap, and walked up the street to the county park. I sat under a sycamore tree and tried to think the thing through. After about twenty minutes, I realized that I couldn't stop thinking about the money. Ten thousand would give me clear sailing through the first semester. After I proved myself, maybe I could get a loan or one of those student jobs. I wouldn't have to work during my first semester. I could study, read, spend long afternoons in the lab. It sounded like heaven. Also, if I got on a plane that night, it would mean the end of graveyard shift. At least for a while. I could sleep like a normal human being. Of course, there was also the bonus. That was the kicker. Wanting Maggie again wasn't even an issue. Sure, I was kind of mad at her, but I knew that wouldn't last long once I was back to where I loved to be. I got up and started walking down Canyon Boulevard toward my apartment. Then I started to run.

Chapter Three

I picked up the phone and dialed Maggie's number once again. True to form, she let it ring five times before she picked it up.

"So?" was the first thing she said.

"If I do this," I said slowly, "I might need some coaching. What would you recommend as the first step?"

"You're coming?"

"Let's say I'm going to, unless there's something about leaving tonight that I really don't like."

"Warren, don't be stupid. You can figure it out."

"Come on, Maggie, you're the picking-up-and-leaving expert. Just give me a quick rundown on how you do it. Tell me what you did the day you called and told me that you had fallen in love with someone else."

"That again. Warren, if this is going to be a problem, I think we'd better forget the whole thing. I'll get on a plane and fly off to some place with a lot of beaches. I'll spend your ten thousand on hotel rooms, fruity rum drinks, and fish dinners. I don't want to right now, but I can do it easily enough. I could leave tonight.''

Neither of us said anything for a few seconds.

''So, I have to pack some suitcases . . .'' I started to say.

''Only two,'' she interrupted. ''One for each hand. If you have a sleeping bag, bring it.''

''Sleeping bag?''

''You never know where you might have to sleep.''

''Great.''

''Call a taxi and have them drive you to a bank machine and get yourself some cash. Then go to the airport, find out who flies into Omaha and use your credit card to buy a ticket for the next available plane. You do have a credit card, don't you?''

''Yes, smart ass. Two of them, as a matter of fact.''

''Good. Take a book because you might have to wait for a while. Or maybe just fly to Denver and work it out from there. When you know what flight you'll be on, call me and I'll meet you at the Omaha airport.''

''It can't be that simple.''

''It really is.''

''What about utility bills, dentist appointments, my car? What the hell am I supposed to do with my car? I can't leave it on the street for a month. They'll tow it.''

''Don't you have a garage?''

''No.''

''So, don't call a taxi. Drive to the airport and leave your car in long-term parking.''

''It'll cost me a fortune.''

''Warren, I think having a job has dulled your brain. You can figure these things out as you go along. I think you're smart enough to get around it.''

''Get around what?'' I asked.

''Paying the long-term parking!''

''You're kidding.''

''Oh, Warren, I think you need me very badly. You're

not as sharp as you used to be. I still use things I learned from you. Little tricks you had. You were great at thinking on your feet. You must be spending too much time sitting on your ass."

"No, I stand by my machine," I muttered.

"That's better. A trace of wit. You see, I'm healing you already."

"Maggie, I want to do this because I need the money. Ten thousand would make everything so much easier."

"Then get on the goddamn plane."

"All right. I'll come. But you better not screw around with me when it comes to the money."

"Why should I? It's worth it to me to have you out of there."

"I hope so."

"There is one more thing you have to do before you leave."

"What's that?"

"You have to go outside and look like you're going to the store or something. See if there are any guys sitting in cars near your place. If there are, call me back and we'll discuss it. If not, call me when you know your arrival time."

With that she hung up the phone.

What Maggie didn't know was that I lived six blocks north of Hollywood Boulevard on a very dark and quiet street. There were always people sitting in cars near my apartment. People who hadn't known each other ten minutes earlier. My roommate liked to say that we didn't live on Foothill Boulevard. We lived on Head Street.

Anyway, I did as she told me. I went down the stairs and the first car by our door had a guy sitting in it. When I slammed our front door another head popped up and snuggled up against him. He gave me a big grin as I turned to walk past the car. I didn't think I had to worry about them. They were the only ones on the street, so I felt pretty safe. I walked down to the supermarket on Franklin, bought some whiskey, and then walked back. The two lovebirds were gone. I went upstairs, downed two shots of whiskey, and started to pack.

Two hours later, I was ready to go. As I got into my car, I realized that I was supposed to be at work in eight hours. I felt guilty about not showing up, but knowing that I would soon be sleeping normally brought a smile to my face. The guilt quickly melted away.

I did exactly as I had been instructed to do. First I went to a bank machine and withdrew two hundred dollars. Then I drove to the airport and parked in the long-term lot. I put the ticket on the dashboard and hoped that I would figure out how to beat paying the full charge. After that, I walked over to the bus bench, sat down, and waited for the shuttle. As I sat there, I looked over at the booth where the cars came into the long-term lot. The ticket was not issued by a person but by a machine. After pressing a button, the ticket would come out with the date and time on it. The guy collecting the tickets was at another booth a couple of hundred feet away. All I had to do was press that button on the day I came back, then make up some story about forgetting something at home. He'd think I'd just come in and I'd probably get out for nothing. I just had to make sure that the guy in the booth wasn't looking when I got the ticket. It probably wouldn't be that hard. It was already beginning to feel like the good old days.

I told the shuttle driver to take me to American Airlines, because I know they fly into Denver. When I got to the ticket counter, I was told there was room on the midnight flight. I would leave exactly when I should have been starting work. They also told me I could make a connection with Midwest Airlines and be in Omaha for breakfast. I put the ticket on my credit card and went over to a phone booth and called Maggie.

"I figured out a way to beat the long-term parking," I said after she said hello.

"See Warren, you're getting undulled already."

"I think it'll be easy."

"How'd the rest of it go?" she asked.

"So far, so good. I'll be on Midwest flight five hundred-eleven at eight thirty-five."

"I'll be there. I'll wear my purple hat."

"I think I'll know you when I see you," I said.

"That would be nice," she replied with a flirty tone in her voice. "I take it there wasn't anybody sitting in a car outside your house."

"Nope."

"No one?"

"Well, a couple of lovebirds, but they left right away."

"A man and a woman in a car?"

"Yeah, my street is a kind of lovers' lane—only the lovers are usually rented."

"Warren, I told you to call me if there was anybody there."

"This goes on all the time on my street."

"Maybe so, but I don't like it. I want you to make an effort to confuse anybody that might be following you."

"Maggie, I didn't bargain for this kind of stuff," I said as I looked around.

"And don't look around," she said quickly. "Warren, you are about to earn the easiest ten thousand dollars of your life. I hope a little effort on your part might be acceptable."

"Maggie . . ."

"You don't have to do anything right now. I take it you're changing planes somewhere."

"In Denver."

"Do you have time in between?"

"Almost two hours."

"Good. What you have to do is leave the Denver airport. Rent a car for an hour. Drive into Denver and then come back. Take some side streets or something. See if anybody is following you. If you think someone is, call me and we'll work up a plan. All right?''

"All right, I'll rent a car," I said with a sigh.

"The chances that someone is following you are very slim. But I know Willem and there's no sense in taking risks."

"Do you really think he'd hire someone to follow me?" I asked.

"He found you, didn't he?"

"True," I admitted.

"So, we have to be careful. Unless I hear from you, I'll see you at eight thirty-five."

She hung up the phone and I stood there talking to the dial tone for a while as my eyes slowly roamed the room. They all looked like travelers to me.

Now I had a lot of hours to kill. I had a shoulder bag with a book, a magazine, and all my shaving stuff. I sat down and tried to read the magazine, but of course I kept looking up at the people around me. My eyes were scanning a story on spiders. Tarantula spiders to be exact. It was about how important their hair is to them. I was reading the words; I may have even mumbled a few of them. But the information was stopping somewhere behind my eyeballs. That's because behind my eyeballs, my brain was going wild. All these alarms were going off. My inner voice was telling me that I was letting the old regime back into power. It wasn't just the return to the scamming world that my inner voice was afraid of. It also feared the decision based on lust. That lust seemed to have been the deciding factor. My inner voice didn't like that the wiener was making the deciding vote.

The irony was that Maggie and I used to talk a lot about this very thing, about all the stupid decisions men make when the wiener rules the head. After one such discussion, Maggie decided that we should take out an ad in the *Omaha News* personals. I still remember how it read:

SINGLE MEN! GET PAID PROVIDING INTIMATE SERVICES
TO LONELY WOMEN! $500/WEEK POSSIBLE. SEND $1
FOR INFORMATION. P.O. BOX 6172, OMAHA, NEBRASKA
68130

The mailbox we rented was one of those big ones. Ten
days after the ad appeared, we went down to the post office
and took everything out of the box. There were over three
hundred envelopes, each with a one-dollar bill inside. We
only went to the post office that one time and we laughed
all the way home.

That was life with Maggie. That was what I was going
back to, and I couldn't resist it. So there it was. Money,
sex, and good times. I thought about the possibility of her
not coming across with the money, but decided that she
would. Obviously, she had a lot at stake or she wouldn't
have offered it. Why shouldn't I take advantage of that? In
a way I was scamming her because I never would have told
that jerk where she was. Having ten thousand fall into my
lap was a lucky break. Money for college. What could be
more noble than that? After all, I didn't take this guy's opals.
I was just earning money from Maggie. As long as no one
was following me, this was going to be a piece of cake.

So I had to act like everything was fine. Make anybody
who was following me feel sure that I wasn't aware of them.
I went back to reading about the spiders. Then on to a story
about bug-eating plants. I also did my best to keep myself
from looking around the room. I did all the usual things
during the time I had to wait. I went to the bathroom, watched
a few planes land, ate a hot dog, and bought a hat. I figured
the hat would be a nice touch. I'd make it easy for someone
to follow me when I wanted them to and then I'd take it
off when it was time to lose them. Sort of lull them a bit.
I was thinking up a storm and really enjoying it.

At twenty to twelve, I got on the plane. We were in the
air in no time and soon I was downing a decent-tasting plate

of pasta. After a drink, some more reading, and a snooze, we were coming in over the Rockies. I could see the mountains in the moonlight. The masses of green forest looked silky, and the lakes would suddenly light up like a flashlight in a dark mirror. I was coming into this adventure under a full moon and couldn't help but wonder if it had gotten its hands on me. I did feel like I was being pulled along on some tide. It was the tide of events and I had decided to ride it for all it was worth. Thinking that made me smile. I was going to live by my wits for a while. Since I'd come to California, I had been cloistered. I was on my mission to hunker down and save every penny I could. Delayed gratification, my roommate called it. I was delaying, all right, but it was dull as hell. I think I may have taken the word *sacrifice* and made some kind of god out of it. It was time to bob and weave again.

When we landed, I took off my hat and headed for the rental car area. I got a car and fifteen minutes later was driving down the freeway to Denver. I pulled off near downtown and drove along one of the city streets. One car behind me got off at the same exit, so after a few blocks, I pulled into a deserted parking lot and let them go by. I sat there for a few minutes and waited to see if they came around again. They didn't. Then I started the car again and zigzagged my way through some back streets while I kept my eyes on the rearview mirror. The coast was definitely clear. I drove back to the airport and turned in the car. Forty minutes later they called my flight, and I was the first one aboard. We were soon flying into the rising sun. The plains of Nebraska looked golden and rich in the dreamy morning light.

I was sound asleep when the flight attendant woke me and told me to put my seat belt on. I walked off the plane and into the terminal, still not completely awake. At the gate, I stopped and looked around for Maggie but didn't see her anywhere. Then I scanned the crowd a second time, looking for a purple hat, and again was disappointed. I wasn't sure what to do, so I went down to the first level and waited for my luggage. When the two bags arrived, I went to the restroom and changed my shirt. After slapping some cold water on my face, I walked out and went to the cafeteria and got a cup of coffee. I was stirring in the milk when Maggie appeared at the table and sat down across from me. She didn't say anything. Just sat there with a big smile on her face. She looked great.

"What happened to the purple hat?" I asked.

"Decided against it," she said with a shrug.

"I was beginning to get worried."

"I was watching you," she said. "Going into the bathroom was perfect. It gave me a chance to see if anybody hung around waiting for you to come out."

"Did anybody?"

"I wouldn't be sitting here if they had."

"So, we're home free."

"Maybe. Just to be sure, we'll head west out of the airport. Get out on some country roads and then double back."

"You're really worried about this, aren't you?"

"This is the big time, Warren. Mistakes are very costly."

"I went for a ride in Denver. I don't think we have any problems."

"I know, but humor me for a little longer. One screwup at this point and we might kill the golden goose."

"I'd like to hear more about the golden goose," I suggested.

"There's not a lot I can tell you about that. Right now, I'm your golden goose. That's what should be important to you."

"It is, believe me," I said.

"Well, you've had a good stare. How do I look?"

"I hate to say it, but you look younger."

"Nice thought, but I'm afraid not," she said with a wave of her hand. "I think I may still be wearing the flush from my recent success."

"Willem?"

"Yes. It's been awhile now, but it really was a marvelous con."

"You must be well flushed."

"I am," she said with a big smile. "I must say, you look older."

"Six months of graveyard shift. I'll look more like my old self when I'm sleeping normal."

"How could you do that to yourself?"

"It suited my needs."

"Bullshit. You're too smart to be stuffing envelopes."

"I was too poor not to."

"So, you're going to college, huh? Going to join the rat race?"

"If you must put it that way, yes."

"What are you going to study?"

"Entomology."

"Bugs?" she said with disgust.

"Yes, bugs. All my life I've been fascinated by them. I used to scan the TV listings for shows on insects and watch as many as I could. I loved biology in high school. I remember sitting in my backyard when I was a kid and watching a mud wasp build its nest. I was mesmerized. Until recently, it never occurred to me that I could go to college and study insects. I wish some guidance counselor or somebody would have pointed that out to me. Would have saved me a lot of time."

"Oh, come on, Warren, think of all the fun you would have missed out on. Without your misspent youth, we never would have met."

"That is something to consider," I said with a laugh.

"You better do more than consider it, buddy," she said as she playfully kicked me. "Well, the best I can say is, good luck with your bugs."

"Thanks, Maggie."

"You like saying my name, don't you?" she asked with a sparkle in her eye.

"Yes, I do," I confessed. "You've ruined the name for me. Other Maggies just don't measure up."

"That's nice to hear."

"Obviously, my name pops into your head now and then."

"Yes. Sometimes with unfortunate results."

"God, I'd love to hear how that conversation went," I said with a laugh. "How did you come up with Grandfather Doctor Warren Allison from Los Angeles?"

"I was working a mean shovel that night," Maggie said as she shook her head.

"What have you gotten yourself into?" I asked. "We did things for a few bucks. This stuff sounds dangerous."

"It *is* dangerous, but the payoff is worth the risk. Warren, you don't really know me as well as you think you do. What you and I did were exercises. Sort of like an athlete keeping in shape. I've always been after bigger game. I've been plucking the golden goose since I was twenty. Two more years to go and that's it."

"Sounds like a graduate program."

"It is. In two years, I graduate to a life where I never have to work again."

"If I remember correctly, you'll be thirty in two years."

"That's right, and I'll have a million dollars in the bank."

"Jesus."

"I figure I can get at least six percent for it. That means, sixty thousand a year for the rest of my life."

"What will you do?"

"Go to sunny places. Eat lots of good food and probably get as big as a house."

"I don't think so," I said.

"What do you mean?" she asked.

"Because nothing turns you on like a good scam. You get all flushed and beautiful. I don't think what you and I

did were little scamming exercises. I think it had more to
do with obsession. You're not happy unless you're getting
away with something. I predict that retirement will not suit
you."

She stared at me for a few seconds and then nodded her
head.

"I have wondered about that," she said. "I worry that
I'm hooked on the hustle. But common sense says the law
of averages will catch up with me. If I keep going, I'll get
busted sooner or later."

"What you need, Maggie, is a loving husband and about
six kids."

"Oh God," she said as she rolled her eyes. "I thought
you wanted to be serious."

"I do!"

"Finish your coffee. Let's get out of here," she said as
she got up from the table.

We drove out of Omaha and headed west down one of
the state roads. After about ten miles of cornfields, Maggie
pulled onto a dirt road and turned the motor off.

"So what did Willem tell you?" she asked.

"Maggie, if somebody is following us in order to get
their hands on you, isn't it pretty stupid to be sitting alone
in the middle of nowhere?"

"We're not being followed. I'm sure of that."

"I probably threw them off in Denver," I said with a
smile.

"Tell me what Willem said."

"Well, Willem seems to be under the impression that you
and he were about to enter into holy matrimony. However,
shortly before the appointed day, you took off with his opals.
He had some detectives trying to figure out who you were
and all they came up with was me. He flew to Los Angeles
to see me. Which should tell you that he is pretty serious
about this. In about an hour, he's going to be sitting in a
restaurant waiting for me. He was going to show me a police

report and then I was going to tell him who you are. If he caught up with you and the jewels were recovered, I would get a reward."

"Did he ever say how much the reward would be?"

"No."

"I can guarantee you that it wouldn't have been anywhere near ten thousand dollars."

"Then I made the right choice," I said.

"I can't believe Willem is being this persistent. He'll make up for what I took in a couple of months."

"He's worried about the jewels, but more than that, I think he'd like to beat on you for a good long while."

"They told me he might be a problem."

"They?" I asked.

"Warren, this isn't just me going out into the world and picking up some rich guy I meet. It's all planned. When I go there, I know a lot about the person. I arrange to meet them. I can even get help if I need it."

"Is this some kind of underground business?"

"Something like that."

"Then why don't you ask for some help? Tell them there's a problem. That one of their marks is on your tail and might cause everybody trouble. Maybe they can take care of it."

"The problem with that is, I'm considered one of the best. I get the plums. If I tell them what's happened, then I have to tell them that I screwed up. They think I'm rather perfect at this."

"Are these people in Des Moines, by any chance?"

"Aren't you the smart one."

"International ripoffs working out of Des Moines, Iowa. Who would have ever guessed."

"That's one of the beauties of it."

"How did you get involved?"

"No more questions. I've already told you too much."

I started to object but broke into a yawn instead. Maggie smiled over at me and then reached down and started the

car. We drove back to Omaha and then across the Missouri
River into Iowa. Weaver was thirty miles to the northeast
and we got there in about half an hour. Maggie pulled the
car into a driveway next to a white clapboard house. She
went up and unlocked the front door as I got my bags and
carried them into the house.

"A whole house!" I said as I put the bags down in the
living room.

"Not great, but it will do for now. It costs me a whopping
three hundred a month."

"Ah, the Midwest," I said as I gave myself a quick tour
of the downstairs.

"I don't even use the second floor," Maggie said from
the kitchen.

My tour told me that there was only one bedroom on the
first floor. I wasn't sure if I should assume anything at this
point. So I went into the kitchen and sat at the table while
Maggie made some toast.

"Where do I sleep?" I asked after a while.

"For now, you sleep upstairs. There's three bedrooms up
there, but only two of them have beds. You can take your
pick. There's sheets and blankets in the closet by the bathroom. Why don't you go make up the bed of your choice
and then get some sleep. You look pretty wasted."

"I will in a minute. There's one thing we have to go over
before I do anything else."

"What's that?"

"The money. You promised me two thousand dollars
when I got here. I'm here, so where's the money?"

"I'll go to the bank and get it while you're sleeping."

"I'd like to see it before I go to sleep."

"Come on, Warren. You don't have to worry about it. I
promised you the money and you'll get it," she said with
a hurt look on her face. "I like you—I have always liked
you, and you're helping me out of a jam. I'm not going to
try to cheat you. That would be stupid."

"Okay," I said, as I raised my hands. "Don't get all offended. As long as I get it today."

With that, she turned her back and proceeded to butter the toast. The sunlight was coming in through the kitchen window and hitting the top of her head. Her black hair sparkled. It reminded me of the moonlight hitting the mountain lakes. In the old days, this would have been the moment when I came up behind her, wrapped my arms around her stomach and pressed up against that lovely rear. But, these weren't the old days and I wasn't sure how I would be received. It was so easy to see why guys around the world would fall for her and, in the process, let their guard down. They would so want to believe that she was in love with them. Her shining beauty was the kind that affected a man's judgment. She turned around, gave me a big smile, and then brought the toast over to the table. She got us both some orange juice and then sat down.

"Were you staring at my butt?" she asked.

"More like, thinking upon it," I said with a smile.

"I thought maybe you were on your way over to give me a hug, but it never happened."

"I wasn't sure."

"Of what?"

"Of you. Besides it being a long time, I'm not sure about what you are."

"What do you mean by that?" she asked with an icy stare.

"You're part of some program, some professional organization. It scares me."

"Warren, I was always a pro. When we were dating, I was just in between things. That's why I left. I had an opportunity in England, so I took it."

"Sounds like you're wreaking havoc on the British Empire."

"Unfortunately, that is one of my limits. I can only speak

English. I've had to pass up some good opportunities in Germany and Italy.''

"How many women work for this organization?"

"A select few."

"You must have very interesting Christmas parties."

"Try not to be cynical. I've already told you more than I should. Just enjoy your month and collect your money. That's all you have to do."

"Are we going scamming, like we used to?"

"No, I'm not allowed anymore. I have to wait around for the big fish."

"Orders from corporate?"

"That's right."

"I'll believe it when I see it," I said with a laugh. "So if there is no scamming to be done, what are we going to do for a month?"

"I thought we might do a lot of screwing," Maggie replied. "I could use a good, lustful month. Now I'm not so sure. You seem to disapprove of me. If that's the case, then we'll go to the movies, eat out, and go for long walks. That kind of thing."

"I always had the impression that the scamming was what turned you on."

"I suppose it does, but certain men do, too."

"Like me?"

"You did. Probably could again."

"I hope so," I said with a smile.

"That's what I like to hear," Maggie said as she reached over and patted my hand. "It will make the time so much nicer."

"Am I part of the job?" I asked.

"No, you're not part of the job, Warren. You're a good-looking man and you're also very smart. I'll be going to bed with you because I find those things attractive."

"I guess I can live with that."

"Good. Now, I'm going to the bank to get you the two

thousand dollars. Make up your bed, get some sleep, and I'll see you this afternoon.''

"I think I'd better make some phone calls first.''

"Fine. There's a phone by the couch.''

With that, Maggie got up and put her glass in the sink. She came back over, kissed me on the forehead, and then gave me a big smile. She got her keys and walked out the front door. I sat there for a few minutes, drinking my orange juice and thinking about the whole arrangement. I thought a lot about Maggie's saying that she found me attractive. I really wanted to believe it.

I finished my toast and juice and then called the people at my work in Los Angeles. My supervisor was still there and I told him that my father was very sick and I wasn't sure how long I would have to stay home. He said he would allow me to use the first two weeks as my vacation time. After that, he would have to hire someone else if things got busy. I then called my roommate. I left a message on his machine, telling him the same thing. I promised him that I would send a rent check at the end of the month. I wanted to call Martha but decided to wait a few days. I then went upstairs and picked the larger of the two rooms and made up my bed. I got undressed and was asleep in no time.

Chapter Four

I woke up with a start six hours later. I had to sit there for a few seconds, remembering where I was and how I had gotten there. When my head cleared, I lay back down and enjoyed the warmth of the late-summer sun coming in through the window. I could hear Maggie moving around downstairs. It sounded like she was working in the kitchen. At this point all I could think was, so far so good.

I got up and walked to the window. The backyard was quite large and the grass had the tired-green look of a long, hot summer. There were two willow trees in the backyard, which gave the place a weepy, sentimental feeling As I pulled my pants on, I noticed an envelope lying near the door. I walked over and picked it up. Inside were twenty one-hundred-dollar bills. They were all new and crisp. On the outside, she had written, "FOR WARREN AND HIS BUGS." I couldn't help but laugh. I resolved right then and there to enjoy Maggie and to forget about the other part of her life. Guys like Willem were on their own. They were big boys and had to look out for themselves. Maggie was right. I was doing this for me and my bugs. I was doing it for a life of classes, reading, long afternoons in the lab, and peace of mind. Plus, normal sleep.

I finished dressing and went downstairs. I found Maggie in the kitchen cutting up vegetables for a salad.

"Get your bug money?" she asked with a twinkle in her eye.

"You bet. We thank you."

"Well, Mr. Entomologist, how does a nice salad followed by chicken and corn on the cob sound?"

"Great. It's been awhile since I've had good Iowa sweet corn."

"Sleep all right?"

"Like a baby."

"If I know you, you've been thinking real hard about all this. Have you reached any conclusions that I should know about?"

"Maggie, I just want to relax and enjoy myself. I promise not to lecture or pry into your life. Let's just have a pleasant month together."

"Now you're talking."

I sat down while Maggie finished making the salad. When she was done, she got the chicken out of the oven, the corn out of the pot, and then sat down opposite me.

"I could have said my grandfather lived in Seattle or Dallas, or any other city in America, and you wouldn't be sitting here right now," Maggie said after a few bites of salad. "The odds against me picking the city you were in are pretty long."

"I'm just lucky, I guess."

"Had you ever told me you were going to Los Angeles? I wonder if, in the back of my mind, I had made some connection and it just came out of my mouth."

"I don't remember ever saying that. How did you happen to need to come up with a grandfather?"

"It was at a picnic with Willem's parents. They wanted

to know all about my family history. Wanted to make sure I was pure enough to carry on the family line. You were my mother's father. A nice, respectable doctor who had retired to the sunny climes of Southern California.''

"You were supposed to marry Willem and live happily ever after Down Under?"

"That's what he thought. I told him I just wanted to be wherever he was.''

"Ouch," I said with a grin.

"Don't feel sorry for Willem. He's rich and he's spoiled. This ex-farm girl was just redistributing the wealth a little. You see, some of it is even going to a good cause like the Warren Allison Scholarship Fund. Willem should be proud of himself.''

"What do you think he'll do now?"

"He'll probably hang around Los Angeles for a couple of days, trying to find you. Then he'll tuck his tail between his legs and fly home. In a few months, he'll have another big bag of black opals. Sooner or later, he'll find himself a nice Aussie girl and settle in for a long, rich life.''

"I don't think he'll ever have any great love for Americans.''

"Probably not. It all works out for the best. It's funny; his parents approved of me when I lied, but if I had told them the truth, they would have thrown me out of there.''

"Your grandparents weren't quite up to being doctors, I take it.''

"God, no. They were hillbillies. My mother and father are actually second cousins. My grandfather on my mother's side ended up in the Louisville State Mental Hospital. He spent the last ten years of his life mumbling about all the people he was going to get even with. It was weird to listen to him.''

"So you decided to break the mold.''

"That's right. I don't want to spend my life slaving away on some farm or in some factory. My parents tried to get away from all that. They came here so they could change their lives, but very little changed. They stayed poor. They tried several different ways to break through, but something always happened to keep them down. I don't want to fight that battle. I don't want to look sixty when I'm forty. This family of mine needs to make some economic progress and I'm just the one to do it. I'm smart, I'm good-looking, and I aim to have a lot of money in the bank.''

"Why don't you do it the way I am? Get an education. Improve yourself that way."

"No thanks. I'd be bored to tears. Warren, you can't imagine how exciting this stuff is. When you pull off one of these big deals, it makes you high. I've never found anything that was half as much fun as pulling off a good con. I live to be one step ahead of the other guy.''

"I remember," I said. "Nobody knows better than me how it turned you on."

"That was just the small-time stuff. Doing the big ones makes me kind of wild."

"You should call me the next time you pull one off."

"Maybe I will. I'll come home by way of Los Angeles."

"It's a date," I replied with a big smile.

"You don't scam at all anymore?" she asked. "You're completely straight?"

"Pretty much."

"What happened? What scared you? What sent you running off to Los Angeles and turned you into an honest man?''

"Well, after you disappeared, I hooked up with this guy I met at the racetrack. He used to get temporary jobs and then steal things from the companies he was temping for. I became his helper. One day he got this job unloading a truck full of Jack Daniels Whiskey that had turned over on Interstate Eighty. The temp agency sent him and three other guys out there to move the whiskey to another truck. During the course of the job, he found out where they were going to keep the new truck while they waited for a driver. So that night, we went out and stole the truck. I helped him unload the whiskey into a garage behind his house. We waited a month and then started going around and selling the whiskey to the bars in Omaha. It was the biggest thing I had ever gotten into. We were making a fortune. I went over to his house one Saturday morning and found him hanging from the wall of his garage. They had nailed his hands to the wall and then beat the shit out of him. All the whiskey was gone. He was alive, but just barely. I called the paramedics and then went home and packed my bags. I hid out in Lincoln for a couple of days but then decided to get out of Nebraska. I came back to Omaha, finished up some business, and then got into my car and drove to Los Angeles. While I was in Lincoln, I decided that I'd had enough. I'd been thinking a lot about going to college and suddenly it sounded like a nice, safe thing to do."

"You weren't afraid to come back here now?"

"I think it'll be all right. Let's just stay out of Omaha."

"You might have gone through all that for nothing. They might not have even known you were involved."

"I doubt it. After they drove the nails through his hands and punched him a few times, I bet he told them everything they wanted to know. I would have."

"And here you were, making such a fuss about picking up and leaving Los Angeles."

"That was different. I have a job now. I have relationships that I care about. I have plans, a future. More important, no one was after me in Los Angeles."

"Relationships?" Maggie asked.

"There's one woman I've been seeing. We've only been out a couple of times, but I really like her."

"What did she think of your leaving so quickly?"

"She doesn't know yet. I guess I'm going to call her and give her the same song and dance that I gave my boss."

"Are you in love?"

"No, I'm in like. Serious like."

"Sure it isn't serious lust?"

"Well, yes, there's always that," I said.

Neither of us said anything for a few minutes as we finished the meal. Maggie got up, put her dishes in the sink, and started to wash them. I finished my corn and walked over to the sink and stood next to her. I reached over and rubbed the back of her neck. She bent her head down and let out a soft moan.

"The things you miss when you live alone," she said.

I reached down and took her arm and turned her toward me. She smiled as she looked up.

"Are you going to kiss me now?" she asked.

"I thought I might. Since we didn't have any dessert."

"There's ice cream in the fridge," she teased.

"Too cold," I whispered.

I leaned down and softly kissed her. She didn't respond at first. I kissed her beautiful lips slowly as she stood there with her hands at her side. Remembering her weakness, I put my arms around her waist and began to lightly kiss her ear. Then I slid my tongue down the side of her neck and nestled in for a long stay. I felt her take in her breath and place her arms around my neck. The warm water and soap on her hands dribbled down my back. I worked my way up under her chin and back to those lovely lips. We had a good long kiss and then she broke away and turned back to the sink.

"You dry," she commanded.

"Are you?" I asked with a laugh.

"I was on my way," she said with a sexy smile.

"See, you don't need a scam to turn you on. You just need the right kind of lover."

"Sex is good," she said. "Sex that makes you rich is even better."

"Shit," I muttered.

We washed and dried the dishes as I started humming the song, "Money." Maggie knew the words and started singing as I hummed along. When I joined her singing the chorus, she immediately slipped into a lovely harmony.

"I forgot how good a singer you are," I said as we put away the plates.

"Used to sing in the church choir, way back when. I think that's the only thing church was good for. They taught me how to sing harmony."

"Yeah, I went to church when I was young and didn't even learn that. Just learned that there was some old guy up in the sky watching everything I did. Gave me the creeps."

"Bad ideas. Great music," Maggie said.

"My church didn't even have that. Just a bunch of people in robes who couldn't carry a tune. It was pretty awful."

"That's too bad. We had a wonderful choir leader. I fell in love with him when I was thirteen. My first serious crush. He knew it, too. Used to flirt with me all the time. I think he may have taught me how to flirt, as well as teaching me to sing harmony. So you see, church was very useful to me."

"Well, Miss Church Flirt, what are we going to do this evening? We've still got a lot of daylight left."

"I was thinking we could go into Omaha. Do some shopping, go to a movie. But since you don't want to show your face around there, I guess we'd better give it a miss."

"Give it a miss?" I asked. "That's a funny way to put it."

"It's something they say in Australia. Guess I picked it up."

"Well, you're right. I think we should give Omaha a miss the whole time I'm here."

"That was my idea for the evening. Since you don't want to do that, you think of something."

"Remember how we used to go on our joyrides through the cornfields? I'd like to do that. Get out on some country road, feel the sun, and listen to the wind blow through the corn. That's something I've missed."

"Really?"

"Yes, really. Let's find some little hill and sit and watch the sun go down."

"You're not going off looking for bugs, are you?"

"Why should I, when I have you by my side?" I replied with a straight face.

"I'm not sure how to take that," she said as she squinted at me. "But all right, nature boy. We'll go watch the sun go down."

We finished our kitchen chores, hopped in her car, and headed out east of Weaver. It was only a matter of minutes before we were surrounded by fields of very tall corn. I rolled down the window and took a deep breath.

"Corn's high this year," Maggie said. "The good old boys will be able to hang out at Ruth's Lounge all winter, waiting for their CDs to mature."

"It smells great," I said as I took in another deep breath.

"You smell the same," Maggie said as she looked over at me.

"Do I?"

"Sure. Every man has his own smell. Once I've been with him, I never forget it. I could not see you for twenty years and I would know you by the smell of your hair and neck. Haven't you ever noticed that with the women you get close to?"

"I notice their particular scent, but I don't think I'd remember it after twenty years."

"I would."

"Would you know your old choir leader if you had the chance to smell his hair?"

"God, no, I was only thirteen. He did kiss me once, at New Year's, but that wasn't enough to sink in."

"Oh, they have to sink in," I said with a smile.

"Warren, I know it's hard, but try not to be crude."

"Just trying to understand this fetish of yours."

"It's not a fetish; it's a talent, and can we please change the subject?"

"Fine," I said with a shrug. "I see you still don't wear your seat belt."

"Old habits die hard."

"Hate to see that pretty face of yours get smashed up against the window."

"Seat belts make me nervous. I don't like being all tied in like that."

The wind was coming in the window and blowing her hair back. Her summer tan made her look like a picture of health. A true all-American girl from the heartland. A girl who went into other people's heartlands and took them for everything she could get. The picture was beautiful, but the reality was shocking.

"Warren, I know the perfect place to watch the sun go down," Maggie said as she slowed to make a turn. "It's about five miles from here. There's a tree-covered hill that's surrounded by cornfields. My mother and I used to go there every spring, looking for morel mushrooms. You walk through these beautiful dark woods and then come to this little meadow on top of the hill. It's the perfect place to watch the sun go down."

"Sounds great," I said. "I can watch the sun go down and you can smell my hair."

She looked over at me and shook her head. We drove along the road for a while and then I saw the hill on the horizon. It was exactly as she had described it. Maggie pulled the car over when we got near the hill and we both got out. We had to walk through about a hundred yards of corn to get there. She walked down one row and I walked down the row next to her. It was like being in a tunnel with the sun filtering through in thin bars of light. Every now and then we'd hear a little mouse scurry away as we came rustling by. The smell of the corn was overpowering. I got the feeling that if the ears stayed on the stalks much longer, they would burst open. When the wind blew, the silk waved and shone. It felt as if I had entered into a completely different universe.

"The old John Deere will be ripping through here any day now," Maggie said as I stopped to listen to the wind.

"Hard to believe this will be open ground in a few days."

"I wonder how many mice will get ground into the mix?" Maggie asked.

"And rabbits," I added.

"We gobble all," Maggie said as we started walking again.

In a few minutes we came out of the corn and into a small, open strip between the corn and the oak trees. The open space was wet and muddy. I made it over in two leaps while Maggie danced over it in little, light ballet steps. Soon we were under the trees. There wasn't a path, but the thickness of the canopy had prevented much undergrowth. We walked quietly on the mossy ground.

"We used to find hundreds of mushrooms in here," Maggie said as we made our way up the hill. "My mother would fry them in lard. All spring we'd have chicken or pork and fried morel mushrooms. I hated them by Memorial Day."

"Do you still eat them?"

"I haven't had a morel mushroom in ten years and I don't care if I never do again. I don't like thinking that I used to have to go out into the woods and gather my own food."

"Did you have a garden?"

"A huge one. It was my job to mix the horseshit in with the soil. Great big wheelbarrows full of horseshit. We used to drive around to farms that had horses and ask them if we could shovel up their horseshit."

"Sounds lovely."

"I hated it. It was humiliating. Can you imagine, going around begging for horseshit?"

"Does it work in the garden?"

"Oh, yeah. We used to grow gigantic tomatoes. I'd be

eating my salad during the summer and I'd think about what was around the roots of those plants and I'd want to vomit.''

"All the time I knew you before, you never told me this kind of stuff.''

"I don't tell a lot of people about my early days. I like to concentrate on where I'm going—not where I've been.''

"They go together, don't you think?'' I asked.

"Sure, one leads to the other. Just because the past is in my head doesn't mean that it has to come out my mouth.''

"True,'' I said. "But it still comes out in your decisions.''

"Sure it does. My sister was pregnant and living like my mother by the time she was twenty. I'm really glad I had an older sister. She let me see where I was headed.''

"And you said no thanks.''

"Yeah, and let me out of here. Now I have more money than the whole bunch of them combined.''

"I never knew you had a sister.''

"She lives in Minnesota now. Poor as a church mouse. I don't see her very often.''

"I bet some farm boy got his heart broken when you decided to shift gears.''

"Yeah. His name was Vince. He wanted to get married the summer after we got out of high school.''

"What happened to him?''

"He married one of my girlfriends. They have a farm near Grinnel. Last I heard they had four kids.''

"Kind of scary. Could have been you.''

"No way. I told Vince I was off to seek my fortune. Within a week, I was on my way to Des Moines.''

"Not too many people seek their fortunes in Des Moines.''

"Hey, I would have tried Omaha, but it was too close.''

I laughed out loud and Maggie laughed with me. The spongy ground under our feet seemed to soak up the laughter as it left our mouths. In a few more steps we came out of the woods and into the little meadow at the top of the hill. We ran to the top.

The shadows were getting long and the sun was just beginning to turn from bright yellow to a soft orange. Maggie sat down in the grass and I sat down beside her. We leaned against each other and neither of us said anything for a long time. We were on the only hill for miles. The country all around us was a carpet of corn. The green of the corn was not the fresh, vivid green of spring, but the deep, dusty green of September. The clouds were big and full and they caught the orange color from the sun and showered it down on us. Maggie's face took on a wonderful glow.

"You look like an angel," I said as I gazed over at her.

"I'm hardly that," she said with a grin.

"I said you look like one. I didn't say you were one."

"I guess that's why the game works," she said as she stared at me very seriously.

"Warren, do you remember that I used to go to Des Moines every Tuesday and come back on Wednesday?"

"Yeah."

"I still do. I'll have to take off pretty early tomorrow morning. I'll stay overnight and come back on Wednesday afternoon."

"Where do you stay?"

"Different hotels. I try not to stay in the same place too often."

"What do you do while you're there?" I asked.

"Help out. Read some of the reports. Make plans. Hear about other people's experiences."

"How'd you get hooked up with these guys?" I asked as I looked out at the sinking sun.

"When I went to Des Moines, I got a job as a waitress and I hated it. Everybody kept telling me that I should get into modeling, so I decided to give it a try. After a lot of work, I got with a decent agency and was able to give up slinging hash. The modeling was pretty dumb stuff. Underwear ads in the newspaper. Standing around new car models. I was even on the Hastings Ranch Feed Store calendar."

"I'm impressed," I said.

"I wasn't. Then I met this man who told me he had something a little different that I might like to try. It sounded pretty exciting and very lucrative, so I told him I was game. He set me up for my first profitable romance and it went very well. I've been working for him ever since."

"Who is this guy?"

"Warren, I can't tell you that kind of stuff."

"It's hard not to be curious."

"I know, but surely you can understand why I have to keep my mouth shut."

"Of course. It's just hard to believe that this is an actual business. That it's all organized and planned."

"I never would have believed it myself."

"You don't ever feel guilty?"

"Remember how we used to talk about slipping into neutral?"

"Sure."

"That's what I do. Did you feel guilty about selling stolen whiskey?"

"Not really."

"Then why should I feel guilty about taking opals from Willem? I just slip into neutral."

"It's just that your way of stealing is so much more personal. I mean, you sleep with the guy. That's different from stealing a truck."

"Neutral is neutral," Maggie said casually. "It's all a matter of style. I don't steal trucks. I romance my victims. It's just life, Warren. People come and go and you take what you can from them."

"God, that's cold. It makes me feel like you'd turn on me in a second if it was to your advantage."

"Then the trick is to know where the advantages lie, isn't it? Right now it's to my advantage to keep you here while Willem flounders around in Los Angeles."

"So I'm safe for now?"

Gil Roscoe

"Sure. Don't worry about yourself, Warren. You're smart enough to figure out which way the wind blows."

"I hope so."

"You can take care of yourself. You may be a little rusty, but deep down, you're still a scammer at heart. Isn't this a type of scam? What you're doing right now? Coming to Iowa. Getting paid to disappear. Didn't you pull a bit of a scam on Willem by telling him that you'd meet him and then not showing up?"

"I suppose you could say that."

"You and I have something in common. We both left Willem hanging in the breeze. You're an assistant in this deal, whether you like it or not."

"I don't know if I'd put it that way," I protested.

"I would. We're partners again, old buddy. You're stuck with me and my dishonest but lovely ten thousand dollars."

I looked at Maggie for a few moments and then turned and looked at the orange ball falling to the horizon. Maggie reached over and put her hand on the inside of my thigh. I put my arm around her and she leaned up against me. We didn't say anything for a while as we watched the sun. Maggie's hand moved a little further up my thigh. I looked down at her and she smiled. She then took her hand off my thigh, reached up, unfastened my belt and pulled my zipper down. Before I knew it, I was sitting there with my jeans and underpants down around my ankles. Maggie then pulled away and stood over me.

"You know Warren, you're not exactly Tiny Tim," she said as she looked down at me.

"I guess that's a compliment," I replied.

"Of course it is. You're a very desirable man. I bet you forget that sometimes."

"Why don't you remind me once a day?"

"Maybe I will."

As she said that, Maggie bent down and untied her shoes and kicked them off. Then she took off her jeans and her panties. She quickly pulled off her sweater and stood there gloriously naked. She was so beautiful, I swear, I would have been happy to just look at her for a while.

"The sun is setting between your legs," I said.

"Rises there too," she replied with a laugh. "Now, Warren, I don't want you to do anything. I want you to lie there and let me do you. You've done me a great favor coming all this way, and I want to show you how grateful I am."

I started to talk, but Maggie leaned down and put a finger over my lips. I put my hands behind my head as she lowered herself onto me. It was very hard not to move against her. Every time I did, she'd lean over and bite me on the neck.

"I'm doing you," she'd whisper in my ear.

"I lay on that late summer grass and watched her move on top of me. I felt like I was being milked. Her movements were so graceful and smooth that I was hoping it would never end. Slowly she increased the rhythm, and shortly after that, I was beyond the point of no return. When she knew I was close, she went wild. When my moment came I felt a wonderful tightening. I moaned, but she screamed. It was as if her pleasure was based on mine. When it was over I felt her muscles relax. It was as if I was being released. She leaned over and kissed me and then lay down on top of me as she tried to catch her breath.

"Best sunset I ever saw," I said.

Maggie laughed long and hard when I said that. Her laughter and her sweet breath poured all over my neck. I felt great.

Chapter Five

Maggie wouldn't let me sleep with her that night. It seemed crazy to me, after our splendor in the grass, but that's what she wanted. She said that she needed a little more time to get used to me again before we could spend a night in the same bed. I tried to talk her into it but got nowhere. When the time came, I trudged up the stairs to my room. It felt awfully lonely up there. I read one of my science magazines for a while and later faintly heard Maggie talking to someone on the phone. I wasn't happy with the sleeping arrangement, but here it was Monday night and I was going to be sleeping normally. Remembering that I could have been home, getting ready for work, made me feel a little better.

I got up the next morning, went downstairs, and found a note on the kitchen table. She had already left for Des Moines. The note told me to relax, watch TV, and eat whatever I wanted.

I didn't have a car, so I really couldn't go anywhere. Weaver was too small to have a movie theater, so I couldn't

even go to the movies. I watched a lot of television that day
and took a long bath in the middle of the afternoon. I had
a nice nap and when I got up, I called Martha and left a
long message on her answering machine. I told her the same
story that I had told my boss. I also told her that I missed
her and would be back in Los Angeles as soon as I could.
I didn't leave her Maggie's phone number, but I did tell her
that I'd call again next week. When I hung up the phone, I
realized that when Willem figured out that I had taken off,
he might try to track down Martha. That thought made me
very uneasy. I closed my eyes and slowly replayed the scene
in the restaurant. I couldn't come up with anything that led
me to believe he would be able to find her.

I had a nice dinner of soup and a chicken leg and then
went for a walk just as the sun was going down. It was
cooling off outside, but I did feel my body temperature rise
as I thought about what I'd been doing twenty-four hours
earlier. I walked to the end of the town, which didn't take
very long. Then I walked along the railroad tracks that
headed out of town to the west. I walked the rail for a while
and then sat on it and listened to the stream that ran next
to the tracks. The sound of the water was so pure and clean.
It made me feel very relaxed. There was still a small part
of my brain that was screaming at me. It was there, but
definitely fading. I decided it was the voice of fear. That
this whole circumstance was a gift of fate and that I should
accept my good luck. I knew Maggie was using me, but the
reality was that we were using each other. She was right
when she talked about people doing things that were to their
advantage. I'd get what I wanted, she'd get what she wanted,
and that's all there was to it. It wasn't my business to worry
about her morals. It was my business to look out for myself.
The screams in my brain faded even farther away. Pretty
soon, all I could hear was the sound of the stream and a
few birds chirping as they settled in for the night.

I fell asleep in front of the TV and woke up at three in

the morning. There was an old World War II movie on and
I sat there bleary-eyed, watching the Yanks storming foreign
beaches once again. When the movie ended, I went upstairs
and got into bed. I slept until nine. I was already more rested
than I had been in the past six months. It was as if my body
was telling me, yes, this is how you're supposed to do it.
It was going to be very hard to go back to the graveyard
shift after a month of normal sleep. Those first few nights
were going to be murder.

I had breakfast and went for another long walk along the
railroad tracks. I turned over a few rocks by the stream to
see what kinds of things might turn up. Unfortunately, there
wasn't much, except for the usual beetles and grubs. When
I went back to the house, I got the idea of just moving all
my stuff into Maggie's room. I would have liked to see how
she handled that. But I didn't do it. If I forced things, I
would probably blow it. It was obvious I'd be in there soon
anyway. I had lunch and another nap. After I got up, I went
downstairs and made some tea. I was sitting there drinking
it when Maggie's car pulled into the driveway. She came
in all flushed and smiling. She was carrying several bags
that looked like they contained new clothes.

"Water still hot?" Maggie asked as she looked at my
teacup.

"Sure," I said, getting up to kiss her.

"Pour me a cup, will you?" she said. Then she went into
her room and dropped the bags on the bed.

"Milk and sugar?" I asked after her.

"Both. You may want to put a shot of whiskey in each
of them."

"Why is that, Maggie?"

"It's under the sink."

I could hear her in there, changing her clothes and hanging
up what must have been her recent purchases. She came out
wearing her usual jeans and sweater and sat down at the
table.

"Did you put the whiskey in?" she asked as she smelled the tea.

"I don't think I want to until you tell me why I need it at three o'clock in the afternoon."

"You know what they say, takes the edge off."

"I've had a very relaxing couple of days," I said as I pushed the bottle across the table to her. "I have no edge."

"Come on, Warren, there's always an edge," she said as she poured herself a double.

She slid the bottle back to me. I put a token drop into the tea and placed the bottle back on the table. She sipped hers and gave me a big smile.

"Warren, do you have a passport?" she asked.

"Why would I need a passport?" I asked back.

"Because having one might lead you to enough money to keep you in college for a long time."

"Really?"

"You could study your bugs and not worry about paying the rent."

"Just by having a passport?" I asked sarcastically.

"No more graveyard shift. No more envelope-stuffing," Maggie teased.

We stared at each other over our teacups. We both sipped and stared, each waiting for the other to say something.

"Let me guess," I said after a few sips. "You've got a fish on the line and you need some help reeling him in."

"Something like that."

"I thought you were resting."

"Break is over," Maggie said as she put her teacup down.

"What about my money? I still have eight thousand coming."

"Jesus, Warren, we can work that out. I'm trying to turn you on to a much bigger score."

"Tell me about it."

"Answer the question first."

"Leaving soon, are we?" I asked. "Going to slip away on me again?"

"You don't know it yet, but I've gone way out on a limb for you. Now do you have a passport or don't you?"

"I took a vacation in Costa Rica several years ago. Yes, I do have a passport."

"Do you have it with you?"

"No, it's back in my apartment, in Hollywood."

"But it's still valid?"

"For many years to come."

"We'd have to stop and pick it up."

"Really?" I said.

"Warren, I know you. I also know what you want. When I fill you in on the details, you will want to be part of this."

"So, fill me in on the details."

"All right. When I got there yesterday, I got called into the office and shown a file on a guy in New Zealand. Stuart said that he thought this one was just right for me and would I look it over and tell him what I thought."

"Is Stuart the brains behind this thing?"

"Yes, he's the one that brought me into the business."

"He must be a piece of work."

"He's very smart. One of those computer whizzes. If you decide to help me, you'll have to go to Des Moines and be interviewed. He has to approve you."

"You and I would be partners? We'd go to New Zealand together?"

"That's the general idea. Stuart gets forty percent of the money and you and I divide the rest."

"We go to New Zealand for how long?"

"As long as it takes. I was in Australia for eight months."

"Eight months!"

"Look, you were going to go back to California and stuff envelopes for at least another eight months. Why not do this and make a lot more money? When we're done, you can go right on to college. You'd have plenty of money and wouldn't have to worry about a thing.''

"How much money?'' I asked.

"I don't know,'' Maggie said with a shrug. "It depends on what happens.''

"Didn't the computer whiz give you an estimate?''

"He tells me how much he thinks the guy is worth. What I get out of it depends on my scam.''

"How much did you get from Willem?''

"Come on, Warren, I can't . . .''

"It will give me a better idea of what we're talking about here.''

"All right, if it will help convince you. I ended up with a hundred and eight thousand dollars.''

"Jesus!''

"It was a lot of opals.''

"That's not including what Stuart got?''

"No, that's how much I put in the bank after expenses and everything.''

"You think this guy in New Zealand is worth more?''

"He's definitely worth more. It remains to be seen if I can get more.''

"What kind of split would you and I be doing?''

"I'd give you thirty percent of whatever I make.''

"That's already decided, huh?''

"Warren, there are several women who do this. They almost always work with a partner. I did once, but I didn't like it. I think it would be different with you. We know each other. We've done some small stuff before. Besides, Stuart doesn't like it that I work alone. He thinks it's too dangerous.''

"So if I had been working with you on this Willem thing, I would have cleared over thirty thousand?''

"Something like that. The partner always gets thirty percent of what the operative makes.''

"You're called an operative?'' I asked.

"Yes."

"Sounds like spy stuff."

"That's the way Stuart likes us to think of it. He used to do that kind of work. I've asked him about his past, but he won't talk about it. The rumor is that right after he left the government, he did some time in jail. Whatever the case, he's real good at getting financial information on people."

"You hang with an interesting crowd."

"Don't I, though? Warren, this could be a big one. If it is, it will be the last con for me. If we pull it off, you'll be able to go to college and I'll find myself a nice beach. I'll eat lots of rich food, get fat, and be very happy."

"Who's the guy in New Zealand?"

"Do you want to do it?" Maggie asked firmly.

"Tell me more about the mark. Where did he get his money?"

"I can't tell you any more until you talk to Stuart. He usually assigns the partners himself, so he's not used to doing things this way. I've told him about you and he says he'll trust you if I do. All you have to do is convince him that you're smart and hungry and you'll be in. He has a lot of faith in my judgment."

"Is there a plan in place? Do you know how you're going to get to this guy?"

"No, that's what you and I do. Stuart gives us all the information he has. Then we go there, learn whatever else we can, and then make a plan."

"Do I stay in the background or do I get to know him, too?"

"Could go either way. You could end up being my brother, a business associate, even my husband. Sometimes the partner just supports. Does a lot of research, watches people, keeps close in case I have to be pulled out."

"Pulled out? Has that ever happened to you?"

"Let's just say I won't be going back to Ireland for a long time. If you really want to know the details, I'll tell you some other time. Right now we have to decide about this. If you want to do it, we have to go to Des Moines tomorrow."

"I only have until tomorrow morning to make up my mind?"

"No, I have to call tonight. Stuart said he'll be in the office until six. You've got a little over two hours."

"Oh, man," I muttered as I stared into Maggie's eyes. "Jesus, look at you."

"What?" she asked.

"You're glowing. You really love this stuff, don't you?"

"I guess I do."

"You're never going to be able to give it up."

"In a few years I'll be too old. Stuart turns you loose when you hit thirty. Company policy. I just need one more big one and I'll have my million."

"You're right about one thing. Around you there is always an edge."

"Come out on the edge with me, Warren," Maggie said as she leaned in on the table. "Think of the adventure. We'll make a bundle and have a hell of a time doing it."

"I don't know. This is a big decision."

"If we go to New Zealand now, we go from summer to spring. Doesn't that sound great? Oh, yeah, you'll love this part. The guy lives in a city named Christchurch."

"I've heard of it. That's the home base for a lot of scientific expeditions to Antarctica."

"So, what's the answer, Warren? How about a little scientific expedition for you and me?"

"I have to think. This is an awful lot at once. I want to go for a walk. Run all the information through my mind a few times. I'll be back in an hour and give you an answer then."

"All right. Have your walk. You think it over real good. Think about the money most of all. If we do this right, we'll each walk away with a lot of money."

"We could also come away with zip."

"That's right, too. High stakes equal big chances."

Maggie stared at me long and hard. Her eyes were full of challenge. I went up to my room, got my shoes on, and came back downstairs. I looked into the kitchen as I walked toward the front door. Maggie was pouring some whiskey into a shot glass. She looked at me and lifted the glass. She smiled, toasted me with the drink, and then slugged it down.

"We'd make a great team," she said.

I walked out the front door, down the steps, and headed for the railroad tracks. At first, I walked quickly with my hands pushed down in my pockets. When I got to the tracks, I slowed down and walked the rail. I did that for about a hundred yards and then sat down in almost the same spot as earlier. I could see the rocks that I had turned over down by the stream. I threw a few small stones into the water and listened to the splash. Several frogs jumped in from the opposite bank.

Maggie and I would go to New Zealand and nail this guy. I'd probably help set him up. Maggie would get into his head, into his heart, and finally into his pockets. We'd find the weak spot and then go for it. Like wolves culling the herd. I didn't like it and I loved it. I was in love with the high I knew I'd get if we pulled it off. A time a few months down the road when I'd have forty or fifty thousand dollars sounded like a wonderful dream that might come true.

I wondered if I could make myself feel nothing for this guy in New Zealand, if I could easily slip into neutral again. No harm intended, old sport, we just need a chunk of your money. We're going to teach you a valuable lesson. Show you that you have to be more vigilant. The frog that learns to leap the quickest survives, right? Yeah, I was going to scam this man because Darwin told me to do it.

God, what a bunch of bullshit. I'd be doing it to make my life easier. I also wanted Maggie for as long as I could have her. That part was not to be forgotten. I'd have to slip into neutral one more time. I'd do it and then get out for good. I'd do it for me. For the importance of what I wanted.

I got up from the rail and started to walk back toward the house. The only thing that still bothered me was Maggie's need for a partner. She said she liked to work alone. Why not this time? Why divide the pot with me? In the back of my mind, I couldn't help thinking that there was something going on here—maybe something related to the eight thousand she still owed me. With us in New Zealand, Willem was no longer a threat. If he was no longer a threat, then I was no longer an asset. I was afraid Maggie might pull her vanishing act on me once again.

When I got back to the house, Maggie was taking a shower. I sat in the living room and listened to her singing a very sweet tune. When she came out, she was still humming. She was wearing a new robe and when she saw me she stood still and gave me a questioning look.

"Sounds like you're having a good time in there," I said.

"A shower is always nicer after a few drinks," she replied.

"Is that a new robe?"

"Good for you. You noticed. How do you like it?" she asked as she spun around.

"I'd like you better without it."

"Oh? Do we have something to celebrate?"

"Yes and no."

"You mean you'll go as far as Hawaii?" Maggie asked with a laugh.

"What I mean is yes, I want to do it, but there is a question and a condition."

"What's the question?"

"Why do you want a partner now? You said you've done this type of thing with a partner before and that you didn't like it."

"Stuart won't let me do this one alone. He says if I want it, I have to have a partner. He wants to team me up with the same man I worked with last time. I didn't like the guy.

He has no charm and I don't think he's smart enough. I don't like depending on him."

"So you told Stuart you had an old partner in town and nominated me for the job."

"That's right."

I got up and walked out into the kitchen and poured myself a drink. Maggie followed me and leaned on the doorway.

"Does that answer your question?" she asked.

"Yes."

"Well, then, what's the condition?"

"If we do this, we have to leave in the next few days, right?"

"The sooner the better."

"In that case, I want my eight thousand before we leave. When we stop in Los Angeles, to get my passport, I'll put it in the bank."

"Afraid I'm going to stick you?"

"I'll still be holding up my part of the deal. I won't be home for a month."

"Then why can't I keep my part of the deal? I can still give you two thousand every week."

"Let's call it a good-faith payment."

"How do I know you won't take the eight thousand and run?"

"Because I want more."

"That's a good answer," Maggie said with a big grin.

"That and you are the only answers."

I walked over to her and pulled on the silky belt that held her robe closed. She just stood there and watched me do it. I gave it a good yank and the knot came undone. The robe fell open and Maggie's freshly cleaned breasts peaked out through the opening. She suddenly took the robe off and threw it across one of the kitchen chairs. I reached down around her waist and pulled her to me. We had a nice long kiss and then she broke it, leaned back, and looked at me.

"I'll tell you what, Warren. You pass the interview with

COMPANY OF THIEVES   71

Stuart and I'll get you your eight thousand tomorrow. When we get back to Weaver."

"Good," I said.

"Since we're talking about conditions, I have one, too, that you should know about."

"What's that?"

"From the time we leave the office in Des Moines, until the project is over, I'm the boss. You offer advice and assistance, but my decisions are final. It's my ass that's going to be on the line. So my brain is the one that counts."

"All right," I said. "But one more question occurs to me."

"What is it, partner?"

"Why does Stuart feel that you have to have a partner for this one?"

Maggie laughed and then hugged me close. She kissed my neck slowly, then moved up and nibbled my ear.

"Because our mark is the prime minister's son," she whispered.

Chapter Six

We got to Des Moines just after one o'clock the next afternoon. Maggie drove to an eight-story building not far from the Capitol and parked in the underground garage. She shut the engine off, turned, and looked at me.

"Nervous?" she asked.

"Not especially," I said with a shrug.

"Good. The most important thing is that you look cool under pressure."

"Anything else I need to know?"

"Well, whatever you do, don't tell him that you want to quit after this. Don't tell him about your bugs. Try to make him believe that you look forward to a nice, long life of scamming."

"All right."

"Don't imply that you and I are anything more than friends."

"He wouldn't like it that we are?"

"No. He's very careful. Doesn't like people getting their emotions and their jobs confused. He likes the partners to be smart, efficient, and kind of nondescript. Try to look like you would easily blend in with the scenery."

"Like one of my bugs?"

"That's right. I go out on a limb and you're the stick bug blending in with the branches."

"That was almost poetic," I said with a grin.

"Wasn't it, though," she said as she smiled back. "Enough with the poetry. Let's go do some business."

We took the elevator up to the eighth floor and walked down the hall until we came to a large wooden door that said "COYOTE ENTERPRISES." Over the words was a picture of a very healthy coyote. The coyote had a mischievous look on his face. I had to guess that this Stuart guy had an interesting sense of humor. We walked in and the woman behind the desk smiled and looked up at Maggie.

"Good afternoon, Susan," she said.

"Good afternoon, Emma. Stuart is expecting me."

We went in through another set of doors and down a long hallway. We walked by various offices, but all the doors were closed.

"Susan?" I whispered as we walked down the hall.

"No need for the help to know our names," Maggie whispered back.

"Can I be Raul?" I asked.

"If you want," Maggie said with a laugh.

"This place must be very confusing for the IRS," I joked.

"I think Stuart has the IRS very confused about a lot of things," Maggie said as we stopped in front of a large door at the end of the hall.

Maggie knocked and then walked in. I walked in behind her and closed the door. Stuart wasn't behind his king-size desk but over at a computer, studying the screen. He looked to be in his late forties. He had a very distinguished-looking gray beard and wore wire-rimmed glasses. He wasn't wearing a suit, just some slacks and a blue sweater. When we walked in he looked up from the screen and smiled at Maggie. Maggie walked over to him.

"Stuart, this is Warren," Maggie said as we shook hands.

"Why don't you both sit down," Stuart said as he turned back to the computer. "I just need another moment here."

We went over and sat in a couple of chairs facing the big desk. Stuart studied the computer for a few minutes and then printed out a spreadsheet. He got up, tore it off the printer, and then looked it over. He walked to a filing cabinet and put it away. He then came over and sat behind the desk.

"So, Warren," he said, "which drawer in the file cabinet did I just put the spreadsheet in?"

"The third. Toward the back," I said quickly.

"That's right," he said as he leaned back in his chair. "Do you have any questions right off the bat? Anything you need cleared up right away?"

"Why *coyote?*" I asked.

"Old Apache legends. Coyote is the trickster. The one who often brings the high and mighty down a notch or two. You have to keep your eye on old Coyote."

"Good choice," I said with a nod.

"Any other immediate questions?"

"Not really."

"I take it that Margaret has filled you in on our general mode of operation."

"Oh, yes," I replied. "This is very unique."

"Not really," Stuart said casually. "Romance bunko, as the police like to call it, is as old as the human race. We're just more organized."

"Should we discuss benefits and retirement plans?" I said with a laugh.

"Sure," Stuart said with a smile. "A nice retirement is very possible in this business."

"That's something to shoot for," I said.

"That it is," he agreed. "Now, Margaret, if you don't mind, why don't you go down to the restaurant across the street and have a nice lunch. Warren will join you in a little while."

"Fine," Maggie said as she got up and walked out of the room.

"So, you and Margaret used to work together?" Stuart said as the door closed.

"Yes, a couple of years ago."

"Were you screwing her at the time?"

"No."

"Are you screwing her now?"

"No."

"I find that hard to believe," Stuart said with a very skeptical look.

"I have a girlfriend back in California."

"Then you'd say, you and Margaret have a thoroughly professional relationship?"

"I would say so, yes."

"Good. What have you been up to lately?"

"I've managed to get a job with Pacific Bell in Los Angeles. A friend and I are using phone company computer information to track down people who have ignored certain debts. We get a percentage of what is collected."

"Why are you back here?"

"My father is very sick, so I came back to visit. I wondered if Maggie was resting, so I called and, sure enough, she was here. We got together, talked about the old times over dinner, and promised to keep in touch if anything came up. Yesterday she called me and here I am."

"I get the feeling you're making this up as you go along," Stuart said as he shifted in his seat.

"No . . ." I started to say.

"Don't apologize," Stuart said as he held up his hand. "You need to be a good liar."

I took a deep breath and was about to wing it again when the phone rang. Stuart picked it up and told the person on the other end that he'd be available shortly. I wasn't sure if that was a good sign or a bad sign. He hung up the phone and looked over at me.

"You not only have to be a good liar, you have to know when to stop. It's important to be able to tell when the other person is beginning to have doubts."

"Are you having doubts?" I asked.

"About some of the things you've told me, yes. About whether you can do the job, no. Margaret has told me a lot about you and I trust her judgment. It sounds like you've had a lot of experience, even if most of it was small-time. Actually, some of it was very clever."

"It was. I did it mostly for laughs at first."

"This, however, is not small-time. As a matter of fact, it is very big-time. Margaret is the best I've got. Listen to her. She can teach you a lot."

"I think I'll pick it up pretty quick."

"I also think you're screwing her, and that makes me nervous. She's very easy to get attached to. That's one of the reasons she's so good at this."

"You're worried I'll get emotionally involved?"

"Yes."

"I will do my job. I'm tired of small-time stuff. I want to move up to the next level."

"I understand that. So tell me, are you emotionally involved?"

"No."

"I hope that's the truth."

"It is."

"Good. I'm going to let you do this job because you seem to be the right type. However, I suggest that once you get to New Zealand, you stop having sex with Margaret. You'll need a cool, clear head. If things go as we want them to, she'll soon be screwing somebody else. I don't want you having a problem with that."

"All I have to do is think about the money."

"Good answer. Very good answer," Stuart said with a smile.

"Thanks."

"This job may take awhile, so I hope you're free to stay down there for as long as it takes."

"Maggie said six to seven months."

"That's just a guess. Could be more or less than that. Margaret works very quickly sometimes."

"The quicker the better," I said.

"Just remember, she's done this a lot. She knows a million things that you never even thought of. When you're out there, she's the absolute boss. Forget everything else. You do what she tells you. You can offer advice, but she decides. Don't ever forget that."

"All right."

"One more thing. Don't even think for a minute that you can scam the scammer. If you pull anything like that, I will see that you are very sorry."

"I know better than that. Maggie told me the splits and they're fine with me."

"This one could be very lucrative for all involved, so don't get greedy."

"No chance."

"Good. I may come down for a visit to see how things are going."

"Fine. I'll show you the sights."

Stuart smiled when I said that. He stood up and reached his hand across the desk. I stood up too and shook his hand.

"Oh, I almost forgot," he said. "I need to take your picture. It's wise to have more than one passport in this business. I'll have a phony one made up for you. We'll send it along later."

He reached into a desk drawer and pulled out a camera. I went over and stood against the wall and he took my picture.

"Good," Stuart said after he had taken three shots. "Now,

go down to the restaurant and tell Margaret to come up here when she finishes her lunch. I'll probably see you in New Zealand."

"All right."

"Good luck," he said as I walked out the door.

I walked down the hall and through the outer office. I took the elevator down and found Maggie eating a salad and reading a newspaper in the restaurant across the street.

"That was fast," she said.

"He's very sharp," I replied as the waiter handed me a menu.

"You have to be to put this kind of operation together."

"He knows that you and I are more than friends."

"Really?"

"Yeah. He says we have to stop screwing when we get there."

"Oh, I don't know about that," Maggie said with a wink.

"He wants to talk to you when you finish your lunch," I said with a big grin.

"We have to go over some things. He'll give me the file, our airline tickets and some seed money. Did he say he might come down and check on us?"

"Yeah. Does he do that?"

"He's done it twice with me. In Scotland and South Africa."

"You went to South Africa?"

"Sure, that was my first one. Beautiful country. Brought some of it back with me."

"What do you mean?"

"Oh, you know. Those clear rocks they have in the ground there."

"Jesus. So, are stones your specialty?"

"Whatever I can carry. I try to stay away from cash. Too bulky."

"What does this guy in New Zealand have that you want to carry away?"

"That's what we have to find out. Rich people love to have small things that are worth a lot of money. We can depend on that."

Maggie finished her salad right after I ordered my hamburger. She gave me the newspaper she'd been reading and then went back to the office to talk with Stuart. I watched her cross the street and then looked down at the newspaper. It was the *Wellington Times*. After looking over the front page, I realized that the paper was from New Zealand. There was a story there about the prime minister. New Zealand had just signed a trade agreement with Singapore. Something about wool and mutton going to Singapore and electronics coming to New Zealand. The article implied that the prime minister was a master at making trade deals. That he was really helping his country out of an economic slump. I read over the rest of the paper and got some glimpses into life in New Zealand. From the comics, I could tell they definitely had a different sense of humor. After about forty-five minutes, Maggie came back to the table and ordered some pie for dessert.

"Get the plane tickets?" I asked.

"You bet. We leave Omaha tomorrow with an eight-hour layover in Los Angeles. That'll give you time to pick up your passport and whatever else you need."

"You guys don't mess around, do you?"

"Warren, I go halfway around the world like most people go to the supermarket. It's really no big deal."

"What did Stuart have to say about me?"

"He's a little nervous about it, but he trusts me. He also said something I think you'll like."

"What's that?"

"He said we should make an effort to move fast on this one. He's a little afraid the father might start checking up on me. Stuart can cover us for a while in that area, but not for anything real thorough. He wants it to be a mad affair and a quick ripoff. The father and mother are living in

Wellington and the son is in Christchurch. That's in our favor. I think we can count on Stuart showing up within the first month. He may even stay around and help out for a bit.''

"I thought he had other stuff to manage.''

"This one is kind of special for him. He likes to stick it to people connected with government. That's his real love.''

We finished our desserts and walked down to the parking garage. Maggie drove the car to Weaver while I read the files on our target. His name was Peter Newton and he managed a big car dealership in Christchurch. His father had made a fortune coming up with the idea of importing shiploads of used cars from Japan and selling them at reasonable prices. The father had become an expert on international trade, which led him into government and eventually to the office of prime minister. Our boy Peter was thirty years old and had never been married.

"I hope he's not some kind of jerk,'' I said to Maggie.

"I don't think so,'' she replied. "He's just wrapped up in his business.''

"The women in New Zealand must be all over this guy.''

"Probably. He's not bad-looking either.''

"I hope you can do it.''

"Warren, I am an expert at figuring out what men want to hear and then feeding it to them. Something else you may not realize is that American women are very exotic to men in other countries. They love the idea of having an American.''

"That's good to hear,'' I replied.

I went through the file and then read everything I could in the Wellington newspaper. Maggie played the radio and sang along with the songs as we drove through the endless cornfields. I still had my head deep in the newspaper when we pulled into Weaver. When Maggie got about a block from her house, she suddenly pulled the car down a side street and turned the engine off. I looked up from the paper and then over at Maggie.

"What's up?" I asked.

"There's a car down by my house," she said. "Not right in front, but near enough. It's got Nebraska plates and there are two guys sitting in it."

"Who do you think it is?"

"I don't know. There was a sticker on the back bumper. I think it's a rental car."

"You don't suppose . . ."

"Don't even say it," Maggie said as she started the car.

She drove to the other side of town and then looped around until we came down the street the next block over from her house. She parked in front of the house behind her house.

"Did Stuart give you a little lecture about me being the boss?" she asked.

"Yeah."

"Well, it starts now."

"All right," I said with a nod.

"We're going to sneak through the two backyards and then along the west side of my house. We're going to look in all the first-floor windows and see if anybody is in there. If there is, we'll meet behind the house and talk. If not, we'll go in the back door, pack as fast as we can, and then drive to Omaha. Got it?"

"Jesus, Maggie . . ."

"Have you got it?" she demanded.

"I've got it," I said as I took a deep breath.

We got out of the car, ran across the two lawns, and crouched down in the bushes on the west side of the house. We looked in the kitchen windows and didn't see anybody. Maggie told me stay put and then she crawled up and peeked into the living-room window. She crawled back and then looked up at me as she shook her head.

"It's Willem," she said.

"Shit," I said in a loud whisper.

"He's sitting there, staring at the front door. Just waiting for me to walk in."

"So, what's our plan?" I asked.

"First thing is, we have to think about his plan. He's got two guys sitting in the car out there. He's probably told them to sit tight until they see me come into the house. Right now he's living for the moment when I come through the front door and see him sitting there. After I go in, the guys in the car are probably supposed to come running in for support. So what we are going to do is go in the back door, overpower him, tie him up, pack our bags, and slip out the back door again."

"Just like that?" I asked doubtfully.

"See this little container?" Maggie said as she held up her key chain. "It contains pepper spray and it will make Willem unable to function for half an hour. We'll sneak in the back door and through the kitchen. I'll go to the right through the kitchen and you go to the left. I'll pop into the living room first and he'll either turn to me or jump up. As soon as he moves, you step in from the dining room. He'll turn to look at you. I'll step in and when he turns back to me, I'll nail him with the pepper spray. There are a couple of extension cords in the living-room closet. You get the cords and tie his hands and legs while I start packing. I'll gag him while you pack, and when you're done, we'll go out the back door and run to the car. There's no time for questions or comments. I want you to just do it."

We both crawled to the back door. Maggie sat on the porch and took her shoes off, so I did the same. She slowly opened the back door and we both crept into the house. We moved carefully across the kitchen floor. When we got into position, she gave me a nod and stepped into the living room.

"Hello, Willem," I heard her say.

I heard Willem stand up and start to say something. When he did, I ran into the living room and called his name. He turned to me for a second, and when he turned back, Maggie let him have it right in the face. He immediately fell to his knees and then down on his side. Maggie took one look at

him and ran into her room. I got the extension cords out of
the closet and tied him up. I then ran upstairs and started
throwing clothes into my suitcase. Ten minutes later, I came
down with my suitcases and my sleeping bag. I ran into
Maggie's room. She had one suitcase full and was working
on another.

"Go through his pockets. Take all his money and anything
else that looks valuable," Maggie shouted at me.

I went back into the living room and found Willem still
squirming on the floor. I went over to the window and peeked
through the curtains at his two buddies. They were sitting
in the car, laughing about something. I went back to Willem
and went through his pockets. His wallet had a couple of
hundred dollars in it. I took the cash and threw the wallet
on the floor. In his other back pocket I found an envelope.
I opened it and inside was a computer printout of the phone
calls from my apartment for the past month. Maggie's number was circled in red.

"Gag him," Maggie said as she threw me a long white
sock.

I tied the sock around his head and then walked into
Maggie's bedroom and showed her the paper with her phone
number on it.

"How'd he get that?" she asked as she threw clothes into
a suitcase.

"Probably paid some clerk for it. Maybe got some detective agency to come up with it."

"I can't believe I never thought of that," Maggie said
with disgust.

"He's going to trash your house," I said as I tore up the
paper.

"It's a rental," she said as she slammed her second suitcase shut.

We both grabbed our stuff and went out the back door.
We sat down on the back porch and put our shoes on. Then
we ran through the two yards. A woman in the house behind

Maggie's stared out her window as we ran by. Maggie opened the trunk and tossed her suitcases in. I put mine on the back seat and got in on the passenger side. Maggie got in and started the car, and off we went.

"Like taking candy from a baby," Maggie said as we hit the edge of town and got onto the state road.

"I don't think you'll be able to live in that town again," I said as she turned on the radio.

"If we pull this next one off, I won't have to." She looked over at me and smiled.

"What now?" I asked.

"I think, directly to the airport. We'll see if we can get these tickets changed for the next flight to Los Angeles."

"Is there anything in the house that might lead him to the office in Des Moines?"

"Nothing. I kept very little of anything in that house. It was just a place to rest."

"Hell of a rest."

"Warren, think about what just happened. We had a serious problem. We made a plan and executed it. We thought fast, acted fast, and now we're on to bigger and better things. We just had a success. I was right about us making a good team."

"Maybe Willem will finally give up."

"I hope so. I guess I underestimated his determination."

"I think what you underestimated is how much he hates you."

"Maybe I did," Maggie said quietly.

Chapter Seven

"If you were Willem, what would you do right now?" Maggie asked as we drank coffee and waited for our new flight to Los Angeles.

"Pack up and go home. Realize that I'm up against a superior opponent," I said with a smile.

"He *is* up against a superior opponent," Maggie agreed. "I'm not sure that guarantees that he won't keep trying. So, short of his completely giving up, what do you think he'll do?"

"First of all, I'd be hoping that those guys in the car will get a little curious and figure out that something is wrong."

"The longer he lies there, the madder he's going to get," Maggie said with a hint of a smile.

"I'd say the amount of damage he does to your house is in direct proportion to the length of time those guys spend sitting in the car."

"Thank heaven I've been putting my money into bank accounts and not into worldly goods."

"After the rent-a-cops untie him, I imagine he'll go looking through the house for any clues to who you might be and where you might be going.''

"Good guess," Maggie said as she nodded her head.

"If he finds anything, he'll pursue it."

"Makes sense."

"So, the question of the hour is . . ."

"Is there anything that might do just that?"

"Exactly."

"The answer is no. There is not a thing. I was very careful about that. I've learned to plan for quick escapes."

"Willem seems to have a special relationship with the phone company. I don't suppose you ever called Stuart from home?"

"Never. I call him from the phone booth down by the gas station."

"What about your mother? Did you ever call her?"

"Well, yes, I did call my mother."

"She may get a visit."

"Don't worry about Mom. She won't tell him a damn thing."

"Maybe not, but he could get very nasty about it."

"One of my brothers would shoot him so fast there'd be no fun in it."

"Really?" I asked.

"You bet. I told you, I'm a hillbilly once removed."

"Willem may dislike Americans, but he may really come to hate Iowa."

We both laughed when I said that. I had to admit we were feeling rather goofy after our narrow escape.

"Maggie, something occurs to me," I said as I looked over at her. "I never got my eight thousand dollars."

"I was wondering when you were going to bring that up."

"So what's the story? Is that part of the deal now canceled?"

"I have a bank account here in Omaha. I could easily get

the eight thousand out and give it to you. The trouble with that is, we'd have to wait until tomorrow to do it."

"Maggie, that was the deal."

"No, Warren, the original deal was that you would get two thousand a week. I think we should stick with that. I'll give you two thousand every Monday."

"You'll be able to do that in New Zealand?"

"I'll have Stuart send me the money. He'll just take it off my split."

"I'll tell you what," I said. "I'll go back to the original deal if I can have the second two thousand right now. Wouldn't that be a fair compromise?"

Maggie sighed, got up, and walked to the ladies room. She was gone for five minutes and when she came back, she handed me twenty crisp hundred-dollar bills. They were still warm.

"Happy now?" she asked.

"Not only am I happy," I said with a grin. "I think I like where these have been."

"They were up against my belly. A place you're not going to get to visit again unless you start to trust me," she said as she sat back down. "Warren, this con isn't going to work if you don't trust me."

"I trust you, Maggie," I said as I put the bills into my bulging wallet. "I trust you with everything except money. In that department, you can expect me to trust no one."

"I can't say that I don't understand that point of view," she said, leaning back in her seat.

"Good."

"Now I owe you six thousand. You'll get it over the next three weeks. Is that good enough?"

"It's a deal."

I wasn't completely happy with the arrangement, but I knew that Maggie was right about getting out of Omaha as soon as possible. I would put three thousand in the bank when we got to Los Angeles and take the other thousand with me.

It would be a big improvement in my savings account, and I hadn't exactly busted my balls earning it. Just having all that money in my wallet made me feel very good.

We had an awful flight to Los Angeles—a crying baby in front of us and a couple of drunks behind us. When we finally got off the plane, we got our luggage and then went to the long-term lot to bail out my car. Since it had only been a few days, I just wanted to pay the fee and get out of there. Maggie wouldn't hear of it. She insisted that we put my plan into action and that she help out. So she went over and asked the man in the booth about the local restaurants while I walked over and hit the button for a fresh ticket. I then drove to the booth and told the guy that I had just pulled into the lot, but discovered that I had left my passport at home. He tore up the ticket and away I went. I picked Maggie up at the bus stop around the corner.

"Easy as pie," she said as she got into the car.

We stopped at the bank and I deposited the three thousand dollars. We then drove to my apartment. Maggie waited in the car while I went upstairs. My roommate was home. I told him my father was better, but that I had to go away for a while. I wrote him a check for the next month's rent, and when he asked me where I was going, I told him Canada, to visit a friend. I got my passport and a few things to add to my suitcase and then went back down to the car. We had plenty of time, so Maggie and I drove down to that Italian restaurant on Melrose and had a two-hundred-dollar dinner on Willem. After a couple of hours of eating, we went back to the airport and parked in a different long-term lot. Our tickets for New Zealand were for the eleven P.M. flight, so we still had a few hours to wait. We sat in a bar, watched a Dodgers game, and got rather drunk. As our flight time neared, we got washed up, bought some aspirin, and half-stumbled onto the plane. We found our seats and settled in for the sixteen-hour flight.

We were flying first class, so as soon as the plane leveled

off, the drinks and food started coming. Pretty soon we were re-drunk and restuffed. After the meal they started a movie and we put our earphones on and watched. Maggie nudged me with her elbow about halfway through the movie and signaled for me to take my earphones off.

"What did you do with the New Zealand newspaper?" she asked.

"I think it's still in the backseat of your car," I said.

"Shit," Maggie muttered.

"Oh, come on," I said. "He'd have to figure out that we were going to the Omaha Airport. He'd also have to figure out that your car was in long-term parking. Then he'd have to figure out which car was yours and break into it. Even if he did all that, he'd still have the whole country of New Zealand to deal with."

"It's not that big a country. He saw us with the suitcases, so the airport might not be that hard to figure out. He could easily find out what kind of car I drive. All he'd have to do is ask around Weaver. Plus, don't forget he's got two rent-a-cops to help him."

"It's too long a shot," I said as I shook my head.

"Any longer than me putting you in Los Angeles and you being there?"

"That was a freak. If I were you, I'd worry about your phone calls. If he can get his hands on a printout of my phone calls, then he can probably get one of yours. If I were you, I'd carefully review everybody I called in the last few months. See if there are any weak spots."

"I hardly ever use the phone."

"Then it should be easy."

"There is one thing. The guy at the gas station knows I go to Des Moines every week. I stupidly told him once that I had to go there a lot on business."

"Our ship has a few leaks," I said.

"Yeah, well, thanks for calling me from your home phone."

"Well, thanks for using my name while you were out there ripping off the world."

"And thank you for moving to goddamn Los Angeles, where you weren't supposed to be."

We stared at each other for a few seconds and then Maggie smiled. She leaned over and kissed me on the cheek.

"We're not perfect, partner," she said, "but stick with me and you'll be farting through silk."

I laughed and shook my head as she put her earphones back on. When the movie was over, we were immediately served a three-course meal.

"We sure are eating well lately," Maggie said, diving into her prime rib.

"Not to mention all this wonderful travel," I added.

"This is definitely the life," she said as she chewed her meat. "So, Warren, tell me what you remember from the file on our mark and his family."

"Is this a pop quiz?"

"That's right."

"Okay, let's see. Mr. Newton, Peter's very loaded dad, has a successful car dealership in Christchurch. Back in the seventies he and his wife go on a vacation to Japan. While there, he notices that the used-car lots of Japan are full of cars that don't look very used at all. Upon further investigation, he discovers that many Japanese turn their cars in for new models after only thirty or forty thousand miles. He does some research on shipping costs and comes to realize that he can ship vast quantities of used cars to New Zealand, sell them at reasonable prices, and make a healthy profit. The Japanese are so excited about the idea that, when he presents it to them, they throw in some tax breaks and other incentives. Making the profits even healthier. Fast-forward ten years and Mr. Newton is bringing thousands of cars into New Zealand every year. Other dealerships are going out of business and he's making more money than he ever dreamed possible. He opens dealerships in every major city in New Zealand and even branches out to Australia. By now, Mr. Newton and his company are one of the economic powerhouses of the South Seas. However, he gets bored with it all and starts hanging around with political types. Because of his connections, Mr. Newton is able to cut a deal with the Japanese for them to buy New Zealand wool. He becomes an economic hero and someone puts his name up for Parliament. He wins the election and proceeds to get very involved with international trade. After a few years, he becomes leader of the Conservative Party and before you know it, the Conservatives are in power and he is the prime minister. Of course, he has to distance himself from his car dealerships, so he turns the entire operation over to his son. His son, who has been running the dealership in Christchurch, is now in charge of a multimillion-dollar company. That's how it stands, as of now. Dad is in Wellington running the country, and Peter is in Christchurch running the company from his new office building behind the dealership.''

"God, Stuart is good. Don't you agree?'' Maggie asked.

"Yes,'' I said.

"He is a whiz at getting that kind of information. The trouble is that Stuart's files don't contain much about the people themselves. Their hobbies. Their weaknesses. All the good stuff that might offer us a route to their money. He says that's for us to figure out.''

"You can make certain deductions, can't you?'' I asked. "I mean, the father is obviously a go-getter.''

"That doesn't mean the son is. He could be a slug who has had everything handed to him.''

"I don't think go-getter Dad would hand his precious business over to a slug, even if he was his son.''

"You're probably right. So, let's make an early plan of action. You get a New Zealand driver's license, rent a car, and follow the son for a couple of days. Keep track of everything he does. We'll take whatever information you get about him and see if it presents us with a way for me to get into his life."

"What will you be doing while I'm following him around?"

"I'll be finding a place to live, for one thing."

"A place for both of us?"

"Warren, don't be stupid. We can't live together. We have to try very hard to not even be seen together."

"No more fooling around, huh?"

"Well, maybe we can. In the beginning. Once I hook up with our boy, you have to stay out of the picture. I have to be a model of devotion."

"I suppose that makes sense," I said with a sigh.

"Of course it does. Now, have you ever followed anyone before?"

"Yeah, you," I said as I went back to my meal. "To the ends of the earth."

We both fell asleep shortly after we had eaten and were awoken by the captain's voice on the intercom. He apologized for disturbing us, but there was something he had to let us know. He said there was a very small electrical problem, and though it was nothing to worry about, they were going to make an unscheduled stop in Fiji to have a look at it. If all went well, we would only be on the ground for a little while.

"Great," Maggie said.

"So, how long can you tread water?" I asked her.

"Very funny," she replied as she looked around. "I guess, as first-class passengers, we should set an example by remaining calm."

Just then, a man in a uniform came down the aisle. He kneeled down next to my seat and threw back the carpeting. He opened a small trapdoor in the floor, leaned over, and looked inside with a flashlight. Maggie and I sat there watching him, as did everyone else in first class.

"Nothing to worry about," he said as he closed the trapdoor and put the carpeting back. "Just a minor problem."

After he left, Maggie and I turned and looked at each other. "I need a drink," she said.

We ordered drinks, and this led to an immediate run on the bar. There were a lot of jokes about insurance and not being able to swim, but underneath it all, I could tell that people were frightened.

An hour later we landed in Fiji. The airport had been cleared of all other traffic, and the runway was lined with fire trucks and ambulances. When we landed without a problem, the emergency vehicles turned off their flashing red lights and returned to their garages. We sat on the ground for an hour while men in overalls walked around under the plane. Finally the captain came on the speaker again. He said that they were going to have to take a close look at the landing gear, which meant that we were going to have to stay in Fiji for twenty-four hours. We would get off the plane, claim our luggage, and then be bused to a hotel. The airline would pick up the bill and we would resume our flight at about the same time tomorrow.

"Twenty-four hours in Fiji," Maggie said when the captain was finished. "Worse things have happened to me."

"Maybe this is the retirement tropical isle you've been looking for."

"We'll see," she said with a smile. "But also think about this. Twenty-four hours in Fiji. All those tourists. All those people who will never see us again."

"Don't you think we'd better lie low?" I asked. "We need to concentrate on what's ahead. You wouldn't want to get busted here for some small-time hustle and have it mess up our shot at the big game."

"I'm like an athlete," Maggie said as she got up. "I have to keep in shape."

"Count me out," I replied. "I'm going to sleep, sit around the pool, and eat lots of fresh fruit."

"You do what you want, Warren. I'm going to make some money."

We got off the plane and got our luggage. After a half-hour bus ride, we checked into a large hotel near the beach. As soon as we got to our room, I lay down for a nap. Maggie changed her clothes and went back downstairs, looking for a scam. She woke me up three hours later.

"Let's screw," she said as she started pulling her clothes off.

When she was naked, she jumped on the bed and pulled the blanket back. I had been sleeping in my underwear and she had them off me before I was really awake. She then got on top of me and started kissing me very passionately. She went down and played a little tongue game with my belly button. After about a minute of that, I was as awake as I had ever been. When I grabbed for her, she pulled away and jumped off the bed.

"Catch me," she taunted.

I got up and chased her around the room twice and finally tackled her on the bed.

"Uncle," she said as she lifted her legs in the air.

After fifteen wonderful minutes of rolling and moaning, we jumped into the shower together. As I rubbed the soap on her breasts, she leaned back, smiled, and hummed a tune.

"You are so turned on," I said as I soaped her down. "I get the feeling that somebody is a lot poorer than they used to be."

"Not yet," she said as she opened her beautiful brown eyes. "But it will be a piece of work if I pull it off."

"What did you do?" I asked.

Maggie got under the water and rinsed herself. I followed and then we both dried off. As we were lying naked on the bed, she leaned over, kissed me softly on the lips, and then fell back and laughed.

"I went down and sat in the lobby by the registration desk," she said. "I just wanted to hear people's names. Hear what they said to the desk clerk. So, I'm sitting there studying a map, and in comes this woman with two porters behind her. Between them, they are carrying seven suitcases."

"I can hear the alarms going off from here," I said.

"Exactly. She checks into the hotel. Then she opens one of her suitcases, takes out a small jewelry box, and asks the clerk to put it in the safe. He does it, fills out a receipt, gives it to her, and she goes off to her room."

"Oh boy," I said with a laugh.

"I heard her say her name. It was Mrs. Landsburg. She was very clear about the spelling. She wanted to make sure the clerk spelled it with a *u* and not an *e*. So, while you were up here snoozing, I came back up and emptied one of my jewelry boxes. I went for a walk and found a stone that fit into it real nice. I went out by the pool for a while and waited for the clerk behind the desk to be relieved. As soon as he was, I went up to the desk and checked in my jewelry box."

"I don't have to guess what name you used," I said as I shook my head.

"You're so clever," Maggie shot back.

"Now, all you have to do is wait for a third clerk to appear and go claim your jewelry box. You've got a fifty-fifty chance that you'll get hers."

"Oh no, Warren. Fifty-fifty would never do. I got to flirting around with the clerk. I told him I'd be here for three weeks and hoped I'd see him around. Then I asked him to put my jewelry box way in the back of the safe. I pretended I was real worried about it. He opened the safe and had me watch him as he reached past everything else and placed my box way in the back. So as soon as I see a third clerk behind the desk, I'll go reclaim the box. It'll be like Christmas. Who knows what she's got in there?"

"I think you're addicted," I said.

"I don't mind that," she said casually.

"You'll never be able to give it up. Someday you're going to be a little old lady scammer."

"I don't think so," Maggie said.

"You know what you should be?" I suggested as I reached over and stroked her stomach. "A spy."

"What?"

"Sure. Get trained in international intrigue. You should find out what a person has to do to get into the CIA. Or learn to be a corporate spy or something like that. You'd be a natural."

"Scam for Uncle Sam," Maggie said thoughtfully.

"You wouldn't have to give it up. You'd go legit."

"That's not a bad idea, Warren."

"Plus, if any of your old marks happen to catch up with you, you'd have some protection."

"I'd probably have to go to college first."

"That's not a bad thing. What kind of grades did you get in high school?"

"I got tons of A's, but I cheated all over the place."

"Why doesn't that surprise me?" I asked.

Maggie laughed when I said that. We tickled each other and rolled around on the bed for a while. After we laughed ourselves silly, we got our bathing suits on and went down and had a swim in the pool. The airline had given us vouchers for a couple of meals at a nearby restaurant, so after our swim we changed and headed off to eat. On our way through the lobby, Maggie looked at the clerk behind the desk and then leaned over and whispered in my ear.

"Same one," she said.

We walked down to the restaurant and ordered dinner. While we waited for the food, we sipped huge tropical drinks whose color resembled that of the pool we had just been in.

"What was your very first scam?" I asked Maggie as she stirred her drink.

"Besides cheating in school?"

"What grade were you in when you started doing that?"

"Seventh. When I got away with it once, when I realized that God wasn't going to strike me dead, I became a maniac.

For a while I cheated on everything, just for the thrill of it. Then I slowed down and saved it for the important stuff.''

"When was the first time you scammed for money?"

"Actually, the first time wasn't for money. It was for records."

"Really?"

"Yeah. It was one of those record club things that you see advertised in magazines. All my friends had these great record collections and I had nothing. I decided to join one of those clubs. I got to pick several free albums and then they sent me lists of other records to choose from. The only thing was, when I filled out the application for the club, I didn't quite spell my last name right. I didn't quite get the address right either. It didn't matter because we had this real friendly mailman who made sure everybody got their mail. He figured the stuff must be for me, so he'd deliver it every time. After about six months the record company sent out a bill collector. He wandered around the neighborhood for a while and eventually made his way to our house. My mother simply told him that nobody lived here by that name and that he had the wrong address as well. What could he do? The records stopped coming, but by then I had a real nice collection."

"Your mother went along with this?"

"She yelled a little and told me that if I ever did anything like that again, she'd beat the daylights out of me. I had trouble taking her seriously, though, because she liked the albums more than I did. She still plays them."

"And so begins a life of fraud."

"Well, that man coming to our house really scared me. I stuck to just cheating in school for a while. Then a couple of years later, I read a story in the newspaper and it led me back into it."

"A newspaper story?"

"Yeah. It was something that happened outside of Chicago. There were a couple of guys going door to door with some

phony land deal. Land in New Mexico or something like that.
Whatever it was, the buyer was required to make an immediate
down payment. A few of the people realized right away that
they'd been taken, so they called the cops. The cops then went
into several homes in the area and explained to the citizens
what the scam was all about. Then they asked the good citizens
if they would allow them to wire their houses, so they could
record the bad guys and then use the tapes in court. Several
of the people agreed to do it and sure enough, one of them
gets a visit from the phony salesmen. He has them sit on the
couch by the microphone, just as he was instructed to do. Then
he goes into the kitchen and turns on the tape recorder. The
salesmen give their pitch and the guy falls for it! He wrote
the check right then and there. When the cops later asked him
how he could have done that, he said he didn't want to miss
out on a good deal.''

"You're kidding."

"That's what it said in the newspaper."

"Unbelievable."

"After I read that story, I thought to myself, that guy
deserves to lose his money. If people could really be that
stupid, I was going to make it my business to take advantage
of it."

"And you have," I said as I nodded my head.

We finished our meal and walked back to the hotel while
a yellow half-moon came up over the ocean. Maggie and I
held hands as we walked along the road. We may have been
up to no good, but at that moment it felt like we were a couple
of innocent honeymooners.

We walked down to the edge of the water and sat on
the sand. There was a nice, warm breeze, and the moon's
reflection made a light trail along the tops of the waves.
Maggie's hair blew out behind her and it made her look like
a glamorous model. I leaned over and kissed her neck. There
was no one else on the beach, so I reached around and cupped one of her breasts in my hand.

"No sex on the beach," she said as she reached up and pushed my hand away.

"Come on," I whispered. "It's such a great night. We're on a beach in Fiji. No one's around. Don't you feel the romance in the air?"

"Yeah, the last time I felt the beach romance in the air, I ended up also feeling a ton of sand in my vagina."

"Jesus Christ," I said, laughing out loud.

"Go ahead and laugh, buster," Maggie said seriously. "But I was sore for days. It was like he was wearing a sandpaper condom."

"I'll be careful," I said softly.

"That's what the last guy said," she replied with a snarl.

I laughed again and Maggie gave me a dirty look. She got up and started walking down the beach. I quickly got up and started after her. When I caught up with her, I put my arm around her waist.

"I'm sorry I laughed," I said.

"Oh, it's all right. I suppose it is a funny story."

"Why didn't you tell him to stop?"

"When it really started to hurt, I knew that I could use it. I knew I could use the pain to make him feel guilty later. That I could use his guilt to get closer to what I wanted."

"Boy, you are hard-core."

"Of course I am. I might add that it worked like a charm."

"That wasn't Willem, by any chance?"

"No, it was the guy in South Africa. He gave me a diamond to make it up to me, and that's how I found out where he kept them."

"Amazing," I muttered as I shook my head.

Suddenly Maggie stopped in her tracks and looked me square in the eye.

"Warren, I just had an idea," she said excitedly. "I want to make a deal with you."

"What kind of deal?"

"I owe you six thousand, right?"

"Yeah."

"How about a little gamble?"

"Gamble with your own money, honey. I want the six thousand."

"Don't get all mad," she said as she took my arm. "Hear me out."

"All right. Go ahead."

"Neither of us knows what's in that lady's jewelry box. It might be something worth two hundred dollars or something worth twenty thousand. How about if we make a deal: that if I get the box, I give it to you and you accept it as payment in full?"

"How do I know that you didn't hear Mrs. What's-her-name tell the clerk what was in the box?"

"Because I swear to you I didn't. Besides, why would she do that? It wouldn't make any sense."

"Forgive my lack of trust, but I just can't help but feel that you have some little piece of information, that I don't."

"I've told you everything. Warren, this woman had seven suitcases! If I were you, I'd take the chance."

"Sorry, I just can't do it. The six thousand looks too good. I can't take a chance on losing it."

"All right, Mr. Boring. Just thought you might like to have some fun. Think how exciting it would be if you said yes. Think of the anticipation."

"Think of the disappointment," I added.

"You're not the man you used to be, Warren. No wonder you want to go off and study bugs."

"That's right. I'll never be ripped off by a spider."

"No, you'll just sit and watch them suck the juices out of other bugs."

"Very clever," I said sarcastically.

"You're so sure that I'll never give it up and so positive that you will. Wouldn't it be funny if it turned out to be just the opposite?"

"I doubt it," I said.

"I guess we'll just have to wait and see," Maggie said as she stopped walking. "Let's head back. I'm tired."

We walked back to the hotel, and when we got into the lobby we saw that there was a new man behind the desk.

"Well, here goes," Maggie said.

I sat in a chair and watched as she walked up to the desk and turned on the charm. She had the man behind the desk all goo-goo-eyed in less than a minute. She flirted with him while she pretended to search through her purse for the receipt. After she gave it to him, he went over to the safe and disappeared from my view. Maggie quickly turned around and gave me a wink. Soon the man's head reappeared. He walked over to Maggie and handed her a pink box. She offered him a tip and he took it. When she started walking toward the elevator, I got up and joined her. She had already put the jewelry box in her purse. The elevator doors slid open and we got in.

"Bingo," Maggie said under her breath.

We got out of the elevator and walked to our room. When we got inside, Maggie immediately sat down on the bed, took the jewelry box out of her purse, and placed it in the middle of the bed. I sat on the other side and we both stared at the box.

"I'll give you one more chance," she said with a sparkle in her eye.

"I can't do it, Maggie," I muttered as I shook my head.

"All right, then," she replied with a shrug.

She reached over to open it but then stopped and looked up at me.

"Why don't *you* open it?" she said.

"You just want to see a grown man cry," I said as I picked up the box.

I opened it and then placed it back down on the middle of the bed. The inside was covered in soft black velvet, and in the middle of the velvet sat a silver bracelet with at least a dozen good-sized diamonds on it.

Gil Roscoe

"I don't suppose they're fake," I said with a moan.

"Are you kidding?" Maggie said as she lifted the bracelet out of the jewelry box and put it around her wrist.

"Do you know anything about diamonds?" I asked.

"I learned a little on my expedition to South Africa."

"So go ahead, break my heart. Tell me what you think it's worth."

"I can't be sure, but offhand, I'd say you have missed an opportunity to triple your money."

"You mean to tell me that woman is traveling around the Pacific with an eighteen-thousand-dollar bracelet?"

"There's no way to explain these things, Warren. There are only ways to take advantage of it."

Chapter Eight

After we ordered breakfast the next morning, Maggie got up and went to call her mother. She got back just as the food arrived.

"What did you tell her?" I asked.

"The usual. That break was over and I'd see her in a few months."

"What did she say?"

"Don't get caught."

"She knows what you do?"

"Vaguely."

"What does she think of it?"

"It's like the thing with the record club. She doesn't really like it, but she doesn't turn down the rewards either. I gave her a check for five thousand dollars just before you breezed back into my life. She really needs the money."

"What about your father?"

"He's back in Kentucky, doing some dumb job during the day and drinking with his pals at night. We've pretty much agreed to stay out of each other's lives."

She spent most of the rest of the meal teasing me about my financial loss on the bracelet scam. I finally had to tell her to shut up about it. After breakfast we went upstairs, packed our bags, and caught the bus out to the airport. The plane had been repaired and we were soon on our way again.

"I'd like to see the look on that woman's face when she gets her jewelry box," Maggie said as we watched Fiji disappear over the horizon.

"Yeah," I grunted.

"You always miss that part," Maggie said a little sadly. "I bet it will be quite a scene in the old hotel lobby. However, I must say, the stone I put in the box was really quite pretty."

"Well, then, maybe she won't mind at all," I said.

Maggie laughed as if I had told the greatest joke of all time. After she caught her breath, she reached over, squeezed my hand, and smiled at me. When she did that, I looked at her and let out a hopeless sigh. She was so damn beautiful. She had her glow on again. It was like she was a pirate, sailing away from a wrecked ship. It was the glow of victory. Maybe it was only a victory over a desk clerk and a lady with seven suitcases, but it was victory nonetheless.

Maggie leaned back in her seat and closed her eyes. I stared at her for a few seconds. She must have felt it, because she opened her eyes and looked over at me.

"What are you thinking about?" she asked with a sly smile.

"Lots of things," I replied with a shrug.

"Like what?"

"Oh, your father, for instance."

"My father? *I* don't even think about him. Why should you?"

"Curious, I guess. When did he go back to back to Kentucky?"

"Warren, you're not going to psychoanalyze me, are you?"

"Sorry, but it's interesting."

"Girl goes bad because Daddy didn't love her. So she

spends the rest of her life ripping off males. Is that what you're getting at?''

"I doubt it's that simple.''

"You're right about that, and in case you forgot, I just stole a very expensive bracelet from a member of my own sex. I'm an equal-opportunity thief.''

"Did he leave when you were little?''

"No, Doctor Freud. He left my senior year in high school. He wanted to go back to Kentucky and my mother didn't. When he couldn't convince her, he went by himself. I'm sure he thought she would follow him, but she didn't. After a few years, she filed for divorce.''

"Was he a good father?''

"That doesn't matter, Warren. *I'm* responsible for my life, not him. He wasn't the greatest father who ever lived, but so what? He longed for the mountains of his youth and he went back to them. I long for the world and all I can get from it. I doubt there's a connection.''

"All right,'' I said. "I just wondered.''

"Well, don't. If you want to think about something, think about what we have to do. Start getting focused on that. We'll be in Auckland before you know it.''

Maggie gave me a stern look and then settled back into her seat.

"Auckland?'' I asked after a few seconds. "I thought we were going to Christchurch.''

"Didn't you look at your ticket?'' Maggie asked. "Haven't you heard the pilot say Auckland at least three times?''

"Sure, but I assumed that we were landing in Auckland and then catching another plane to Christchurch.''

"No, we're driving to Christchurch.''

"Why?''

"It's one of my rules to never land in the city where I'm going to work. It gives me a chance to get acclimated to the country, and makes it harder for people to figure out where I came from.''

"Makes sense," I admitted.

"Actually, you're going to need a few days to practice your driving."

"I don't need to practice my driving," I said with a grunt.

"Really?" Maggie asked. "Have you ever driven in a country where they drive on the left-hand side of the road?"

"Oh. I forgot about that."

"Believe me, it takes some getting used to. Wait until you make your first left-hand turn. It feels very weird."

"Jesus, I'm supposed to follow that guy around."

"Exactly. Now are you beginning to think I know what I'm doing?"

"Yes," I said with a big sigh.

"Good. We'll use the time in the car to go over the file. We'll quiz each other on the facts."

I nodded humbly. It was obvious that Maggie was way ahead of me. I decided to do what she recommended and get focused on the task at hand.

When we got close to New Zealand, Maggie went into the bathroom and hid the diamond bracelet in her clothes. After we landed, we went through customs and the men in the blue uniforms went through everything we had. Maggie looked at me and smiled as the customs man unrolled my sleeping bag. After they were convinced that we were not bad people, we took our luggage and caught the bus into the city. When we got into Auckland, we stored our luggage at the American Express office and then went to work.

"First thing for you is a driver's license," Maggie said as we stood on the steps of the American Express office. "Then go rent us a car. After that, we'll have a nice meal and then head south."

"What will you be doing?" I asked.

"Getting this jewelry out of my underwear, for one thing Then I'll find us a good road map. After that I might try to see if I can find out how much your favorite bracelet is worth."

"Do me a favor and don't tell me," I mumbled.

"Not a chance," Maggie said with a laugh. "See that restaurant over there with the red roof? Let's meet there in a couple of hours for lunch."

I went back into the American Express office and they directed me to a building next to the Department of Labor where I could get an international driver's license. It was only a few blocks away, so I walked over to the office and studied the test booklet for an hour. I took the test and passed it very easily. After I got the license, I found a car rental agency, got a car, and arranged to drop it off in Christchurch. While driving the car to the restaurant, I discovered it was indeed very tricky to suddenly have to drive on the left-hand side of the road. Maggie was sitting at a table in the restaurant studying a book of maps. As I walked to the table, she looked up and gave me a big smile.

"I don't want to know," I said as I sat down.

"Of course you do. It'll teach you a lesson about playing it safe."

"All right, get it over with. How much is it worth?"

"Twenty-three thousand New Zealand dollars. Which is approximately sixteen thousand American."

"Shit," I muttered, shaking my head.

"The jeweler offered to buy it. He said it was in excellent condition."

"Did you sell it to him?"

"No, I've decided to hold onto it. I may need to look elegant in the coming weeks. Besides, if that's what he offered, it's probably worth more."

"Sixteen thousand dollars, just like that," I said, snapping my fingers.

"Or more," Maggie teased. "Too bad, could have been yours."

"Let's talk about something else."

"All right, sore loser."

We had our meal, picked up our luggage, and then headed

south. Maggie was so very right about the driving. It was like the whole world had reversed itself. Once I was going straight, it was fine, but every time I had to make a turn, I really had to slow down and think about it. A lifetime of driving instincts had to be constantly suppressed. We slowly made our way out of the city and found the main highway south. Soon we were in open country with green rolling hills. Everywhere I looked there were sheep. Maggie didn't pay much attention to the scenery. When she was sure that we were on the right road, she got out the file and started going through it. She read everything out loud so I could hear it. I had read some of the information in the car coming back from Des Moines, but there was a lot of stuff that I hadn't gotten to.

"He has his own apartment," Maggie said. "His sister lives alone in the family house."

"He has a sister?" I asked.

"That's what it says."

"How old is she?"

"Twenty-eight."

"Maybe she could be your in," I suggested. "Become friends with the sister, she introduces you to her brother. Might work."

"That's a very common approach."

"You've done it that way before?"

"Not with a sister. One time I worked it out so the mark's brother introduced us."

"How did you arrange that?"

"I found out that the brother and his wife worked with a conservation group. They would go out building and repairing hiking trails. I showed up one week with a shovel and volunteered. After a few Saturday afternoons of work, I got invited to a party they were having and that was that."

"Maybe we should work this one the same way. I'll follow the sister and find out what she likes to do. Then you jump into whatever it is and become her friend."

"What if our mark hates his sister's guts? Or what if they travel in completely different social circles? You can't just jump into a thing like this. You've got to do your research."

"I see what you mean," I said with a nod.

Up ahead there was a gigantic herd of sheep crossing over the road. We stopped and watched as a couple of black-and-white dogs worked the sheep from one pasture to another. I was totally absorbed in watching the dogs when a man, who I thought was a member of the crew, came over and leaned down on my open window.

"Name's Neville McIntyre," he said as he reached in a big, rough hand.

"I'm . . ." I started to say.

"I'm Susan and this is Thomas," Maggie said as she quickly reached over and shook his hand.

"Nice to meet you, Susan and Thomas. Yanks, are ya?"

"That's right," I said.

"Well, I hope you're enjoying New Zealand."

"We are so far," I said. "I love watching your dogs work those sheep. They seem very smart."

"Ah, yeah," Neville agreed. "Part of the reason they look so smart is that the sheep are so bloody stupid."

Maggie and I both laughed. I could see that Neville was very pleased that he had amused us.

"Actually, they're not my dogs," he said. "I'm waiting here to get by, just like you are."

"Oh," I said as I looked over at Maggie.

"You folks wouldn't be going by Taupo, by any chance?"

"I don't know," I replied. "We're headed for Wellington. Hope to spend the night there."

"Then you'll be going right by Taupo. I could sure use a lift. I've got to do the late shift at the mill tonight."

"You work at night?" I asked.

"You bet. Saw up pine trees all night long."

I looked over at Maggie to see if she wouldn't mind.

Neville realized that I was looking for her approval, so he leaned down and looked across to her.

"I won't be no trouble, Miss. I can talk a mean streak or shut up. Whatever you like. I've been up to Auckland, trying to find a better job for myself, but didn't have any luck. I've walked the last ten kilometers and I'm wore out."

"If we put my two suitcases on top of each other, he could fit back there," I suggested.

"All right," Maggie said with a shrug.

"Thank you both," Neville said with a big grin.

I rearranged the suitcases as he walked around to the other side of the car.

"Might be a good idea," Maggie said as she put the file away. "Part of getting to know the country."

She got out and let Neville into the backseat. We chatted for a few minutes while we waited for the endless line of sheep to cross in front of us. Maggie told him that we were tourists and had just two weeks to see New Zealand. Neville made a few recommendations of sights we shouldn't miss and we said we would take his advice. Finally the last of the sheep crossed and we started out again.

"I work the night shift myself," I said as I went through the gears.

"Do ya, now?" Neville said from the back seat. "Bloody hell, isn't it? I never have gotten used to it. I've lost ten pounds and feel like I'm in a fog all the time."

"I know what you mean."

"Ever work at night, Miss?" Neville asked Maggie.

"No," Maggie said. "I'm not too fond of working during the day, either."

"I hear ya," Neville replied. "My mates and I have decided that work mostly interferes with living."

"That's a good way of putting it," Maggie said with a laugh.

"What would you do if you didn't work?" I asked him.

"Improve myself. Get better educated. Travel some. It's a big, beautiful world and I probably won't see any of it."

"You never know," I said. "I never thought I'd get to New Zealand, but here I am."

"That's why I was up in Auckland. I can't see myself sawing trees for the rest of my life. I had an interview to work in one of the big hardware stores up there. You see, I know my tools and my plumbing and carpentry. I'd like to manage a hardware store. I reckon I'd be good at that."

"You want some advice?" Maggie asked.

"You know the hardware business?" Neville asked back.

"No. I just know about getting what you want. Those things apply to any business."

"You're right about that," Neville said seriously.

"If you want a job in a hardware store in Auckland, then pack your bags and go there. Don't stick your toe in the pool to see how the water feels. Go down to the deep end and jump in. Success belongs to the people who know how to take what they want."

"Take it, Miss?"

"Aren't there a lot of men in Auckland right now who have jobs in hardware stores?"

"Sure enough."

"Well, those men have what you want. You have to go up there and take it."

"How do I do that?"

"That's what you have to figure out. That's how you have to be smarter than the other guy. You have to go up to Auckland, knowing that when you get there, you'll come up with the answers."

"Pardon my saying it, Miss, but that sounds a bit risky to me. I might end up living on the street."

"As long as you think like that, you might as well stay where you are," Maggie said harshly.

"Aren't you being a little rough on the guy?" I asked.

"No, don't worry about that," Neville put in quickly. "She's given me something to think about. Maybe I'm being too cautious.''

"Exactly," Maggie said.

Nobody said anything for a while. I turned on the radio and we listened to a debate about letting nuclear-powered ships into New Zealand harbors. I noticed that the country around us was changing from rolling green hills to mile after mile of pine trees. Every once in a while, there would be a dirt road leading back into the trees. At one of the dirt roads, Neville asked us to pull over and he got out of the car. He thanked us for the ride and then turned and walked off into the pine forest. His walk looked rather sad. I pulled out onto the highway and noticed that Maggie was looking back toward Neville.

"The very simple dream of managing a hardware store and he'll probably never get it," Maggie said.

"How do you know?" I asked.

"Because he's at least thirty-five years old and the thought of really going after what you want is a new idea."

"You can be a tough one," I said.

"No, he's a soft one. People like him make me want to puke."

"He's just some guy."

"That's right," Maggie agreed. "Just another schmuck. The world is full of them."

"I guess you don't figure on the meek inheriting the earth," I suggested.

"Give me a break," she replied.

"I'm not that different from him."

"Come on, Warren, you're not like him at all. I've seen you in action. You may not want to admit it, but you've got the tiger in you. Once you taste the meat, it's hard to go back to being one of the sheep."

"What about you? You said this was the last one."

"Maybe it is and maybe it isn't. But you can bet I'll always have my eyes open. Like the thing in Fiji. If some woman is dumb enough to travel around with a diamond bracelet worth sixteen thousand dollars, then I'm going to take it from her."

"A few days ago you were talking about the law of averages. Don't you think that sooner or later you'll make a mistake? That someone like Willem will catch up with you?"

"Who knows? I'm on a new trail now and I can't think like that."

"Well, I believe in the law of averages. I figure that every deal I pull off brings me closer to the one that doesn't work. The one with the very high price."

"Please, don't think like that, Warren. At least not for the next few months. If you start to worry, I want you to think about one thing and forget about everything else."

"What's that?"

"The money. We're here for the money. Lots of money— that will make your life a whole lot easier. Whatever you do, don't forget that."

"I won't," I said quietly.

"Good."

She got the file out again and started going over the information with me. We did that for about half an hour, then Maggie lifted her head out of the file and looked over at me.

"I've got an idea," she said. "Stop at the next place where we can pick up a newspaper."

We stopped at the next café and got a newspaper from the machine out front. While we were there, we decided to go in and have something to eat. We both ordered some pie and coffee and then sat down at a table near the front window. Maggie read the paper and I stared through the window at a distant snow-covered mountain. The mountain stood all by itself off to the west and was perfectly shaped. I stared at it and tried to imagine a nice, clean stream bouncing down the rocks. I was feeling a great urge to just go somewhere and listen to something pure.

"Good," Maggie said as she put the newspaper down and started in on her pie. "Parliament is in session. We'll get to Wellington tonight and go visit the Parliament building tomorrow. Maybe we can get in and watch for a while. It might be interesting to watch the old man in action. You never know what you might pick up from something like that."

"Like father, like son?" I asked.

"Maybe. It might be educational to see Papa under pressure."

"Sounds interesting," I said, still staring off at the mountain.

"Look, Warren," Maggie said as she reached over and touched my hand. "I'm sorry if I seem so hard. I'm sorry if you don't like it. I'm using these few days to get my game face on. I'm slipping into neutral. I suggest that you do the same. This is no time for philosophy class. You're in, so get in. Don't ever stop thinking about the money."

"All right," I said, and I looked over at her and smiled.

We drove on to Wellington and got a room for the night. The next morning we got up early and went to the Parliament building. There was a line to get in, but after an hour we got a couple of seats in the gallery.

I could tell that this was no ordinary day. There were a lot of reporters present, and the air was full of tension. Just like the people on the radio, they were debating about the visitation rights of nuclear-powered ships. Our man was not doing very well. Members from the opposition were shouting him down and the support from his own party was not enthusiastic. But our Mr. Newton never shirked. He took the shouts and arguments in stride. He answered clearly and with a conviction that I had to admire. Despite the grave situation he was in, he still had an air of dignity and intelligence that could be felt all the way up in the gallery.

"If the son is half the man the father is, we're going to have to stay on our toes," Maggie whispered to me as we got up to leave.

"Maybe we got lucky," I replied. "An issue like this might keep old Dad occupied for a while. Maybe he won't have time to go home."

"I hope you're right," Maggie said. "I'd be very happy to never meet him."

We drove down to the harbor and booked onto the ferry over to South Island. We had to wait a couple of hours for the next boat, so we parked the car in line and went for a walk around the harbor. It was a nice, clear spring day, but there was a steady wind blowing. Maggie's cheeks soon had a rosy glow. She had on a pair of tight jeans and a very attractive sweater.

"Maggie, can I do a little experiment?" I asked.

"What kind of experiment?"

"I want to watch men react to you."

"What?"

"Just walk ahead of me. I want to hang back and see what happens."

Maggie shrugged her shoulders and kept walking as I stood still and watched her go. When she was about fifty feet in front of me, I started to follow. The results were amazing. I watched every man that approached from the opposite direction. The reaction was always the same. At first they stared at her and then they stole glances as often as they thought they could get away with it. About half the men turned after she had passed and had a look at her going away.

I guess I'd been wondering about Maggie's ability to roll into a strange city and instantly get the attention of the man she had picked out. There were a lot of things that might be in doubt about our mission to Christchurch. However, there was one thing that could never be in doubt, and that was Maggie's allure.

After a while, she stopped walking, leaned against the railing and looked out over the water. As I caught up with her, she turned and gave me a big smile.

"So?" she asked as I got close.

"Do you feel it, Maggie? Do you feel the way men look at you?"

"Sure," she said, and her smile got bigger. "You know, Stuart did the same thing when he was thinking of hiring me. I walked around the streets of Des Moines and he followed."

"I bet that was the day you got the job."

"That's right. Do you feel better now?"

"Yes."

"Good."

"Do you like that kind of attention?" I asked.

"I more than like it. I depend on it."

"So I guess it's true, that beautiful women get whatever they want."

"That's right, Warren," Maggie said as she put her arm through mine. "Everything but younger."

Chapter Nine

When we got back to the dock, we saw that a circus had
pulled in right behind our car. They were waiting to cross
to South Island, just like we were. It wasn't a very big
circus—about eight trucks in all. One of the trucks had a
hole in the roof, from which extended the long neck of a
giraffe.

"Do you think riding a ferry with a giraffe is good luck
or anything like that?" Maggie asked.

"Better be," I said with a laugh.

Maggie and I walked along the line of trucks and looked
at the animals and the people. There was a woman, dressed
very much like a gypsy, down by the last truck. She had a
table set up and was moving shells around with lightning-
fast hands. Several people were betting on where the pea
was. We went down and watched for a while. The gypsy
woman asked Maggie if she wanted to play, but Maggie
just smiled at her. The woman gave Maggie a long look and
then smiled herself.

"Comrades in arms," Maggie whispered to me.

"In a way," I whispered back.

"Yup. No sense sitting in the truck when there are suckers with money all around you."

The ferry docked and the cars started loading fifteen minutes later. After we got our car on, we went upstairs to the café and each got a cup of tea. The crew from the circus were at one end of the room making a lot of noise. The gypsy woman sat off by herself, flipping through a deck of cards.

"Let's go see if she'll read our fortunes," Maggie said. "It'll be fun."

We walked over and stood next to the table where the woman sat. She looked up at Maggie and smiled again.

"Well, sister, do you want your fortune read?" the gypsy asked.

"Sure," Maggie said as she reached into her wallet and put a ten-dollar bill on the table.

"Do you want him to hear?" the gypsy asked, looking over at me.

"Why not?" Maggie said as we both sat down.

The gypsy lady had Maggie shuffle the cards and then laid seven of them on the table. We all stared at the cards for about thirty seconds. After that, the gypsy gathered them up and had Maggie do it again. We studied the cards once more and then the gypsy asked to see Maggie's left hand. After rubbing the hand with her thumb and studying it for a full two minutes, she sat back and looked at us both.

"What are you two?" she asked.

"What do you mean?" Maggie asked back.

"I think you are lovers, but yet you are rivals. It is very strange."

"We are lovers," Maggie said quickly.

"Of convenience."

"You might say that," Maggie agreed.

"Why is it so convenient?" the woman asked.

"Business," Maggie said with a shrug.

"Monkey business, I'd say," the gypsy muttered as she looked back down at the cards.

"Why would you say that?" Maggie asked with an offended air.

"Because I think you are me twenty years ago."

I saw a shiver run through Maggie as she sat straight up in her chair. Nobody said anything for a few seconds, and then the gypsy looked over at me.

"Are you sure you want him to hear this?" she asked.

"Warren, go take a walk around the deck," Maggie said without looking at me.

I took my tea, went out, and looked at the water and receding North Island. Every once in a while, I turned and looked through the windows into the café. The two of them were always in serious conversation. One time they both sensed my staring. They turned at the exact same moment and looked at me. I quickly went back to studying the water. Soon after that the wind came up, so I went back inside. I bought a newspaper and read it. I decided to keep my back to the two of them so I wouldn't be tempted to stare. Half an hour later, Maggie came and sat down next to me.

"You certainly got your money's worth," I said.

"It's a shame a woman like that has to do shell games on the dock to make a living. She has an amazing talent."

"So tell me, what did she say?"

"Well, a lot of it wouldn't make any sense to you, but one part would."

"Yeah?"

"Willem. She didn't mention him by name, but that's who she was talking about."

"What did she say about him?"

"That he is very determined. That he will turn up again."

"That's not exactly good news."

"It isn't news at all, Warren. It's the musings of a circus ripoff artist. I wouldn't worry too much about what she says."

"She was an amazing talent a moment ago."

"I exaggerated."

"That's why you spent a half hour talking to her."

"It was an amusement."

"Sure drained your rosy cheeks. You're awfully pale for someone who just had a good time."

"Come on, future scientist. Don't make such a big deal out of a bunch of hocus-pocus. She's a little spooky, that's all."

"I'll say."

"If by some chance we run into Willem, we will handle it. We'll outsmart him again and that's all there is to it."

Maggie looked at me and shrugged her shoulders. After a few minutes of sitting in silence, we went out and walked around the deck. When South Island appeared on the horizon, we went up front and watched the land come into view. After we docked, we drove off the ferry and headed down the east coast toward Christchurch. As we pulled away, I looked in the rearview mirror and saw the truck with the giraffe sticking out of it fall into line with the other circus trucks. The gypsy was looking out of the truck's window and watching us as we drove away.

The road down the east coast started off dramatically. The ocean was on our left and a range of fairly large mountains were on the right. The road traveled on the green plain between the two. We went through several small towns that seemed to be made up of farms and fishing boats.

"Reminds me of Ireland," Maggie said as she gazed out the window.

"Never been there," I said.

"It's like this in the spring. Everything is so green and fresh. Makes you want to settle down and start a family."

"You?" I asked.

"Not really, but it's a nice feeling. Believe me, I'd make a lousy mother, I know that much. It's a job I'm totally unsuited for. What about you? Think you'll ever be a dad?"

"Yeah, I think I'll have kids some day," I said. "Find me a nice Nordic type with big hips. Have her shoot me out a couple of little Warrens."

"How romantic. I can see you and the nippers out looking for bugs together."

"Sure. We could have our vacations in the Everglades. We'd have a hell of a good time."

"What if you have daughters?"

"Who knows, they might like bugs. There are lots of female entomologists."

"True," Maggie agreed.

"I'll tell you what, if I have a daughter, maybe I'll name her after you. Margaret Allison, how does that sound?"

"Fine, just don't call her Peggy."

"I never understood that one," I said. "How did they ever get Peggy from Margaret?"

"I don't know, but they tried to brand me with that name when I was a kid. Then I saw Elizabeth Taylor in *Cat on a Hot Tin Roof*. She was Maggie and she was beautiful. After that, I insisted that everyone call me Maggie. It took awhile to train them, but I stuck with it."

"I would have never gotten away with something like that. I hated Warren. But I was Warren Junior, so being critical of my name was dangerous territory."

"Where were you from originally?" Maggie asked. "I don't remember if you ever told me."

"I'm from the third-largest city in Nebraska," I said seriously.

"Which is?"

"Grand Island. Don't tell me you've never heard of it."

"I've heard of it. I just didn't know it was ranked up there with Omaha and Lincoln."

"Well, it is and we're mighty proud of it."

"I can see that," Maggie said with a laugh. "What does Warren Senior do?"

"He's a supervisor in an onion ring factory."

"You're kidding."

"Absolutely not. As a matter of fact, that's where he met my mother. He was the supervisor and she worked the line. They fell in love over the onion rings and produced three wonderful children. Mom went back to work a couple of years ago. Now she drives a forklift. She loads boxes of onion rings into trucks all day. I did the same job myself one summer. I think it's what drove me to a life of crime."

"I guess I never thought of people getting up every day and going to make onion rings."

"Sure. There's production quotas, quality control, bonus programs. Just like anywhere else."

"Amazing," Maggie said, shaking her head.

"Ever see me eat an onion ring?"

"Not that I recall."

"Believe me, you never will. Just the sight of those things can send me into shock."

"Just think of it," Maggie said as she gazed out the window at the beautiful scenery. "There are people who spend their days making potato chips, jelly beans, pretzels, things like that."

"What about goobers? You know, those chocolate covered peanuts? How'd you like to tell people you make goobers for a living?"

"I eat them all the time at the movies," Maggie said.

"There you go. You're a supporter of the goober industry."

"I don't know how they do it," Maggie said.

She let out a big sigh, leaned back and closed her eyes. After a while, I could hear the steady breathing that told me she had dozed off. I quietly hummed old rock tunes to pass the time. When Maggie woke from her nap, she rolled down the window to get some fresh air. She tried to stretch out her arms and legs, but the car was too small.

"Let's stop somewhere and go for a short walk," she said with a yawn.

After a few minutes, we came to a sign that said, "KAI-KOURA BIRD SANCTUARY, 5 KILOMETERS."

"How'd you like to walk around a bird sanctuary?" I asked.

"Sounds nice," Maggie said as she yawned again.

We came to the turnoff and drove down a one-lane road toward the sea. After about a mile, there was a small parking lot and I pulled the car in. At the end of the parking lot, there was a sign that directed us down a path to the sanctuary. We walked down the path and after about a hundred yards, we became aware of a noise that sounded like a bird riot. We walked around a huge boulder by the edge of the sea, and the screeching got even louder. After we went around another point of land, we came to the birds. Just a few yards offshore, there was a rocky island about the size of a football field. The island was literally covered with birds. There were thousands of them and it did look like there was some kind of riot going on. When we got closer, it became obvious that it wasn't a riot at all. It was a gigantic bird orgy.

"Jesus, they're all screwing," Maggie said as we got closer.

"Or trying to," I added.

"Males fighting over females," Maggie said. "How delightful."

"Hey, it is springtime," I replied. "You know what bird-ies do in the springtime."

We stood and watched for a few minutes. It was hard to believe there was any actual mating going on. As soon as one of the males was able to climb aboard a female, another male would come along and try to chase him off. The two males would then fly at each other. After a couple of charges, one of the males would retreat and the winner would go back to his reward. He'd no sooner get in position than another male would come along and the whole thing would start all over again. It looked as if the only males who were getting laid were the ones who could screw in about a second.

"Let's get closer," Maggie said.

"Maybe we should go down there and show them how it's done," I suggested.

We walked down to the edge of the rocks. As soon as we got down by the water, something happened in the bird colony. A great deal of the noise stopped, and about a thousand heads turned to look at us. A few seconds later, dozens of birds took off and flew right at us.

"Let's get out of here," I said as I grabbed Maggie's hand and turned to run up the trail.

Birds immediately started diving for our heads. We had to duck and run at the same time. Some of the braver ones got low enough to peck at us. Maggie screamed when one of them got her on the back of the neck. We were trying our best to get away, but the rocky footing made it difficult. The attacks let up for a moment, and then a whole new flock descended on us. The new wave did not swoop down and try to peck at us. They were content to fly over and shit on us. There was a steady line of birds coming off the island, and every one of them took a dump when it got over us. Maggie was swearing a blue streak, but I thought it wiser to keep my mouth shut. When we finally ran back around the big boulder, the birds flew back to their orgy. When we realized they we gone, we stopped and looked at each other.

"Shit!" Maggie screamed.

"That's what it is," I said dryly.

When I looked at Maggie, I couldn't help but laugh. She was covered with the stuff. It was dripping off her hair and onto her shoulders. It was running down her cheeks and all over the back of her neck.

"Better keep your mouth closed," I said as Maggie started to laugh.

"You should see yourself," she howled as she covered her mouth with her hand.

We started walking again, but had trouble not looking at each other and laughing.

"Those birds sure do like their privacy," Maggie said.

When we came to the parking lot, there was a small truck parked near our car. A man in a brown uniform was doing some work on one of the fences. He took a look at us and a big grin grew on his face. He put his tools down and walked over to us.

"Got a good close look, did ya?" he asked seriously.

"Does this happen a lot?" Maggie asked.

"Ah, yeah. This time of year, it happens nearly every day."

"Ever think of putting up a sign?" I suggested.

"Nope. We love sending them Aussies and Poms down there for a good close look. Helps break up the boredom. I kind of like you Yanks, though. I would have warned ya if I'd seen ya. You are Yanks, aren't ya?"

"Yeah," I replied.

"What do people in our situation usually do?" Maggie asked.

"Generally, they take the other path there up to the campground. They pay my wife a dollar each and then they get to use the hot showers we have for the campers. After that, they often like to go back down by the sanctuary and watch some other poor sods get the whitewash."

"The shower part sounds real good," I said as Maggie and I started walking over to our car.

We each got a change of clothes and lots of soap and shampoo out of our suitcases. We walked up the path toward the campground as the hot sun started to cake and dry the bird shit.

"Lovely custom, don't you think?" I said in my best English accent.

"Want to save a dollar on the showers?" Maggie asked with a twinkle in her eye.

"I don't know if Mrs. Forest Ranger is going to go for that," I said.

"So what," Maggie replied.

"Maggie, these are probably public restrooms. You know, ladies' room, men's room."

"Warren, we've been shit on!" Maggie said, as if that should end all objections.

We came to the campground and sure enough, there were a couple of green buildings underneath the trees. One was for men and the other for women. There was a small house at the other end of the campground with "OFFICE" painted on the wall near the door. Maggie and I walked over and knocked on the door. A woman soon appeared and immediately broke into a big smile when she saw us.

"You'll be wanting a couple of showers, I suppose," the woman said.

"No, not a couple of them," Maggie said as she handed her a dollar. "One will do just fine."

The woman stood there with her mouth hanging open as Maggie grabbed my hand and walked away. Maggie went to the building marked for men. I went in and looked around and then came back out and told her that the coast was clear. As I went into the building, I saw Mrs. Forest Ranger come out of her house and head down the path toward the parking lot. I went in and put my stuff on the floor near one of the sinks and then ran some water to wash my face. When I lifted my face out of the towel, Maggie was standing there without a stitch on. It was quite a sight to see. There was all that beautifully tanned skin and all that bird shit on top of it. I quickly got undressed and we both stood there nude, looking at ourselves in the mirror. After having a good laugh, we walked over to one of the showers and got in.

"You wash me and I'll wash you," Maggie said as she squeezed out some shampoo.

So, we scrubbed each other down. Though the bird shit was mostly on her head and neck, I made sure I washed every inch of her. She did the same and even gave me some special attention in the best of places. By the time the scrubbing was over, I was very turned-on. Maggie got out of the shower first, and when I came out, she was sitting on one of the sinks.

"Let's pretend we're birdies," she said as she gave me a wink.

I walked over to her and she wrapped her legs around my hips. Pretty soon she was rocking back and forth on the sink and making those sweet little moans that I loved so much. Just when her moans were starting to increase in volume, a voice came in through the window.

"You oughtin' to be doing that in there," said Mr. Forest Ranger. "It really isn't decent, you know."

"If your birds can shit on our heads, then we can fuck in your bathroom!" Maggie screamed without missing a beat.

I started to laugh, but didn't get much of a chance because Maggie put her arms around my neck and moved off the sink. The next thing I knew, I was standing there holding her as she started screaming at the top of her lungs. I was having trouble holding her, so I slowly backed up and leaned against the wall. When I fell out, she screamed as if she'd been robbed. When we got everything back into place, Maggie finished off with a crescendo that left my ears ringing.

"Yanks," the ranger muttered from outside the window.

"Stayed to listen, didn't you?" Maggie shouted at him. "The Mrs., too, I bet."

With that, we heard the two of them turn and walk away. Maggie and I both laughed at the same time.

"That was wonderful," she whispered in my ear.

"I think we should stop here on the way back," I suggested.

"That would be nice," she said as we got unwrapped "But we'll probably be in a bit of a rush at that point."

"That's right," I said, picking up my towel. "If all goes as planned, we'll be on the run."

"That reminds me: one of the first things we have to do

when we get to Christchurch is find out how to get out of there in a hurry. Trains, bus stations, all of that.''

"Aren't we going to keep the car?''

"Probably, or get another one. It's usually not a good idea to leave town in the same car you've been using.''

"Makes sense," I agreed.

"When I'm working alone, I sometimes avoid having a car. Makes me sort of helpless. Always needing a ride, if you know what I mean.''

"Man, these guys don't have a chance, do they?''

"I hope not," Maggie said with a smile. "Remember, when it's time to run, we shouldn't do anything that's logical. When I left South Africa, I flew to Calcutta first. They were right on my tail coming down-country, but I swung to the left instead of the right. They were probably scouting every plane that left for America.''

I finished dressing before Maggie and watched her as she buttoned up her blouse. She went over to the mirror and brushed out her hair. When I saw her reflection, I knew something was different. I got the feeling that this fling in the bathroom was going to be it for a while. Maggie caught me staring at her reflection. She put her brush down, turned around, and looked me in the eye.

"We're almost there, Warren. We're at the beginning of the hunt. We've had a good time, but now it's business.''

"Into neutral, right?''

"You got it," she said as she turned back to the mirror.

Chapter Ten

We got to Christchurch in the late afternoon and found ourselves caught up in the homeward-bound traffic. Five minutes after we were in the city, a police car pulled up next to us. One of the cops motioned for Maggie to put her seat belt on. She smiled and did as she was instructed. After the police car pulled away, Maggie had a few choice words for the backs of their heads.

Even though there were a lot of cars on the road, there was still something about the city that was calm and pastoral. The late-afternoon sun slanted down through the trees and gave everything a golden glow. There were flowers everywhere and it truly smelled like spring. A lot of people were on bicycles and many more were walking. The first street we rode down had the name Durham Avenue. It ran beside the Avon River. The river was covered with ducks and surrounded by willow trees.

"This is more England than England," Maggie said as she looked around.

"So, what's the first thing one does upon entering the city of our conquest?" I asked.

"Buy a good city map," Maggie said, as if it were the most obvious thing in the world. "Then a hotel. After that, a good meal and then plan for tomorrow."

We stopped at a bookstore and bought a detailed map of the city. After that, we rode around looking for a reasonable place to stay and settled on the Strathern Motor Court. We booked in for three nights and then went for a walk, looking for a place to eat. We walked toward the city center and came to Cathedral Square. The square was ringed with office buildings and restaurants. We picked a place called the Coachman Inn and sat down to a couple of New Zealand steaks. The booths were very private, and as soon as the meat came, Maggie got down to business.

"Warren, I'm going to spend tomorrow in the library. You can take me there in the morning and pick me up in the afternoon. You've got two jobs to do tomorrow. First, get to know the city. Study the map. Then ride around and look at the street names. When that's done, I want you to get a look at our guy. I don't want you to do much more than that. You need to be able to point him out to me. If you want to follow him for a little bit, that's all right, but keep it loose. We will make a lot of decisions in the next few weeks. We may want him to get to know you and we may not. We need to keep our options open. See what kind of car he drives. If you happen to see where he works or lives, all the better. We don't need to rush this. Just some general information to start off with."

"I'm a little nervous about following somebody," I said. "If I get spotted, I could really blow it."

"So solve the problem, Warren. When you're riding around exploring the city, pick out some people and then follow them. Do it in the car and then get out and follow them on foot. Get a feel for it. Sharpen your alertness. Buy a couple of hats and bring a few different shirts so you can change your look."

"All right," I said meekly.

"Another thing we have to start thinking about is our living arrangements. There's no harm in us staying in the same room for the next three nights, but that will have to be the end of it. You can see why that's necessary."

"I don't like it, but yeah, I understand."

"While you're riding around for the next few days, keep an eye out for a place to live. Sometimes it's good to get a place near a university. Kind of get swallowed up by the college crowd. Even pretend you're a student. I've done that several times. Also, when you get a place, make sure you have your own phone. You and I will need to have private conversations. We'll also need a place where we can meet and talk. A little bar or restaurant—one that's not too popular and preferably rather dark."

"I'm going to be busy," I said.

"This is just the beginning. Sometimes there's a lot to do and other times you just have to wait around. It gets like war. Lots of boredom and then some quick action."

"I'll find a good book to read."

"Sure, study up on your bugs," Maggie said with a smile.

"Maybe I will," I replied.

"Another thing is our names. Stuart is working up some stuff for us. Passports, immunization books, everything we'll need. He'll overnight them to us as soon as I give him an address."

"Do we get new names?"

"Yeah, the ones I used with that Neville character. I'm Susan and you'll be Thomas."

We finished our meal and walked back to the hotel under a lovely night sky. Though there were cars going by and people on the sidewalks, the city still had a very quiet feel to it. I looked up and noticed that the stars were different. I had learned many of the constellations' names when I was younger. It was my earliest draw to something scientific, I guess. Now, all those names were useless. I was in a whole new hemisphere.

When we got back to the hotel, we settled into our separate beds and watched reruns of American TV shows. I fell asleep around eleven, during an episode of *MASH*.

The next morning we were on the road by nine o'clock. I dropped Maggie—or Susan, as I was supposed to call her—at the library. Then I went on a tour of the city. I drove down streets with names like Litchfield and Gloucester. I could tell that the city had been well planned and I quickly got a feel for how it was laid out. I found the bus station and the train station. Even went for a ride out to the airport. I looked on the map and found Canterbury University over in an area called Ilam. I drove there and parked near some apartment buildings just off the campus. There was a red building that looked like it would be just the thing for the students. There was a guy with long hair sitting on one of the stoops, so I got out of the car and walked over to him.

"Hello," he said as I got close.

"Hello," I said back. "I'm looking for a place to stay for a few months. Don't suppose you know if there's anything available in this building?"

"Yank, are ya?"

"That's right."

"What brings you to Christchurch?"

"Oh, I've been traveling for a while. Did North Island and came down the east coast of South Island. Thought it might be nice to stay put for a few months. Get to know a place, instead of just passing through all the time. Might even take a course or two at the university."

"Sounds like a nice life," he said.

"It is," I said with a smile. "I'm Thomas."

"Robert here," he said as we shook hands.

"Know of any vacant apartments, Robert?"

"Nope, place is full up," he said with a shake of his head.

"Too bad."

"Now if you don't mind being somebody's roommate, there might be something for ya."

"I wouldn't mind that," I said. "Who's the person?"

"Fact is," Robert said with a smile. "I don't know if I should offer one of you Yanks such an opportunity."

"I'm a good Yank," I said, matching his smile.

"Her name is Edith. She lives on the second floor. Room two oh six, I believe. Her boyfriend went off to England recently and I know she's having trouble paying the rent. She's probably looking for a woman, but you might try your luck."

"Second floor, you say?" I looked up at the building.

"That's right. Up the stairs, first landing, turn to your right."

"Thanks."

"No worries, mate. I guess I should warn you about something."

"What's that?"

"She's a bloody genius. They can be difficult to live with."

"Might be interesting," I said with a shrug.

"I also know she's not there right now. Saw her go off to class about twenty minutes ago. I'd say come back around five. If you hear piano music, knock real loud."

"Thanks for the tip," I said as I turned to go back to the car.

Just as I was starting the engine, a car passed me with a very heavy woman behind the wheel. I decided to follow her for a bit and see how I did. At first, I followed right behind her. Then I let a couple of cars get between us and I practiced keeping an eye on her. When there were two lanes on my side, I pulled up and actually passed her. I sort of followed her from up front. When she pulled into the parking lot of a department store, I came around the block and found her getting out of her car. I put my baseball cap on and proceeded to follow her through the store. She bought

a bunch of baby stuff and when she pulled out of the parking
lot, I was two cars behind her. I followed her all the way
to what I presumed was her home. I didn't have the least
bit of trouble. Then I followed a man who seemed to be in
a terrible rush. He ended up at a bank, and I even went in
behind him and listened to him argue with the manager. After
that, I parked the car near Cathedral Square and followed a
few people on foot. After lunch, I went to a phone booth
and called the car dealership where Peter Newton kept his
office. I asked for him and was told that he was in a meeting.
I declined to leave a message. I got back in the car and then
drove over to the dealership. It wasn't too hard to figure out
where the employees parked, and I guessed that the Italian
sports car in the number one spot belonged to our boy. I
parked down the street at a spot where I could just see the
corner of the car. It seemed very logical that it was his car,
but I wanted to be sure. So I walked to a phone booth and
called the office again. The woman who answered the phone
said that Mr. Newton was still in a meeting. I told her I was
a car collector and wanted to talk to Mr. Newton about buying his Maserati. The woman just laughed.

"He waited over a year and a half for that car," she said.
"You'll never get him to part with it."

"Sounds like true love," I said.

"Believe me, it is," she replied.

"Thanks for the advice," I said, and I hung up.

I was feeling very clever as I went back and sat in my
car again. I sat there and stared at the back of his Maserati
for nearly two hours. Then, just as I was about to doze off,
I saw the taillights brighten as someone stepped on the
brakes. I got my first glimpse of our boy as he backed the
car out and then headed down the street. I let him get a
good lead and then went after him. He drove about three
miles to an old brick building with a large field behind it.
Above the door was a sign that said "CHRISTCHURCH
CRICKET CLUB." I pulled around to where I could see the

building from the side and ten minutes later, Peter Newton ran out the back door and onto the cricket field. I could tell it was practice and that everyone was glad to see him.

The cricket field wasn't fenced in, so I got out of the car and strolled onto the grounds. I wanted to get closer and get a good look at our boy, but I didn't dare at this point. I stayed up by the trees and watched from a distance. He was tall and thin with very light brown hair. I didn't imagine that Maggie would have any trouble finding him attractive. Or at least, it wouldn't be difficult to pretend.

As the practice went on, several people set up lawn chairs just down from where I was standing. They sat down and began to shout encouragement to the players. I moved down a little closer and heard some of them talking about a big match tomorrow with the team from Dunedin. I walked over and asked one of the spectators what time the match started, and he told me ten in the morning. I knew right away that this would be the perfect opportunity for Maggie to get a first look at her victim. We'd come back tomorrow and blend in with the crowd.

After watching them practice for another half hour, I headed back to Ilam to see if I couldn't secure a place to live. When I got to the old red building, I went up to the second floor and knocked on the door for room 206. There wasn't any piano music, so I did a nice, soft knock. After a few seconds, a woman I guessed was Edith opened the door.

"Edith?" I asked.

"Yes. Who are you?"

"Thomas. I understand you might be looking for a room-mate."

"Ah, yes, Robert told me about you."

"That's right."

"A Yank at that," she said with a sly smile.

"I'm a good Yank," I said quickly.

"That's what Robert said. Come in and sit down. We'll have a cupper and see if this might work out."

She led me into the living room and I sat on an old sofa while she went into the kitchen and started the tea.

Edith looked to be someone who didn't get out in the sun much. Her face was very pale and her dark hair made her look even paler. I could have sworn I saw purple highlights in her hair. Just a quick purple shimmer as she walked past the light. The piano was across the room from where I was sitting. It looked well used. The keys were yellow and music sheets were spread all over its top.

She came back into the living room carrying two teacups. She pulled the piano bench over in front of the couch and placed the cups on it.

"Water will be ready shortly," she said as she sat down.

The sunlight was coming through the window onto the couch. When she sat in the light, I could plainly see that her hair was, in fact, dark purple.

"Do you like my hair?" she asked when she saw me looking. "Purple's my color."

"It suits you," I said.

"Everyone says it goes well with my white skin. I suppose it does."

"Robert says you're a genius."

"That's what they all like to say about me these days. It's because I write music. I've had a few pieces performed at the university. It's quite the rage just now to say that Edith is a genius. I'm sure they'll get on to something else before too long."

"I guess whoever lives here had better like piano music," I suggested.

"Yes, I play a lot," she replied as she gave me a serious look. "The truth is, I've never roomed with a man before, unless there was something special between us."

"I assure you that I'm harmless," I said with a laugh.

"Oh, it's not that, so much. It's more a privacy thing.

It's the idea that I have to give that up. But I must sooner or later, or I'll have no place to live at all."

While the tea was steeping she showed me around the apartment. There really wasn't that much to see. Everything was made out of wood and looked to be very old. We'd have to share the bathroom, which I guessed was part of her privacy concerns. The room for rent was the last one down the hall. It was rather small and had an old mattress on the floor.

"That mattress was here when I moved in," Edith said. "You'd be welcome to use it."

We went back and had our tea, and Edith asked me a lot of questions about why I was here and what I was doing. I told her the same lies I had told Robert. I was beginning to wonder if maybe I shouldn't start keeping notes.

In the end, we decided to make a go of it and she went and got me a key. I paid her the first month's rent and said I'd be back with my things the next day. We shook hands at the door as I left to pick up Maggie.

She was waiting outside the library as I pulled up. She didn't look very happy.

"You're late," she said as she got into the car.

"I've had a busy day," I replied. "Followed our boy for a bit. Even discovered an opportunity for you to get a look at him tomorrow. Plus, I found a place to live over near the university."

"I'm impressed," Maggie said. "You got an apartment already?"

"Yes. I'm sharing with a music student."

"How did you meet him?" Maggie asked.

"I just asked around. His name is Edith."

"Your roommate is a woman?" Maggie asked, giving me a funny look.

"Yes. With dark purple hair."

"Warren, you stay clear of her. Don't get involved in her life. You need to stay focused on why we're here."

"I have no intention of getting involved. You said to find a place to live, so I did."

"If she seems at all nosy, get out. We don't need anybody getting suspicious."

"Don't worry. I know what I'm here for."

"Good."

"How did your research go?" I asked after a short, uncomfortable silence.

"I think we may be overly worried about the fact that his father is the prime minister. There's so little crime in this country that they don't even have a special detail for the prime minister's children. Only for special occasions or if there is a threat. From what I can tell, this is one of the safest places a person could live. The crime rate is next to nothing."

"I kind of like that," I said with a shrug.

"I don't," Maggie said quickly.

"Why not?"

"It's creepy. It's like the place has no edge. Nothing to fear."

"There's always us," I said with a laugh.

"Yeah, and we're not exactly a major threat."

"Unless you happen to be Peter Newton," I added.

"I don't know," Maggie said as she shook her head. "I get nervous if a place is too nice."

"What else did you find out?" I asked.

"There are some amazing facts that I came across today, many of which may prove very useful."

"Like what?"

"Remember what I said about rich people liking small objects with great value?"

"Yeah."

"Well, there seems to be a very hot coin collection floating around in the Newton family. Papa Newton cashed some of it in so he could finance his original car deal with the Japanese."

"That's interesting," I said.

"Isn't it, though. Coins are very nice little items to take home with you."

"They can be very valuable," I added.

"The Newton family has five of the seven Old Globe Sovereigns."

"Is that good?"

"It's excellent. Let me tell you what I read today. It seems that back in 1813 the English government started minting a new coin. A golden sovereign. On one side of the coin was a picture of Elizabeth the First. On the other side was a picture of the old Globe Theatre. When the elders of the Church of England found out about it, they protested to the king. They didn't want the government to encourage theater and other such sinful activities. They got them to change the coins, but several hundred had already been put into circulation. The church offered to buy them for twice their value, and then they melted down all those that were turned in. Only seven are known to still be in existence, and the Newton family has five of them."

"How much are they worth?"

"The book said all seven together would be worth about three and a half million."

"Jesus," I muttered.

"The book I was reading is six years old, so who knows what they would be worth now."

"Having five of them would make us rich."

"Yes, it would. Think of it for a minute, Warren. Wouldn't it be something if you and I come all this way, pull this thing off and then fly home with five coins in our pockets. It's so beautiful, it makes me want to cry."

"Makes it easier to get through customs," I said.

"I'm not talking about customs. Stuart has a guy in Chicago for that. I'm talking about the lightness of it. It would be like loose change in our pockets. All this way for something you can hold in the palm of your hand."

I glanced over at Maggie as I was driving. She had that flushed, turned-on look again. It made her look great, and I swear there was a different smell about her. When she caught me looking, she reached over and gently pushed my face back around to the road.

"Watch where you're going," she said.

"It turns you on, doesn't it?" I said. "I mean literally, physically turns you on."

"Yeah, and you moving out so soon."

"There's still tonight," I replied.

"I was just teasing, Thomas," Maggie said, pouncing on my new name. "We're after the mark now. We can't have any of that."

"I think that's a silly rule," I said. "Especially since we've only just got here."

"There is a very good reason for it. You, in your constant state of lust, have probably failed to think of it."

"What good reason?" I asked scornfully.

"Surely you can see, that this whole thing works better if I'm hungry for it. That makes sense, doesn't it?"

"Yeah," I had to agree.

"You, my friend, satisfy me so completely, that it could start interfering with my work."

That was a hard one to argue.

Chapter Eleven

When we got back to our room, I told Maggie all about the cricket match the next day. She liked the idea of going to the match and told me I was doing a good job. After dinner I tried again for one final night of fun, but she would have none of it. I didn't even get a good-night kiss.

We turned in our rental car the next morning. We then went over to a different agency and rented another one. I drove Maggie over to Ilam and showed her the building I would be living in. We looked around the neighborhood and found a Greek restaurant nearby and went there for breakfast. We decided to make the restaurant one of our meeting places.

"If I say we'll meet at The Greek, you'll know what I mean," Maggie said as she spread jam on her bread.

"What do we do when we get to the cricket match?" I asked.

"Just watch. It might be nice to see if our boy has a girlfriend that I have to do battle with."

"We know he's not married, but what if he's in love or just got engaged or something. Then what will you do?"

"Work harder," Maggie replied with a big smile. "I enjoy a good challenge."

"I wish I had your confidence." I shook my head. "So many things have to go just right."

"Believe me, nothing will go just right," Maggie said sternly. "There is no planned route to those coins. We have to pick our way through the maze. We have to make a lot of good, ruthless decisions."

"It's scary," I said. I took a gulp of my coffee. "Maybe we should pick up some binoculars. It might be a good idea to study our boy up close."

"Excellent suggestion. Let's stop and pick up a pair."

"So, do we just sit and watch?" I asked.

"I'll watch him. I want you to walk around and listen to what people are saying. It'll be the prime minister's son out there. People are bound to be talking about him."

"All right," I said. "I don't know much about cricket, but I do know these matches can last all day."

"We'll stay for a couple of hours. Afterward I'd like to go back to the library, and you can go move in with Miss Purple Hair."

"Sure," I said with a big smile.

"One more thing, Thomas."

"Yes, Susan?"

"Very good. There's one more thing that is very important. We are in fact going there only to watch the match. That's the plan for right now. However, you must at all times, be ready to bob and weave. If an opportunity arises, we must be smart enough to see it and seize it."

"Like what?"

"Like anything. The right move, at the right time, could save us weeks of work."

"Say we got extremely lucky and you got to meet him today. What would you tell him about yourself?"

"I've decided to tell him that I'm a recent divorcée. Out spreading my wings after a difficult marriage. I think that might appeal to him. A woman who isn't looking for a husband."

"Why did you come to New Zealand?"

"Been to Europe. Wanted to see something new. Have a friend over in Australia. Decided to see New Zealand as well."

"Better not make yourself too recent a divorcée. A lot of men will shy away from that."

"Good idea. See? That's why I brought you along. You give good bachelor tips."

We finished our breakfast, got into the car, and headed off to the cricket match. We stopped at a sporting goods store and bought some binoculars and a couple of lawn chairs. We parked a few blocks from the club and Maggie walked over by herself. I followed ten minutes later.

The match had already begun and our boy was out in the field scooping up the ball just as I got close enough to see what was going on. I looked to my right and saw Maggie sitting in a chair, studying Peter Newton. My description of him must have been pretty accurate, because I could tell she had the binoculars pointed right at him. I walked around and tried to listen to what people were saying but didn't hear anything of much value. I saw one man sitting by himself who looked to be taking notes. I plopped my chair down next to his.

"Mind if I sit here?" I asked.

"Help yourself," he said as he looked up from his pad.

"Thanks."

"Yank, are ya?"

"Boy, people around here pick that up pretty quick, don't they?"

"Ah, yeah, it's all the shows on the telly. We know a Yank when we hear one."

"All this time I thought you were the ones with the accent."

"Hardly," he said with a laugh. "Do you know cricket?"

"I know it takes all day. That's about all."

"Maybe I can help you out. My name is Adam."

"I'm Thomas," I said as we shook hands.

"I write for the *New Zealand Cricket Monitor.*"

"Really? This must be an important game."

"Match. We call them matches, and actually it is. Important for the standings. Plus, of course, the prime minister's son is playing. That gives it a certain glamour."

"No kidding!" I said. "Which one is he?"

"The one to the left there with the long brown hair. Needs a bit of cutting, I'd say."

"Is he a good player?"

"Yes, quite good. The club would only be average without him."

"So tell me, what's the prime minister's family like?" I asked as casually as I could. "Any juicy scandals?"

"Now, why would you ask that?"

"Just curious."

"The usual things, really. The father's managed to make a few enemies, but then after all, he is the prime minister. Rumor has it that the daughter drinks more than she ought to. That sort of thing. Say, you're not a reporter as well, are you?"

"No," I said quickly.

"Not here looking for dirt, are you?"

"Of course not."

"I'd be careful if I were you. The Newtons are rather like royalty around here. If you're here to stir the shit, I'd say you'd better move on."

"What is this?" I asked. "I'm just a tourist."

"Bloody wonderful," he said rather loudly.

I got up, folded my chair and walked away. The reporter watched me for a second and then went back to his notes. As I walked away, he mumbled something about Yanks and I don't think it was a compliment. I knew I really hadn't gone about that very well. It looked like I was going to have to develop a more subtle style of information gathering.

The back door of the club was open and suddenly a drink sounded really nice. I leaned my chair against a tree and went looking for a beer. The inside of the club looked exactly as I would have expected it to look. Everything was different shades of brown, and there actually were a couple of guys playing chess. I went up to the bar and ordered my first New Zealand beer. When I got my glass, I was impressed with the nice yellow-brown color of the beer. Unfortunately, it was served warm, and that took a lot of the pleasure out of it. I put some change on the bar for a tip, and soon the bartender came back and looked down at the money.

"What's this?" he asked.

"Your tip," I said with a shrug.

"None of that here," he replied as he pushed the money back at me.

"Really?"

"It's not the custom."

"Oh."

He looked me over and walked away. I put my change back in my pocket and took another sip of the warm beer. I had to admit that I wasn't doing too well today. After another long sip, I looked down the bar and saw a sign near the cash register. "KITCHEN HELP/WAITER WANTED," it said. I wondered if I should tell Maggie about that. Might be a great way for her to meet our guy. But the more I thought about it, the less I liked the idea. Prime minister's sons and waitresses probably didn't mix. I finished my beer and went out and watched the match for a while longer. When everybody broke for lunch, I watched for Maggie's signal. She looked at me and then gave me a head flip, which meant it was time to go. She folded up her chair and started walking toward the car. I got my lawn chair, waited a few minutes, and then followed. I found her sitting on a bus bench around the corner.

"So?" she asked.

"Should we talk here?" I said, looking around.

"It's all right. I don't want to sit in the hot car. Just lean on the bench with your back to me."

"Not much to report," I said, as I did as I was told.

"Me neither, except to confirm that he is quite good-looking."

"Makes it easier for you, I suppose."

"You suppose right," Maggie said with a laugh. "I saw you talking to a man for a while. What did he have to say?"

"Not much. When I found out he was a reporter, I made my exit."

"Good move," Maggie said. "You don't want to have anything to do with reporters."

"He did say something about Peter's sister having a drinking problem. Said it was a rumor. Was that in the report?"

"No, but it's a good thing to know. Might be of some use to us."

"After that I went into the bar. I tried to talk to the bartender, but he wasn't very friendly. I also had a very warm beer."

"Oh, yeah, an old English tradition. You'll get used to it."

"I doubt it," I said with a snort.

"Anything else?"

"Not really. The club is looking for someone to wait tables and work in the kitchen. For a moment, I thought that might be a clever way for you to catch his eye. I dismissed the idea though; I doubt that Mr. Fancy Pants would go for a waitress."

"You never know," Maggie said. "But I think it's better to hold off. If I committed to that and you were right, the ball game would be over."

"So, off to the library?" I asked.

"I've certainly had enough cricket for one day. Why don't we get some lunch and then I'll go to the library. You can go ahead and move into your new quarters."

Maggie got up and walked toward the car. I walked along, about ten yards behind her. As we got in the car, she turned and looked over at me.

"I want you to go back to the club and get that job."

"Me?"

"Yes, something about it feels right. He's obviously there a lot and he's got to be talked about by the people who hang out there. Besides, washing a few dishes might do you some good."

"Are you sure? Aren't we moving too fast?"

"No, I don't think so. It's the kind of move we can always back off from."

"I hate waiting tables," I said.

"Too bad," Maggie replied.

"Damn it!" I got out of the car and walked back toward the club.

The bartender was washing glasses when I came back in. He looked up and gave me a very small smile.

"Another beer, Yank?" he asked.

"No, actually, I was wondering about that job," I said as I pointed at the sign. "I'd like to apply."

"You going to be around for a while?"

"Yeah, I'm taking some night courses over at the university."

"You got a work permit?"

"Not exactly, but I'm a student. Doesn't that make it all right?"

"Haven't a clue," he said with a shrug. "There's no application. You just have to pass the Charlie test."

"Charlie?"

"The cook. You'd really be working for him. You wash his pots and serve his food. Go through the doors there and tell him you want the job. If he likes you, you're on."

I went through a pair of swinging doors and into a pretty good-sized kitchen. A small man with white hair was working a piece of beef back and forth on the slicing machine.

"Charlie?" I asked.

"That's right. Who might you be?"

"Thomas, your new helper."

"Is that a fact?"

"I'm a good worker and I can start tomorrow."

"Ever waited table?"

"Sure."

"Don't mind scrubbing pots and washing dishes?"

"No."

"You're a Yank, ain't ya?" he said after a second.

"That's right," I said with a sigh.

"Well, I kind of like the idea of ordering one of you Yanks around," Charlie said with a big grin. "I might just give you a go."

"I hope you will."

"We'll try you tomorrow. Be here at eight sharp and look nice. You'll get four dollars an hour and a meal for every four hours worked. Got it?"

"Got it."

"See ya tomorrow, Yank," Charlie said as he went back to slicing the meat.

I turned and walked out of the kitchen. As I walked past the bar, the bartender gave me a questioning look.

"See you tomorrow at eight," I said.

"Charlie don't like Yanks, you know," he whispered.

"I'll survive."

"Good on ya," he said with his first real smile.

I walked back to the car and got in. Maggie watched me start the car and then turned and looked out the front window.

"You got it, didn't you?" she said.

"Yeah. Working for a man who doesn't like Americans."

"Well, they get on my nerves sometimes, too," Maggie said with a smirk.

Chapter Twelve

Maggie was right about always having a sleeping bag. That's what I was thinking as I rolled mine out on the very used mattress in my room. After I was done with the unpacking, I went down the street to the market and did some food shopping. When I got back, I made myself some noodle soup and then settled in on the living room couch with one of Edith's books. I was hoping she'd come home so I would have someone to talk to, but she never showed up. At around ten o'clock, I started to feel very tired. I went down to my room, crawled into my sleeping bag, and was soon sound asleep.

I was awakened at six the next morning by beautiful piano music. I got dressed and walked down the hall to the living room. Edith had a cup of steaming tea sitting up on one side of the piano and a plate of toast sitting up on the other side. She wasn't paying much attention to either of them. She played like she cared about every note. Her eyes were closed and she moved her body in smooth circles to the sounds that sometimes met with her approval and sometimes didn't. One passage really frustrated her and after three tries, she let out a disgusted sigh and reached for a piece of toast.

"Sounds good," I said from the doorway.

"Jesus!" she said as she quickly turned around.

"Sorry," I replied.

"Oh, it's you. God, I forgot," she laughed. "Thanks for the compliment. I guess I should have warned you that I like to play in the morning."

"Makes for a nice alarm clock."

"A rather off-key alarm clock, I'm afraid. I can't quite get this part of the piece, and it doesn't help that this thing needs to be tuned."

The living room had two bay windows. One of them had plants in the little alcove, but the other one, near the piano, had cushions to sit on. I walked over and sat down. The morning sun was just coming into the room and my little spot felt warm and comfortable.

"Is this something you're writing?" I asked.

"Yes, but I can't get by this one spot. I keep going back to the beginning and trying to roll right into the transition. Sometimes that works for me, but not today."

"I'm sure you'll get it."

"Oh, I will eventually. I've got lots of time. This is for the Christmas concert that the music department puts on. I've got months yet."

"What I heard sounded wonderful."

"Thanks. What about you? What are you going to do with yourself today?"

"I've gotten myself a job. I'm going to be a waiter and pot washer over at the Christchurch Cricket Club."

"That was fast," she said as she sipped her tea.

"I saw the 'help wanted' sign and seized the moment."

"That's a rather snobbish place. What were you doing over there?"

"I was driving by. Thought it might be fun to watch some cricket."

"At least I know you'll be good for the rent," she said with a smile. "I don't want to be rude, but I want to get back to this. I compose a lot in the morning and kind of need to be left alone. Hope you don't mind."

"No, no," I said as I got up from the window seat. "I understand that kind of thing."

"Good," she replied gently. "Any other time is fine."

When I walked down the stairs to go to work, she was still in there, playing for all she was worth.

I didn't see a lot of Maggie during my first week in Christchurch. I had a phone line run into my room, and we talked every couple of days. She said she was still doing research on the family, but somehow I got the feeling she was goofing off. The job at the cricket club was simple enough. I waited tables, scrubbed pots, and fed dirty dishes into the dish-washing machine. I even helped out with the bartending when things got busy. It was basically a sandwich-and-beer place, so Charlie the cook had it pretty easy. He liked to spend a lot of his time questioning me about American foreign policy. I soon discovered that his greatest love was arguing. I'd give him a good political fight once a day and he loved it. The only thing he didn't like was when I agreed with him about something. I noticed whenever that happened, he quickly changed the subject.

Peter Newton passed through every day on his way to the field. I tried to be out in the bar when I knew that cricket practice was about to begin. On my third day of work, he and a few of his friends stayed for drinks and sandwiches after practice. I waited on the table and tried to listen in on their conversation. Unfortunately, all they talked about was cricket. They fought over the check like good little rich fellows, and in the end, Peter picked up the tab. His friends all took off while I was getting him the change. When I came back to the table, he was sitting there by himself.

"You're new, aren't you?" he asked as he looked me over.

"Just started this week," I replied.

"You do your job well. Just don't let Charlie push you around too much. He needs to be told off now and again."

"About once a day, I'd say," I replied.

"Very good. I think you'll be all right. I'm Peter Newton," he said, and he reached out his hand.

I shook his hand and introduced myself. He then got up and walked out the front door. I felt that at that moment, the game had officially begun. I was already imagining my next conversation with Maggie. I couldn't wait to tell her that I had met the mark.

As I picked up the dishes, I noticed that the bartender was giving me a stern look. As I walked back toward the kitchen, he came over to meet me.

"Just a word of caution, Tom," he whispered. "Be careful around that one."

"I know, he's the prime minister's son," I replied.

"It's not that. He's a bloody poofter."

"A what?" I asked.

"A poofter. A homosexual. Didn't you notice the way he looked you over?"

"You're kidding?" I said as I tried not to drop the dishes.

"I wish I was. He's a great batsman. It's a damn shame."

Suddenly, I couldn't move my feet. The immensity of what I was being told rooted me to the floor. I wanted to say something but found it difficult to get the words out.

"Are you sure?" I stammered.

"Ah, yeah. Don't feel bad. Most people don't know. I was shocked myself."

"Jesus," was all I could manage.

"I know what you mean," the bartender said as he walked away.

My face felt very hot. I went back into the kitchen and told Charlie what the bartender had said. Charlie reluctantly agreed with him. Then I remembered the bad scene with the reporter and that helped confirm it. The reporter had probably felt that he had to protect Peter. I finished my work as fast as I could and then got Maggie on the phone. I told her to get a taxi and meet me at The Greek as soon as possible.

When I got there, Maggie was sitting in one of the back booths eating a salad. I quickly walked over and sat down. I took a deep breath and was about to jump in when the waiter came with a menu. I told him to bring me a glass of beer and then turned back to Maggie.

"What is it, Thomas?" she said with a twinkle in her eye. "Bad day at the sink?"

"I guess you could say that. Actually, it was a pretty good day until your number one target came in and had a sandwich and a beer."

"You met him?"

"That's right, and guess what, Maggie."

"What?"

"You can wiggle that beautiful ass of yours in front of him all you want, but it won't do you a bit of good."

"What are you talking about?"

"Because he's gay. A queer. A homosexual. How's that for a turn of events?"

"You're kidding?" Maggie said as she put her fork down.

"Those were my exact words when I was told. I'm beginning to get the scary feeling that I've come halfway around the world for nothing. Your goddamn Stuart and his computers missed one small little detail. I think I'm going to wring his neck if I ever see him again."

"This has never happened before," Maggie said quietly.

"Oh, well, that makes me feel so much better," I snarled.

"My God," Maggie muttered.

"So, I guess it's just my bad luck to be on the one job that rings up a big fat zero."

"Keep your voice down," Maggie demanded.

"I'm sorry, but I really want to scream right now. I'd like to pull on your hair and shout at the top of my lungs for about an hour."

"Listen, I told you we were going to have to bob and weave."

"Bob and weave? Are you out of your mind? What are you going to do? Grow a dick? You can't bob and weave out of something like this. We're screwed and that is that."

"Maybe not," Maggie said as she gave me a very serious look.

We both stared at each other for a few seconds.

"Don't even let the words pass your lips," I said as I pointed at her. "There is no way I'm going to do that. Do you understand? No way!"

"You'd get the bigger share," she said.

"Forget it."

"I'd do it, if I were you."

"Yeah, but you're not me. I'll get on the next plane out of here before I'll even consider it."

"All right. Calm down. Maybe there's something else."

"Like what?"

"I don't know. Let's just get a hold of ourselves and think this thing through."

"Who I'd like to get a hold of is that asshole Stuart. What kind of research does that jerk do, anyway? How could he not know something like this?"

Just then the waiter came with my beer, and as soon as he put it down I took a slug. Two people came and sat in the booth behind me. Maggie put a finger to her lips to let me know that I was going to have to be quieter.

"I can't believe it," I muttered. "Ten thousand miles for nothing."

"Look, this is a shock to me, too, but we've got to think our way through it. Besides, what if it is all for nothing? You were going to stay with me for a month anyway. You're month is still not up. You'll end up with your ten thousand dollars, plus a nice overseas trip to boot. I'm the bigger loser here, not you.''

"Well, you don't seem very upset about it."

"I am. Believe me, I am. But I'm not going to let my emotions ruin my ability to think."

"Think about what?" I said, louder than I should have. "There's nothing to think about. This whole thing is a bust."

Maggie toyed with her salad while I finished off my beer and signaled for another. After the waiter brought the beer, I took a long drink and then slammed the mug down on the table.

"Goddamn warm beer," I snarled.

"What about the sister?" Maggie asked quietly as she chewed on a tomato.

"What about her?"

"Doesn't she have some kind of drinking problem?"

"That's the rumor."

"What if we regroup. Act as if we just got here and go after her instead?"

"You mean reverse roles? I do the dirty work while you relax in your room?"

"Not at all. I become the partner. I find her and follow her around and see if there's a way to get you into her life. Then you do it and see what happens."

"Maggie, I didn't bargain for this kind of thing. I was going to be the support. I don't know enough about this stuff to do it myself."

"You wouldn't be doing it yourself. You'd have the world's foremost expert on romantic ripoffs coaching you from the sidelines."

"Come on, Maggie, guys fall for you by just looking at you. That's not going to happen with me. I'm no stud."

"You don't have to be. Women are won with charm and humor. You can turn on both those things when you want to. You've had enough experience with ripoffs to take a shot at it."

"I don't know," I said as I shook my head. "I'd really have to think about it."

"Don't forget, the money gets a lot bigger. If you pull it off, you might be able to go right through college. Think about it. She has a drinking problem. We only want five little coins. You get her drunk and then take them."

"Somehow, I doubt it will be that easy."

"So do I. But I bet you could figure it out as you went along."

"What if I screw up? What if we both end up in a New Zealand jail for the next ten years?"

"If that's how much confidence you have in yourself, then maybe we'd better head back to Iowa. I thought you were stronger than this."

"I've got plenty of goddamn confidence. This is just an awful lot all at once."

"Let's just look into the possibilities. What harm could there be in just checking it out?"

"I don't know," I mumbled doubtfully.

"Look, go about your business for a few days. Wash your pots, serve your sandwiches, and leave the rest to me. I'll get a car, find her, and then follow her around. I'll do some more research and see what I can dig up about her. In the meantime, will you please think about the money? You could fly home from this adventure with tons of money. We work hard for a few months and then start the new year with big fat bank accounts."

"I'll think about it," I said quietly.

"Good. While you're thinking, I'll be working," Maggie said as she reached over and patted my hand.

"But if I say no, we get out of here. Understood?"

"Understood. Oh, by the way, since we were meeting today, I thought I'd go ahead and give you your next two thousand."

With that, Maggie reached into her purse, pulled out an

envelope, and placed it on the table. I picked it up and looked inside. I saw that it was another group of hundred-dollar bills. I took the envelope, folded it in half, and put it in my back pocket.

"Thanks," I said.

"You don't have to thank me," Maggie said with a shrug. "We had a deal and I'm keeping my part of it. What you need to think about is how much more is out there if you're willing to trust your abilities."

She slid out of the booth and then leaned down and whispered in my ear.

"Let's meet here for dinner in a few days. I'll tell you what I've found out and then you can make your decision."

She gave me a big smile and then turned and walked out of the restaurant. I picked up my beer and took a sip and then slowly placed it back on the table. I didn't like this. I didn't like it at all. I leaned back against the booth and felt the nice, big bulge in my back pocket. The power of those bills made me relax a little. I pulled them out and had another look at them. Maybe Maggie was right. Maybe it would be easy money. I'd just let my mind process the idea over the next few days and then hear what she had to say. I chugged down the rest of my beer, suddenly liking the warmth of it. I picked up the check, walked to the cash register, and paid for the salad and the beers. I started to walk back to the table to leave the tip when I remembered that I didn't have to. When I stopped, I looked down the row of booths and saw the person who had been sitting with her back to me. It was Edith.

Chapter Thirteen

I thought about Edith all the next morning as I scrubbed Charlie's pots. I was going to call Maggie and tell her about the situation, but I decided to wait and see if I could handle it myself. For lunch Charlie gave me one of his famous beet burgers, and while I sat in the kitchen eating it, I got an idea. I would get Edith's piano tuned. It was a little blatant, but I figured it was better than doing nothing. I knew she would be in classes all that afternoon, so I spent the rest of my lunch calling around trying to find someone who would do the job right away. On the fifth call, I found someone who was available. I arranged to leave the key and the money in an envelope under the doormat. I begged Charlie for an extra twenty minutes for lunch, and when he granted it, I drove home and got everything arranged.

I didn't see Edith that night, but knowing her habit of playing in the morning, I set my alarm for six A.M. I got to bed early and heard her stirring around in the kitchen shortly after my alarm went off. She hit the keys, played a few bars, and then stopped. I couldn't help but laugh to myself. She started playing again and this time continued to the end of the piece. After that, it was quiet for a minute, and then there was a soft tapping on my door.

"Come in," I said as I sat up on my mattress.

She opened the door a crack and looked in to make sure I was decent. Once she was sure I was, she opened the door all the way and leaned on the door frame.

"Someone has tuned my piano," she said, staring down at me.

"Sounds better, don't you think?" I asked lightly.

"Well, yes and no."

"How do you mean?"

"I mean, it depends on why you did it."

"I did it because I think that Robert is right. I think you are a genius. The music you write is terrific. It seems very stupid for you to have to compose on an out-of-tune piano."

"It's not a bribe of some sort?"

"Edith, you're too smart to be bribed. If you have something you want to ask me, why don't you go ahead and ask it."

"All right. What the hell are you up to?"

"You mean, what was I talking about in the restaurant?"

"You know that's what I mean."

"It's private business."

"It sounded like some pretty funny private business to me!"

"Then why aren't you laughing?" I asked with a smile.

"Please, don't get cute. You're not a criminal, are you?"

"I've never been to jail," I said.

"Does that mean yes, but you've never been caught?"

"Look, Edith, I'm here to maybe take a few classes and to work. I'm also doing some business on the side, but it's nothing you have to worry about. I will pay my rent and live here quietly."

"You could bring trouble here."

"That will never happen. Look, why don't you raise the rent a little. Sort of a bonus for putting up with a less-than-perfect roommate."

"I don't know," she said quietly.

"I'll move out if you want me to," I said.

"I can't afford it," she replied. "What you're paying now is more than half the rent."

"Why you little stinker," I said with a grin. "I'm proud of you."

"I need you here and that's the reason. You keep paying what you are and everything will be fine. But the first sign of anything, even just the smell of trouble, and you are on your way."

"It's a deal."

With that she walked out, closing the door behind her. In a few minutes she was back at the piano, pounding away on her piece for the Christmas concert. I got up and showered and shaved as the music rang through the apartment. When I left, I glanced into the living room and saw that she was hard at work writing and playing. It sounded like she was working on something new.

The weekend was a bore. I didn't hear a thing from Maggie and I got tired of waiting around for the phone to ring. On Sunday afternoon, Edith asked me if I'd like to go for a hike with her in the hills by the ocean. I was glad for the opportunity to get out and agreed to go. On the way over, she asked me a few more questions about the things she had overheard at The Greek. Questions that I did my best to dance around. It seemed she was asking them more out of curiosity than any moral outrage. I even got a hint that she was starting to like me. I wondered if maybe there wasn't some romantic side to the mystery of who I was and what I was doing. The pirate, the coyote, and thieves like me. People always love to see us through a romantic light.

Edith was not the kind of person who had to have the air

constantly filled with conversation. While walking in the
gentle hills east of Christchurch, there were long periods of
time when neither of us said anything. I imagined that Edith
was playing music in her head, composing as she walked.
I was involved in a form of composition myself. Trying to
compose an answer for this crazy proposal of Maggie's.

I could steal and I had the history to prove it. I was trying
to change all that, but that didn't mean I wasn't capable of
a little relapse if the stakes were high enough. In this particular case, the stakes appeared to be more than high enough.
That was not the issue. The real issue was whether I thought
I had the guts to go through with it. It was the long-term
part of it that scared me. The elaborate digging into another
person's life. It called for a long haul of terrific selfishness.
Of course, the focus would always remain the same: the
money. Only now there would be a lot more of it. As I
thought it over, I slowly began to think that maybe I could
handle it. If other people could do it, so could I. As a matter
of fact, I began to bet myself that I might be better at it than
most. The horror of only a few days ago started to melt
away. By the end of the hike, I had pretty much decided at
least to hear Maggie out. I would wait for her call, and
unless there was some real problem that jumped out at me,
I would try the first step and see what happened.

Our former mark showed up at the club on Tuesday afternoon with some of his friends. He said hello as he came in
and joked with me as I took orders and served them their
beer. The bartender told me he was checking me out again.
I went over to a corner behind the bar where I could wash
beer glasses and keep my eye on him at the same time. I
was hoping for some evidence to reassure me that the bartender and Charlie were right. I watched for fifteen minutes
and saw nothing. His hair maybe suggested it. The hair was
long and a bit too nice or something. But really, that was
hardly proof of anything. As I was standing there, I couldn't
help but wonder why Maggie had so easily accepted my

word that he was gay. To come right down to it, all I had done was pass on a rumor. A piece of gossip from a bar. We were making an awfully big switch in plans, based on very little information. Peter gave me a big smile on the way out, which I did not return. When he saw that, his smile quickly dropped and he hurried through the door. I suppose that was what I had been looking for, but I still wasn't completely convinced. I went back into the kitchen and told Charlie that the prime minister's son had been checking me out. Charlie advised me to stay away from that "flamer."

Maggie called me Tuesday night and we arranged to meet at The Greek Wednesday for dinner. I agreed and this time promised myself that I would talk a lot more softly. I thought it very unlikely to run into Edith twice in a row. Plus, I didn't want to suggest a change of restaurants and have Maggie ask why.

Something strange had started happening with Edith. She was eating my food. I drew a small line on a carton of milk Tuesday morning, just to see if I was imagining things. Sure enough, when I got back from work, the milk was down over three inches. Also a can of soup I knew I had bought was nowhere to be found. I began to realize just how little money she had. I decided to start buying more food. Maybe it was to be an unspoken payment for her silence, and if it was, that was fine with me. I'd feed her until she was fat if it helped me get what I wanted.

One of the first things Maggie said to me Wednesday night was that she had found a nice place to eat over by her new apartment and that we should meet there sometimes. She said we would call it the Pie Shop. As she wrote down the address, I wondered if Maggie hadn't taken a real liking to their pies. She looked like she had put on a little weight.

"I hope you're not in there eating pie when you're supposed to be out scouting the prime minister's daughter," I said kiddingly.

"Hardly," she answered. "Though it looks like the prime minister's daughter likes pie more than I do."

"Oh, no, please don't tell me she's huge."

"No, not huge. She could lose a few pounds, but it's not that bad. She's got red hair and blue eyes. I don't think you'll have a lot of trouble putting the make on her."

"Did you see her drink? I mean, is it obvious that she has a problem?"

"Sometimes her face matches her hair. Also, her driving got real bad one night. I think she's a late sleeper, which is also a good sign. Basically, she does her day, goes to the theater at night, then comes home and gets potted."

"She goes to the theater every night?"

"Not to see plays—she works on them. She goes to a place called, the Hole in the Wall Theatre. It's a building just off Cathedral Square. She's one of the pillars of the organization. She stage manages almost all of their plays."

"She doesn't work?"

"Doesn't need to. I think I'm safe in saying that she's a night person. I watched her house four times, and she never drove out of the driveway before two in the afternoon."

"Well, I'm the one who is used to late hours," I said.

"Oh," Maggie said as her eyebrows went up. "Are you starting to like our amended plan?"

"Maybe. What exactly is it?"

"I can't give you a complete plan right now. There are too many unknowns."

"Come on, you must have thought of something."

"I have an idea of how to get started. From there the plan becomes whatever it needs to be."

"All right," I said with a sigh. "How do you think it should start?"

"I've already told you."

"I must have missed it."

"Come on, use your head."

"Let's see, from what you've told me, I could sell her a

diet plan, buy her a drink, or suddenly develop an interest in the theater.''

"I like choice three," Maggie said. "As a matter of fact, I called down there yesterday and they told me they always need volunteers. Build the sets, hang the lights, that kind of thing. I'd say you should go down there and see if you can make yourself useful.''

"And if I can?"

"Get her attention and then ask her out, you jerk. Win her heart with your wit and charm.''

"I hope I have enough of those things.''

"You wooed and won me just fine a few summers ago. You did it because you really wanted me. All you have to do is make yourself want her as much.''

"She's not you.''

"No, she's not. She's really a big pile of very attractive money. It's just a project, Warren. You get her to trust you, take some of what she's got, and then get out of there.''

"Then she'll really do some drinking.''

"That's not our problem. So, are you willing to put on your game face, or should I go back to my apartment and pack my bags?''

"It seems so hit and miss," I said after a few seconds.

"It is. If we miss, we go home. If we hit, we go home loaded.''

We got our meals and I picked away at mine while Maggie dove in. I hated it that everything was so unstructured, that I couldn't be sure of more things. Yet it was such an opportunity. I could certainly go down to this theater and see if I could get involved. I could meet her and then take it from there. If I didn't like the situation, I could always back out at that point with no harm done.

"I'll go down there tomorrow night and see what happens," I said.

"Rehearsals start at seven-thirty," Maggie said with a big smile.

"All right. By the way, what's her name?"

"Theresa."

"Terry, for short?"

"I don't think so. She's not the nickname type."

"Is that good?"

"I don't know," Maggie said with a shrug. "You be Thomas, and don't let anyone call you Tom. Thomas and Theresa. Sounds like a lovely couple."

Maggie gave me the address for the theater. We finished our meals and then went our separate ways. I was a bundle of emotions as I thought of the next day. I was full of fear and doubt, but there was also excitement. There was a part of this thing that was very erotic. On the way home, in the car, I actually got an erection thinking about this unsuspecting woman. This unknown Theresa.

When I got home, Edith was swaying away at the piano. A carton of my yogurt sat beside her on the piano bench. The spoon was still in her mouth and her eyes were closed as she weaved to her composition for the Christmas concert. I tiptoed over and sat in the window seat. When she opened her eyes, she tried to pretend that I hadn't startled her, but I knew that I had.

"Sorry to sneak up on you," I said with a smile.

"Home from the hunt?" she asked.

"I never liked hunting," I replied.

"Really?"

"The piece sounds nice," I said quickly.

"Thanks."

"Did you finish it?"

"Yes. I played it for one of my teachers today. She said it was very clever."

"Congratulations."

"I'm eating your yogurt," she said as she lifted it up and showed it to me.

"I know," I replied. "Other things, too."

"That's right. I figure if you're going to steal from one Kiwi, the least you can do is feed another."

"Sounds fair," I agreed.

"Good," she said. "How about buying some wine? I like to have a glass of wine while I'm composing."

"Red or white?" I asked.

Chapter Fourteen

I got to the Hole in the Wall Theatre just before eight the next night. I tried the front door but found it locked. There were several cars in the parking lot, so I knew that people were in there. I walked around the building, looking for another way in. Down on the right side, I came to a door that was propped open with a chair. There was a pinkish light flowing out that felt very inviting. From inside, I could hear an actor thundering out his words. I walked quietly down the steps and peered in the door. I saw that I was right by the edge of the front row of seats. Those few people who were in the audience were all sitting toward the back. I slipped through the door and in only three steps was in front of the corner seat. I sat down, turned, and looked up at the stage. There was a slight rustling in the back of the theater, but no one came down and told me to leave.

I watched what I later found out was the second act of a play called *Arms and the Man*. It was full of blustering military men and flighty women. After the act was over, the actors were told to take a break before they got some notes and did the act again. One of the blustering military men came by where I was sitting and gave me a smile through his huge mustache. I watched him walk outside and light a cigarette. When I looked back toward the stage, there was another man standing in front of me.

"Are you looking for somebody?" he asked.

"Just some good theater," I replied.

"Yank or Canadian?" he asked.

"Yank."

"I'm afraid you're about three weeks early for this one."

"I don't want to just watch good theater," I said in a sincere tone. "I want to help."

"Really?" he asked with a smile. "Have you done much theater work?"

"Not really. I've only recently discovered how much I like it. I'm a quick learner, though. I know my tools and my electricity and carpentry."

"Well, we're pretty much covered in those departments," he said.

"Oh, too bad."

"However, we have decided we want an assistant backstage for this production. We need someone to change the set between the first and second acts. There are some pretty heavy pieces, so we were hoping for a man. The assistant would also set props, pull the curtain, that kind of thing."

"Then I'm your guy."

"Do you live in Christchurch?"

"No, I'm just visiting for a while."

"This may be too long a commitment for you. We rehearse for three more weeks and then run for three weekends."

"I'll be here for at least that long," I said with confidence. "I'm taking some courses over at the university."

"I can only pay you five dollars a show."

"I'd get paid?" I asked. "I was figuring on volunteering."

"Well, you are, really. The five dollars is to just cover your expenses."

"All the better," I said with a shrug.

"Theresa, would you come here for a minute," he said to the back of the room.

I looked to the rear of the theater, and a woman standing in the dark turned from a conversation she was having and looked our way. She bent over the seat near her and picked up a large notebook. After a few more words to her companion, she came down the aisle. As she came into the light, I saw a woman with light, almost blond, red hair. Her face was round and light-skinned. She was a little overweight, but not that much. She certainly didn't look like the brooding problem drinker I had been picturing.

"Yes?" she asked as she got near us.

"I may have found you a scenery shifter," the man said.

"Terrific," she replied.

"Theresa, this is . . ."

"Thomas," I said.

"I'm sorry," he said. "I'm Steven, the director. Forgive me for not introducing myself."

"No sweat," I said.

"American?" Theresa asked.

"Full-blooded."

"Terrific," she said again.

"Why don't you two sit down and go over the rehearsal schedule," Steven suggested. "See if Thomas can come in this weekend so he'll get to know the show. The set will be workable next week; we can give it a try then."

"Fine," I replied.

He then turned, jumped up onto the stage, and began pushing chairs around. Theresa and I sat down next to each other. I had to wipe the big grin off my face. This whole thing had been amazingly easy. I'd been in the building for less than an hour and here I was, sitting next to the mark.

"Let's see," she said as she handed me a schedule. "We're off tomorrow night, but we'll be here Saturday from two to five. Could you make that?"

"Sure."

"I always get here a few minutes early to set up. If you want to come early, you can help me and I'll go over the rest of the schedule with you. I'd do it now, but I have a minor crisis to attend to."

With that she stood up and held out her hand. I stood and shook her hand, and we both smiled. Then she turned and walked up the aisle toward the back of the theater.

"See you Saturday," I said to her back.

After that I turned and slipped out the same door I had slipped in just a short while before.

The next day at lunch, I gave Maggie a call and told her what had happened.

"I can't believe how damn easy it was," I said after I had described the events of the night before.

"What did I tell you?" Maggie said. "Meeting them is often the easy part. Getting them to trust you is something else again."

"Are you sure she's a drinker? She comes off as little Miss Efficiency."

"Efficient people can have drinking problems," Maggie replied.

"I'm supposed to get there early Saturday and help her set up. Should I ask her out for a drink afterwards?"

"Jesus, no! Give it a little time. You're going to be seeing a lot of her, so wait for the right moment. For now, make sure they think you're really dedicated to the theater. She'll probably find that attractive. When the right moment comes, you'll know it."

"All right," I agreed. "This is kind of fun."

"I knew it. I knew you'd get into this."

"There's still a long way to go."

"Of course there is," Maggie said. "Do you think you can pretend to be attracted to her?"

"I don't think it'll be a problem. She reminds me of an Irish girl I went out with in high school."

"Great. Good luck Saturday," she said right before she hung up.

When I got home that night, Edith was sitting at the piano, working on a piece that I hadn't heard before. A glass of my wine was sitting off to the right. I took my usual seat by the window and listened to her play. The music had a very somber part and then it changed into something bouncy and light, almost Western. Then back to somber again. It ended by just gently fading away. We both sat silently and listened to the piano.

"Something new?" I asked as Edith sipped the wine.

"Yes," she said. "It's supposed to be *hiding* music. Did you get that from it?"

"In a way. Are you hiding from something?"

"It's not about me," she replied with a laugh. "It's about you."

"Me?"

"Sure. The great mystery man. The Lone Ranger, out on his nasty but exciting mission."

"Oh. Do you find it exciting?"

"There is a certain cast-your-fate-to-the-wind feeling about it. I admit it makes me very curious."

"Do you by any chance find it attractive?" I asked.

She looked at me for a few seconds and then went for another sip of wine. She drank it down and stared at me at the same time.

"Your socks leave little pieces of yarn all over the hallway rug," she said as she put the glass down.

"What?" I asked.

"Your socks. They shred or something. I'm forever leaning over and picking these little brown specks out of the carpet. It hurts my back to bend over that much."

"I'll get some slippers," I said with a shrug.

"Good," she said as she got up and went to her room.

She didn't exactly answer my question. But then again, she didn't say no, either. I was getting the feeling, that my new roommate was attracted. After all, she had been sitting there composing music about me. That had to mean something.

I got myself a glass of wine and sat back down in the window seat. I leaned back and replayed the scene in the theater from the night before. I closed my eyes and watched Theresa again coming out of the dark at the back of the theater. She is carrying a big notebook. She holds it like it goes everywhere with her—the stage manager and her script. I thought about that image of her and decided that I should have a notebook of my own. A place where I could write down the things I needed to do when I changed the set. I would always have a pencil handy. Then I had a stroke of genius. I would carry my notebook in some kind of book bag. I would have some other books in there, too. One of them would be a book on collecting coins.

Chapter Fifteen

On Saturday morning I went out and bought a coin book. Then I went for a walk on the university campus and found a nice, shady bench. I sat and read the book for quite a while. When I got bored with it, I went to the campus store and bought a notebook and a green book bag. I had a light lunch and then drove over to the theater. After I'd been waiting for a few minutes, Theresa drove up. I got out of my car and walked over to her as she was getting a fancy-looking lamp out of the backseat.

"Let me carry that," I said as I gave my book bag a big over-the-shoulder heave.

"Thanks," she said as she closed the car door.

I followed her around to the side door and we stood there silently as she jiggled the key in the lock.

"Damn thing," she mumbled as the lock finally clicked.

We walked in and were immediately hit with the smell of fresh paint. It was so strong that it made my head snap back.

"Idiots!" she shouted. "Open the windows. Those morons

were painting this morning and didn't leave any of the windows open."

We each ran up a side aisle, opening the windows as quickly as we could. We then went to a room behind the stage and brought out a couple of fans.

"Let's go outside and wait a few minutes until the air clears," she said after we got the fans going.

We went out the side door and stood in the parking lot. Theresa gave me a rundown of my responsibilities. We went over the rehearsal and performance schedules. She had me circle the dates when I would have to be there. After we finished that, she got three aspirins out of her purse and swallowed them dry.

"Damn paint is bound to give me a headache," she said as she worked the aspirin down her throat.

That's what she said, but I had come to a different conclusion. Her eyes were very red and her hands shook just the slightest bit. I was quite sure that she had one hell of a hangover. It may have made her feel bad, but it made me feel very good.

The aspirin never really made it down her throat. We both went back inside so she could get a glass of water. The air was moving by then, and there was only a hint of the paint smell. After she got the water, we pulled some set pieces in from the wings and arranged the stage for the beginning of the play. We were carrying a bed onto the stage when Steven came in the side door.

Shortly after that, everyone was there and they began the first act. It looked pretty good in my opinion, but some of the actors were still unsure of their lines. Theresa and I moved things around between acts, and I made diligent notes of where everything went. During the second act, I was given the script and had the job of yelling out the lines to the actors when they couldn't remember them. After it was over, we all sat around as the director gave his notes. I sat next to Theresa and she occasionally whispered things to me that I would write in my notebook. I could tell that she was very pleased that I was taking notes. Her hands were steady now, and she appeared to be completely recovered from what I assumed was a bout with the bottle the night before.

When the notes were over, everyone left as Theresa and I put away the set pieces. She told me I was doing very well and that she would like it if I could come again on Sunday evening and help the actors with their lines. I told her I would and that was the end of it. I suppose it was a good first time together. She certainly didn't dislike me, so that was a step in the right direction.

I called Maggie when I got home and we agreed to meet at the Pie Shop for dinner. She said she had a surprise for me.

She was sitting in a booth in the far corner when I got there. Her eyes had that Maggie sparkle in them and her cheeks were full of color. As soon as I sat down, she started talking in what sounded like a pretty convincing New Zealand accent. After a few sentences, she stopped and looked at me.

"What do you think?" she asked.

"I don't think you learned it for the fun of it," I said.

"Of course I didn't. Does it sound real?"

"It does to me," I replied with a shrug.

"Good," she said with a satisfied smile. "I have an interview Monday and it needs to be perfect."

"I'm afraid to ask," I said after a short silence.

"Then I'll just tell you. An interview for a job. I can't just sit around while you have all the fun."

"You're getting a job?"

"That's right."

"Doing what?"

"Working in a bank."

"A bank!" I said loudly. "My God. The foxy lady has finally gotten into the henhouse."

"That's a good way of putting it," Maggie said with a laugh. "I've had a couple of dates with the bank manager, so I think I'm a shoo-in."

"Don't you need some identification? A social security number or something like that? They don't seem to mind about that sort of thing if you're washing dishes, but I bet they do if you work in a bank."

"Stuart overnighted me some stuff."

"He approves of you doing this?"

"Yes, because it fits in with the overall plan."

"How?"

"You'll see in a few days. I have to get the job first."

"You will."

"I hope so. Now, tell me, lover boy, how are things at the theater?"

"We were both at rehearsal today. Everything went fine, but nothing special happened."

"That's not to be expected."

"I think she was hungover this morning."

"Really? Oh, that's very good. Probably sat alone all Friday night and got sloshed."

"She doesn't strike me as the type."

"You'd be surprised at all the types out there."

"True," I admitted.

"You know, she's pretty much by herself in that big house. Daddy and Mommy, of course, are up in Wellington. Big brother has his own place, for reasons that are now obvious. This country is so safe and cuddly, they don't need to have secret service types hanging around her house. While I was watching the place, all I saw was a daytime cook and a groundskeeper, who sleeps in a cottage by the pool."

"Makes it easier for us," I said with a smile.

"Yeah, but I don't like these safe little countries where everybody's so damn nice," Maggie whispered.

"Letting you into one of their banks ought to teach them a lesson," I said with a sly grin.

"Makes me warm all over just thinking about it."

"I bet."

"Imagine me, in a closed room, with row after row of safety deposit boxes."

"That's a scary thought."

"Every box a little mystery, waiting to be solved."

"Be careful, you're going to have an orgasm and upset all these pie eaters."

"The orgasm will come when I'm in that room with all that money."

"Well, be careful, dear. I may need a little support now and then. You ain't going to be much support if you're in jail."

"I only do things I know I can get away with," Maggie said with confidence.

"Famous last words. Didn't you say something about having to get out of South Africa in a hurry?"

"Yes, but I got away, didn't I?"

"Don't forget your persistent friend from Australia."

"Don't worry about Willem. Deep down he's a wimp. He's probably given up by now."

"I hope so."

"So what's next with you?" Maggie asked. "Is our little drunkard going to melt in your arms?"

"I have no melting to report as of now."

"It'll come. Just tell me you know you can do it."

"I can do it," I said emphatically. "I feel completely neutral about her."

"That's what I like to hear."

"I want the money as much as you do."

"Good boy," Maggie said with a sexy smile. "You know, Warren, I'd love to take you home with me. I'd love to get you naked. I'm so turned on, I can hardly sit still."

"Well, Jesus, let's go," I whispered across the table.

"No, sweetie," Maggie said with a long sigh. "I can't have you satisfied. It just wouldn't do."

Just then the waiter came up and asked us what we wanted to order. We each got a piece of pie and a cup of coffee. When he left, I reached across the table and grabbed Maggie's hand.

"Maggie, how can you know so little about men? Within twenty-four hours, I'll be a panting beast again."

"Not true," she said with a shake of her head. "Besides, what if your moment happens to come tomorrow? What if she gives you the high sign and you blow it because I've wrung you out?"

"The only thing that's going to wring me out is if you walk out of here without me."

"Sorry, Thomas, I need you to be horny."

"What are you going to do?" I asked. "Leave here and go pick up some guy in a bar?"

"Maybe. I should probably save myself for my new friend at the bank."

"That's just business. You're better off with me, Maggie. I know how to make you scream. A new man isn't going to know how to do that kind of stuff."

"All men can be trained."

"I'm already trained," I said with a smile.

"Don't beg. It doesn't become you. Get us those coins and I'll make it up to you."

"Promise?"

"Promise. Whatever you want."

"I want to go back to that hill in Iowa. I want to see you stand there nude again, with the sun going down between your legs."

"Sounds like fun," Maggie said as the waiter walked up with our pie.

When the waiter left, she got her purse off the seat and pulled the strap up over her shoulder. She got up and smiled down at me.

"You're leaving?" I asked.

"Yes, for your good and mine. Go home, Thomas. Get a good night's sleep and figure out how to get under that woman's skin. The sooner you do that, the sooner you and I will be back on that hill.''

''Easier said than done,'' I mumbled.

'Come on, it's so obvious to me. Figure out why she drinks. If you know why she drinks, you'll know what she needs. You supply whatever that is.''

''What about your pie?'' I said as she turned to go.

''You eat it,'' she replied. ''I need to watch my weight.''

I drove home slowly, thinking about what Maggie had said. I tried to decide if anything that Theresa had done so far had given me any clues to why she drank. Probably it was being alone in that big house all the time. Maybe it was the loss of her parents' attention. Attention, no doubt, was the key word in this whole scenario.

As I walked up the stairs, I could hear the piano playing. I opened the door quietly and slipped into the apartment. I looked into the living room and there was Edith, playing the piano without a stitch on. There were no lights on. She was playing by the light of a couple of dozen candles that she had placed around the room. I leaned against the door frame and took in the view. She sat there with the candlelight dancing off her very white skin. The candlelight also caught the deep purple of her hair and made her seem otherworldly. The music she played was soft and weepy. Her touch was light and her body swayed in little circles. Despite her perfect posture, she looked very fragile and delicate. After a couple of minutes, I could tell she knew I was there. The swaying and the music made the slightest of pauses, then continued to the end of the piece.

''That was beautiful,'' I said.

''Thank you,'' she replied without turning around.

''Am I invading?'' I asked.

''No. Why don't you sit in your usual place and let me play for you.''

She started to play again as I walked to the window seat and sat down. I could see her face now. Her eyes were full of emotion as she looked over at me. Then she closed her eyes and began to sway again. Her skin was so white, it looked ghostly. Her breasts seemed perfectly made for a man to cup his hands under and kiss. I looked down at her stomach and saw a reflection of dark purple from down by the bench. I found that little touch particularly erotic. I hoped that the piece she was playing lasted forever.

When she stopped, she sat there quietly for a moment and then opened her eyes and looked at me.

"I hope you don't mind?" she said.

"Mind? I was hoping you'd play for two or three hours."

"Did you count the candles?"

"With you sitting there like that? You must be kidding."

"Go ahead, count them."

"Twenty-five," I said after I had done it.

"That's right," she murmured.

"Don't tell me it's your birthday."

"Right again, Yankee boy. It was also two months ago today that my love left for England."

"Foolish man."

"Said he wanted to get out into the world. Wanted to go off by himself."

"Does it help to put it into the music?" I asked.

"Oh, yes. I was hoping you'd come home. I wanted you to watch me."

"Why?"

"Because my body is good. I need it to be appreciated every once in a while."

"I've certainly been doing that."

"Good."

"Twenty-five. I thought you were younger."

"Nope. I'm a little old to be in college."

"Just a few years. Did you drop out for a while?"

"Yeah, after my first year. Decided that education was interfering with my piano. I stayed away for two and a half years."

"You played the piano for two and a half years?"

"Pretty much."

I looked down at her breasts and she saw me do it. We didn't say anything for a few seconds. Then she made the slightest of moves toward me. I got up, walked over to her, and cupped one of her breasts in each of my hands. I leaned down and kissed each of them as she slid down to the edge of the piano bench. Then I got down on my knees and reached my mouth up to her breasts. I went back and forth from one to the other, slowly licking the nipples. She wrapped her arms around my head and softly caressed one of my ears. I started to pick up the scent of a familiar perfume. It was one that I had smelled around the apartment before. I followed the scent down her stomach to the inside of her thigh. I moved over to the other thigh and found the same scent waiting for me. She had perfumed the insides of her thighs. She had drawn two lines, like arrows. Edith took her hands out of my hair and laid back on the piano bench. The view past her dark purple pubic hair and up her white body was one of the most erotic things I had ever seen. She closed her eyes and waited. When nothing happened for a few seconds, she raised her head and stared down at me.

"I just want to look at you for a bit," I said softly.

"I'm glad," she said as she lowered her head again.

"Then I'd like to follow this perfume highway."

She laughed, and when she did, her stomach gave little jumps that made her seem so innocent. I leaned up and kissed her stomach and she gave off a slight shiver. After that, I went back down to her thighs and up the perfume highway. I stayed there for a long time.

I had always figured that this part of sex was strictly for the woman, but this time I loved it, too. When she came, she actually reached over and banged her hand down on the piano keys.

When I stood up and looked down at her, she was still breathing deeply. I leaned over and kissed each of her breasts once again. When I did, she reached up and touched my hair.

"Do you want to?" she asked.

"Very much," I said. "But not tonight. Tonight, I just want to give to you."

"Thank you, roomie," she said with a big smile.

"If I had known it was your birthday, I would have gotten you a toaster or something."

"I already have a toaster," she said. "What I needed was for you to find my perfume highway."

"My pleasure."

"Perfume highway," she said again.

"Make a nice title for your next composition," I suggested.

Edith immediately got up, walked out of the room, and came back a moment later wearing a nightgown. She gave me a hug and a quick kiss.

"Go to sleep, Yankee boy. I have work to do."

I walked out of the room as she was sitting down at the piano. By the time I was in my sleeping bag, I could hear the beginnings of a very light but sensuous melody.

Chapter Sixteen

The next week was very busy for me and I didn't see that much of Edith. I knew I wasn't invited to just show up in her bedroom, but I did start dreaming about her sneaking into mine. Unfortunately, she didn't. I began to regret my generosity on her birthday. When I thought about it, I had trouble understanding my own behavior. I had come home, horny as hell, found a nude, beautiful, and willing woman in the living room, and been satisfied with her satisfaction. I wondered what was wrong with me.

She and I smiled in the hall and chatted over quick breakfasts. She was always practicing or running off to class, and I was always running to work or the theater. I called Maggie and suggested that I quit my job at the club now that we had a new plan. She disagreed and said it was a good cover. She also told me that she had gotten the job at the bank. I wasn't happy about continuing as a waiter and pot washer, but I bowed to Maggie's greater experience. Peter Newton came into the club one day and I told him I was working at the theater and had met his sister. It seemed the safest thing to do. When I told him, he just smiled and went back to talking with his friends about the upcoming match against the team from Nelson.

One of the things about my evening with Edith that stuck in my mind was her signal to me that she wanted me to touch her. It was the slightest of moves on the piano bench. A very small slide toward me that said yes. I loved that she had done it, and I loved that I had responded to it. Of course, it was very unlikely that I would ever be in a similar situation with Theresa, but it reminded me that I had to be on a sharp lookout for signals. I wanted to be sure not to miss even the slightest indication that she was interested in me.

Theresa and I were beginning to spend a lot of time together and I was getting to know her. She was very organized and efficient, but underneath, I sensed a gigantic vulnerability. I also began to see some of the ramifications of her drinking problem. She was often hungover. One night when we all went out after rehearsal, I made sure to sit next to her. I noticed that she had four screwdrivers to my one beer. When I asked her if she was all right to drive home, she looked at me like I was crazy.

As we moved closer to opening night, I started sitting backstage during the rehearsals. I sat near Theresa, who was constantly on a headset, talking to the people in the light and sound booths. I had picked up a couple more assignments, which made my job more interesting. At one point I had to run up a ladder and change the colored gel that was in front of one of the lights. I also got to do the offstage voice of someone shouting in the street.

One of the men in the cast was having trouble making a costume change. He kept saying he didn't need any help, but he was always late for his entrance. Three nights before we opened, Theresa came over to me during the second act. She whispered that I should go over to the other side of the stage and be there holding his clothes when he came off.

"Hold his coat for him," she said. "Give him his new costume and take the old one."

As I walked around behind the stage, I realized that she had put her hand on my shoulder as she had leaned down to whisper the instructions. Except for shaking hands when we met, that was the first time we had touched. The hand on the shoulder may have meant nothing. It may have meant everything. I had to do something to find out which it was.

The play went very well that night, and the stubborn actor whom I had helped did make his entrance on time. He took a lot of ribbing about it and did finally admit that it was better with me there. I made a joke about not telling anyone about his skinny legs, and everyone had a good laugh. The mood was high as we got our notes, and as usual Theresa and I stayed late and locked the place up.

During the three and a half hours that we had been in the theater, a very heavy fog had rolled in. As Theresa and I walked to our cars, I made a point of walking just the slightest bit closer to her than I normally would have. When we got to our cars, she turned and said good night.

"Would you like to go for a foggy walk?" I asked as she was about to get into her car.

"Along the road? Wouldn't that be dangerous?"

"We'd only have to go a couple of blocks and then we could walk along the river," I suggested.

She looked around as if checking on the severity of the fog. What she probably was wondering was how long this would keep her from the first drink of the evening.

"Isn't there a pub over by the duck pond?" I wondered out loud.

"Yes," she replied.

"We could walk over and have a nightcap."

"All right," she said as she dropped her notebook on the front seat of her car.

I went over to my car and put my notebook on the front seat, exactly as she had done. When I turned and looked at her, she gave me a smile and then we walked down the road toward the Avon River. The fog was very still and seemed to muffle all sound. It was as if she and I were walking in a very private little space. I walked on the edge of the road and warned her when I heard a car coming. Only a couple of cars passed us, and they were just inching along. When we came to a streetlight, we stopped and looked at the water droplets hanging in the air. I glanced over at her in the light and I could see that her face was shiny and wet. When we got to the park, we walked down the bank to the path along the river. The grass was slippery, and after she almost fell, I put my hand on her elbow and guided her down the hill. When we got to the path, we slowed down and started to talk.

"What are you going to do after you leave Christchurch?" she asked.

"I'm not really sure," I said with a shrug. "I may go over to Australia."

"I've been there several times," she said. "There are a lot of wonderful beaches, and I love the northeast, up around Cairns. If you go over there, you must go up to the north. Don't forget to take a boat trip out to the barrier reef while you're there."

"I'll remember that," I said with a nod.

"So tell me, what makes you such a wanderer?"

"Curiosity for one thing. Plus, I have some things to work out for myself. I'm hoping the long trip will be a buffer zone between some bad events and a new life when I get back. Give me a chance to start over again, if you know what I mean."

"Bad luck in love?"

"No, not that. Family stuff."

"Oh?"

"I have a very strong father. I've had trouble escaping from his opinions. I decided it was time to kick myself in the butt. Put some space between who I was and who I wanted to be. I want to go back to America and have things be different.''

"Sounds like you want an intermission," she said quietly.

"That's a good way of putting it," I agreed.

"It's an interesting idea."

"I hope it works. I can't have things carry on as they were."

"How long are you going to stay away?"

"Hopefully, a year. After Australia, I may go up into Asia. I've always been fascinated by that part of the world."

"I envy you your freedom," she said.

"Anybody can do it. You just have to make up your mind that it's something you want."

We walked on for a few minutes in silence and soon came to the duck pond. All the ducks were huddled on the grass together. They looked up at us as we approached and squeezed even closer together. We stopped and watched them push up against each other. One of the ducks suddenly stretched out and flapped its wings a few times. Little droplets of water flew all around.

"That's me," I said. "Trying to shake off what's landed on me."

Theresa laughed when I said that. Then she shook herself, as if she was trying to imitate the duck. I saw what she was doing and did the same thing. We stood there laughing and shaking as the water flew. The whole group of ducks waddled further away from us.

"I could use a glass of brandy," I said when we stopped shaking.

"That sounds wonderful," Theresa replied.

We turned and walked toward the pub, and when we did, she put her arm through mine. When she did that, I got a glow in my stomach. I was so proud of myself. I couldn't wait to tell Maggie.

We settled into a booth and ordered our brandies. Despite all our shaking, we were still gleaming with fog droplets. I reached over and got a napkin to wipe my face, but Theresa reached out and grabbed my hand.

"I can't do that because it would smear my makeup. If I have to sit here with a shiny face, so do you."

"All right," I said with a smile.

When our brandies came, we both took nice long sips. From the window we could see the ducks. We watched as someone came out the back door of the pub and started throwing pieces of bread to them.

"That's why they're waiting there," Theresa said. "Time for their daily scraps."

"Eat and swim. Swim and eat. What a life," I said as I took another sip of the brandy.

"Animals are lucky," Theresa said, watching the ducks. "We humans have to think all the time. We have to be always figuring things out."

"I think you like that," I replied. "You certainly are the problem solver at the theater. You're the one who makes the whole thing go."

"Thanks."

"It's true," I said with conviction. "So, what other things do you spend your days figuring out?"

"I don't have a job, if that's what you mean. I have a rather large house to look after. My parents come parading home several times a year and I have to have everything just right. All meals are planned with the cook. There's a gardener I have to keep an eye on. You'd be surprised how much time a house takes."

"How long do your parents stay when they come?"

"Usually, just a few days. Dad checks up on the car business, even though he isn't supposed to. He gives a speech here and there. Keeps the home fires burning. I say all this, assuming you know that my father is the prime minister."

"Yes, somebody at the theater mentioned it."

"They love that. They always want to put it in the program notes, but I won't let them."

"You don't like having a famous father?"

"I wouldn't say that. He's doing good things for the country. He works harder than anyone I know. It's probably where I got my problem-solving traits. Unfortunately, he thinks I'm not putting my talents to very good use."

"He's not too happy about your association with the theater, I take it."

"They think it's kind of cute. Like a charity or something. He often wonders when I'll get over it and move on to something serious. I have a degree in economics. He keeps suggesting all these wonderful positions that he could get me, but the truth is, I don't like economics very much. The best thing that ever happened to me was when a friend of mine talked me into stage managing a play she was in. I immediately knew that I had found what I wanted to do. Economics is so damn dry. I love the theater. I love being around creative people. That's just the way I am."

"All you need to do is find a theater where you can make a job of it," I suggested as I waved for the waiter to bring us another round.

"Not even for the money. I don't need the money. I do need to be part of a professional organization. Something with some respect to it. Those kinds of opportunities are rather rare in New Zealand. There are more jobs in Australia. That's why I've been going over there. I have a friend who works in a wonderful theater in Brisbane. She says she can get me a job there."

"So go."

"It's not that easy. I keep thinking, I'll go when my father is no longer prime minister. When he and Mom are back home again. The thing is, he's so damn popular, I can't imagine when he'll be out of office. Until then, we all have to make sacrifices. That's what my mother says when we have our little talks."

"You can't wait forever, Theresa."

"I know, I know; I can't do what I want, because I have

to take care of that stupid house! It makes me crazy. That's the thing about you that I find so, well, interesting. You're free. You needed to go, so you did. I really admire that. I wish I had the ability to do that.''

"You will. When the time is right.''

"I hope so,'' she replied as she started in on her second brandy.

We talked about the play and the people involved. We had a few laughs about the vanity of some of the actors. We had started off with some very meaningful conversation, but it evolved into small talk. It was as if we had approached some sensitive areas and then backed off. Still, it was a very good beginning. She had shared much more than I had expected for a first time out.

Theresa had a third and fourth brandy, but I settled for just the two. By the time she finished the last one, she was talking a mile a minute and I was getting tired of it. I smiled as she ran from one theater story to another—stories in which she usually came out the hero. Earlier, I had started to like being around her. Now, I couldn't wait to get rid of her.

At midnight, they came around for the last call and she had a double. When we started back toward the theater, it had gotten even foggier. Again she put her arm through mine—more from necessity this time.

"So I guess the only reason I'm walking along with you right now is because you and your father couldn't get along,'' she said as we walked along the river.

"It's more complicated than that.''

"No, I think that statement brings everything down to its most basic place.''

When she said *place,* it didn't come out quite right. When she looked up at me, I could tell; I was looking into the eyes of a drunk.

"Couldn't live in the same house, right?'' she asked.

"More like the same town.''

"Just a couple of dogs pissing on the same rocks."

"That's a hell of a thing to say," I said with suppressed anger. I was making all this stuff up, but she was making me mad anyway.

"Wait a minute," she said as she stopped. "You're not some of that American white trash that I've read about, are you?"

"What do you mean by that?" I said loudly.

"Oh, we have those types around here, too. Just go west into the mountains. You wouldn't believe how they live."

"They're probably just poor," I said.

"They're slobs, that's what they are," she said as she tripped over a rock on the edge of the path.

I pretty much gave up after that. Theresa continued to chat on about the inferior classes. She was turning out to be a sloppy drunk with a bit of a mean streak.

Only an hour earlier, I had been thinking I would take advantage of this romantic, foggy evening and give her a good-night kiss. Now the idea was not very appealing. Luckily, it started to rain as we approached our cars. We both made a dash and shouted farewells as we fumbled for our keys.

As I drove home, I thought about what had happened that night. I had to admit that stealing from a lonely woman made me feel slightly guilty. However, stealing from an obnoxious drunk who didn't know when to shut up made it a lot easier to slip into neutral. Since the tentative plan was to get her stinking drunk one night and take off with the coins, I began to think I wouldn't have much trouble doing it.

When I got home, Edith was at the piano working on her Perfume Highway piece. I got a glass of wine and went to my usual place to watch her play. When I settled in, she immediately stopped and looked at me.

"I've just about got it," she said. "I'll start from the beginning and you tell me if it describes my birthday night."

"All right," I replied.

The piece was perfect. I could tell exactly when I walked into the room. There was even a fast little trill that I was sure represented the move on the piano bench that I had thought so much about. The point where I got up and moved toward her was a lovely melody that grew in intensity until I feared the neighbors would start banging on the walls. Then there was this jarring noise as she slammed her right hand down on the piano. I swear, it was the same notes her hand had slammed into that night. Immediately after that, there was a short silence, and then came the musical picture of me leaving the room. Then she did something that I thought was brilliant. The music went back to the place where it had begun. It was as if the end of the piece was her getting the idea for the beginning of it. It was like a circular thing that could be played over and over again.

Maybe it was because it was about me, but I thought it was wonderful. Her ability to musically describe the events of the evening led me to confirm what I had first heard about Edith: she was a genius.

"Amazing," I said as the last notes faded away. "I saw it all."

"I think it's the best thing I've ever done. I'm going to play it at my next recital."

"I'd be honored," I said with a smile.

"You should come."

"I'd love to."

"It's in a few weeks. I'll remind you."

"Great."

"God, I wish I could play it for Brian."

"Who's he?" I asked.

"The man who went to England."

"Oh," I said quietly.

"What about you? Did you leave some poor girl behind when you decided to go to the other side of the world?"

"There was someone I was seeing. We hadn't been going out very long."

"What's her name?"

"Martha."

"What did she say when you told her you were going off to New Zealand?"

"I don't really know."

"What do you mean, you don't really know?" Edith asked after a moment.

"I never got to talk to her about it. I left her a message on her answering machine."

"You what?" she asked as she stood up and stared at me.

"That was the best I could do," I said with a shrug.

"Bastard!" she growled.

She slammed down the cover on the piano and walked over and slapped me hard on the face.

"That's for Martha!" she shouted as she stomped out of the room.

I sat there stunned. I heard her bedroom door slam and a few seconds later, the sound of crying coming from her room. I walked down the hall and stood outside the door and listened. I called her name a few times, but she just kept on crying. When I knocked on her door, she called me a prick and told me to go away.

I went down to my room and got undressed. I sat and thought about Edith for a long time. I could just barely hear her crying through the two closed doors. I had certainly stumbled upon one interesting woman. One part of me was angry at her for hitting me so hard. The other part wanted to go into her room and rock her in my arms. Both parts thought she was wonderful.

When the crying stopped, I got into my sleeping bag and stared at the ceiling. It was very late, but I decided to give Maggie a call. The evening had been such a major break-through with Theresa that I thought she wouldn't mind hearing about it, even at this hour. The phone rang five times before it was picked up and the first thing I heard was music. Soon Maggie's voice came on the line.

"Yes," she said.

"It's me. I just wanted to tell you that I made some great progress with Theresa tonight. We went out after rehearsal. We walked by the river and she put her arm through mine."

"Great," Maggie said.

"She also had six brandies and got drunk."

"Even better. You're on your way, Thomas."

"Thomas?" I asked. "Maggie, is someone with you?"

"Maybe."

"Jesus."

"Now, now, we all have our work to do."

"Let me guess. Someone from the bank, right?"

"My, you are clever," she said with a laugh.

"Let's meet at The Greek tomorrow and go over what's happened."

"What's there to talk about? It's very clear what has to be done. You have your life and I have mine. The fact is, I don't have as much time for you as I once did."

"Is he smiling while you're saying that?" I asked.

"Of course," Maggie said, and then she hung up the phone.

Chapter Seventeen

Opening night for the play was something new and unique for me. The excitement in the air almost equaled that of pulling off a good con. Everyone was running around giving each other presents. The kissing and hugging began to border on the absurd. I got a rose from our leading lady, a pen set from the director, and a book of George Bernard Shaw's plays from Theresa. I felt quite the fool because I didn't have anything for anybody. I confided my embarrassment to Theresa, but she said not to worry about it.

When the news leaked backstage that the critics from both Christchurch newspapers were in the audience, everything reached new heights of frenzy. Ten minutes before the play was to begin, the director called us all together and thanked everyone for their hard work. He then gave us a pep talk worthy of any football coach. When that was done, everyone went to their places and waited for the play to begin.

Besides my shouting from offstage, I had nothing to do during the first act. I had started getting into the habit of pulling a chair over to where the light spilled into the wings.

I would sit there and read until the act ended. During the final few dress rehearsals, I had been bringing in magazines. On opening night, I leafed through a magazine and then got out the book on coins. Theresa was about ten feet away from me and we would often exchange smiles if things were going well. In the final nights before opening, I had caught her staring at me a few times. Tonight, I was hoping she would do just that as I sat there absorbed in the coin book.

She and I had not gone for anymore walks since our foggy evening along the river. Every night, we were the last ones to leave the theater, and I made it a habit to walk her to her car. Two nights earlier, I had put my arm around her as we crossed the parking lot. The next night, we had talked for a while by her car, and when it was time to leave, I leaned over and gave her a good-bye kiss. When I went to pull away, she put her arm up around my neck and kissed me again. The smile on her face afterward seemed to say, "What took you so long?" Tonight, she had squeezed my hand when I first saw her. There was to be an opening night party at the director's house after the play. I thought of it as an opportunity to really give her some attention.

The play went well, and when it was over, the endless kissing and hugging happened all over again. After everyone had reassured each other that the play was a success, they all headed for the dressing rooms to change for the party. Within half an hour, the theater was deserted by everyone but Theresa and me. We talked quietly as we went about our duties.

"Now comes the easy part," Theresa said.

"The party?" I asked.

"No, I mean the run of the show. That's what I really love. We settle in and do the play for three weekends. It gives me purpose. I'm just a happier person when I've got a play going."

"That's not so strange," I replied. "It's what you love to do."

"God, what I'd give to hear that sentence from my father."

"I think you may have to tell him to go to hell one of these days," I suggested.

"That would be a shock for both of us," she replied.

"Come on, Theresa, you've got to stand up for yourself. How can he ever really know what makes you feel good?"

"I'll tell you one thing, Yankee boy, *you* make me feel good. I think I'm going to be sorry to see you wander off."

I walked over to her, put my arms around her waist, and kissed her. She held me tight and gave out a little sigh when our tongues met for the first time.

"Let's lock up and get over to the party," she said when the kiss was over. "If we're late, all the food will be gone."

I followed her over to the director's house, and we walked into the party together. When we came into the living room, everyone looked up from their plates and applauded. Theresa and I did a set of elaborate bows and managed to get a laugh. After our grand entrance, we put our things down and headed for the food table.

My plan to sit with Theresa was immediately thwarted because there weren't any seats together. She sat between two of the actors, and I got a seat next to our host. I complimented him on his home and we did ten minutes of small talk about the play and how well it had gone. After a while, he stopped talking and looked over at Theresa, and I followed his gaze. We both watched her get up from her seat and go over to the bar. The director sighed as she made herself a screwdriver that was half vodka. He looked over at me and gave me one of those helpless little smiles. We both turned and watched Theresa go back to her seat and take a good, long drink.

"Are you and Theresa ready to take over and run the show?" he asked.

"I'm sure Theresa is," I answered.

"I'm going to be out of town next Saturday and Sunday, so she'll be the boss."

"I'm sure she can handle it."

"May I talk seriously with you for a moment?" he asked softly.

"Sure."

"Rumor has it that you and she are getting rather chummy. I don't say that to be a gossip. I say it because I care about her and hope maybe you can help us with something."

"Does it have anything to do with screwdrivers that are half vodka?" I asked.

"Precisely," he said with a nod.

"What can I do?"

"Probably nothing about the actual drinking. I was just hoping you'd be able to keep her off the roads after our parties. When she goes home and drinks, it's fine because she doesn't have to go anywhere. After our parties, we often have this very uncomfortable scene where people try to talk her out of driving. Unfortunately, they never succeed. She's actually gotten quite nasty about it a few times. In the end, she drives home by herself and, I'm afraid, sometimes doesn't even remember doing it."

"I see," I said with a serious sigh.

"If you are developing a relationship with her, you might be able to help with the situation. I would ask you to do what you can to keep her from behind the wheel. Maybe you two could come together so you can drive. That kind of thing. It has gotten so people leave the parties early because they don't want to be there for the promised ugly scene with Theresa."

"I could give it a try."

"Excellent," he said as he patted me on the shoulder. "You didn't by any chance drive her over here tonight?"

"No."

"Too bad. She'll get drunk tonight. We can depend on that. So if you wouldn't mind, for her sake, our sakes, and all those other poor fools out there driving, see if you can arrange to take her home.''

''All right.''

''It's a wonder she hasn't killed herself already,'' he said as he shook his head. ''One more favor: if you don't mind, try to keep an eye on her when she's drinking. She sometimes says very unpleasant things that I'm sure she doesn't mean. Try to pull her out of situations before they go bad. She may not remember these things, but others do. We all love Theresa, and she is a hell of a stage manager, so we want to do our part to help her with this problem.''

After he said that, we looked back to where Theresa had been sitting. We saw that her chair was empty. Like two robots, we automatically shifted our gaze to the bar. There she was, mixing herself another killer screwdriver. Steven turned and whispered in my ear.

''See what I mean?'' he said.

After everyone had eaten, there were a few toasts to various people, and then one final toast to the playwright, George Bernard Shaw. After that, the buffet table and all its contents were carefully lifted and carried into the kitchen. Steven cranked up the music, and pretty soon people were dancing up a storm. I had the first dance with Steven's wife while Theresa danced with the light designer. We found each other for the second dance and rocked and rolled through four straight songs. When a slow song played, we snuggled our warm bodies together and moved slowly around the room. When it was over, Theresa said she needed a drink, so we went off to the bar. I grabbed a beer and she mixed another killer.

''You a vodka drinker?'' I asked.

''Pretty much,'' she answered after a swallow. ''But I really liked that brandy we had the other night.''

''I just liked the other night,'' I said with a smile.

''What a sweet thing to say,'' she replied.

''I hope we can spend more time together.''

"I think that can be arranged."

"Good," I said.

"We're both free Monday through Thursday evenings," she said coyly.

"How about if we go out to dinner on Wednesday night?" I suggested.

"It's a date."

"You'll have to tell me how to get to your house."

"Of course. You'll have to come in for a tour of the empty palace."

"Sure."

Steven came over and asked Theresa to dance, and everybody cleared back and watched them go. The director was an ex-dancer, and the whole point of the exercise was to watch him, not Theresa. The room was all smiles and howling encouragements. About halfway through the song, Theresa came back over to me and Steven went at it on his own. Later, the music was turned off, and a couple of the actors did a very goofy parody of the first scene in the play. By then everyone had had enough liquor to make the parody seem a lot funnier than it was. As soon as the performance was over, Theresa returned to the bar. This time her walk contained a lot of wobble. The music started again and there was dancing for a while longer. Theresa continued to drink, and by then was quite sloshed. My last dance with her was a slow one, and she was unable to follow my steps. At one point, she would have fallen if I hadn't been holding onto her.

"How about if I drive you home?" I said when the music ended.

"Will you take advantage of me?" she asked drunkenly.

"No," I replied.

"Damn," she said with a laugh.

I went to get her purse, and while I was doing that, Steven came over and shook my hand.

"Thanks for coming," he said.

"My pleasure."

"Has our stage manager found a ride home?" he asked.

"Yes, with yours truly."

"Good man, Thomas," he said as he slapped me on the back.

I walked Theresa out to my car as she sang one of the slow songs that we had danced to. I got her into the front seat, and by the time I had walked around to the other side and gotten in, she had passed out. I didn't mind the end of her singing, but now I had a problem. I didn't know where she lived. I found her wallet and got the address from her driver's license. I then looked it up on my map. It was only a couple of miles away and we were there in less than ten minutes. I pulled into the driveway, turned the car off, and tried my best to wake her up. She moaned, said some gibberish words, and then conked out again. I wasn't quite sure what to do with her. There was a water spigot sticking out of the ground by the front porch, so I went and put my hands under the cold water. She woke as I was rubbing the cold water on her face.

"Thomas," she said. "I had a really good time."

"Me too," I replied. "But now we have to get you into the house."

"Did you take advantage of me?" she asked.

"No."

"Good," she said. "I would have hated to miss it."

"Next time."

"Promises, promises," she mumbled with a drunken laugh.

"I'd like to make love to you," I said. "I just need to be sure that you want me to."

"Oh, God," she moaned. "That's the most romantic thing anyone has ever said to me."

She threw her arms around my neck and I took the opportunity to carefully pull her out of the car. We made our way up the steps to the front door. I had to go through her purse

in order to find the key. When I got the door open, I began
to think that this might be a good chance to go inside and
rummage around a bit. Just as I was pulling the door closed,
a voice from out by the driveway shouted up at us.

"Is that you, Miss?"

I poked my head out and was immediately blinded by a
flashlight.

"Who the hell are you?" demanded the voice behind the
flashlight.

"I work with Theresa at the theater. We had our opening
night party tonight and I'm afraid Theresa had too much to
drink. I was asked to drive her home, but now that we're
here, I'm not sure what to do with her."

"Ah, yeah," the voice said sadly.

"Do you live here?" I asked.

"I live in the back. I manage the property."

"Well, maybe you should take over from here."

The flashlight lowered and the man came up the steps.
He had pure white hair and a heavily lined face. I carefully
handed Theresa off to him and he put her down on a couch.

"What's your name?" he asked.

"Thomas."

"I'm Douglas," he said as we shook hands. "Thanks for
bringing her home. She often drives it alone."

"That's what I hear."

"I'll be getting her upstairs now. I'll tell her to thank
you."

"Fine," I said as I started for the door.

"Thomas," Theresa shouted after me. "Don't leave me
alone with this pervert. He grabbed my breast the last time
he tried to help me up the stairs."

"That was an accident, Miss," Douglas said, turning beet
red. "You were about to fall. I was trying to catch you."

"That's what you say," Theresa mumbled.

"I assure you it was accidental," he said to me.

"Of course," I said with a nod.

"That she remembers," he said as he shrugged.

"I want Thomas to take me up to my room," Theresa demanded.

"I'm afraid that wouldn't do at all," Douglas said as he walked over to the door and opened it. "Thomas, not to worry, we have done this procedure many times. I am here at the prime minister's request."

"Just an old soldier doing his duty," Theresa said with a laugh.

"Please, sir, it's very late," Douglas said.

"Sure," I whispered as I went out the door.

I walked back to my car, and when I got into the seat, I saw that several more lights had come on in the house. I was sorry for the lost opportunity to at least learn the lay-out of the place. I decided to wait and watch the lights coming on to see if it gave me a clue to the location of her room. After a couple of minutes, a light on the east side of the second floor came on. The old man came to the window and drew the curtains. I then started the car and headed for home.

The apartment was quiet when I got back. I walked down the hall and stopped outside Edith's room. I put my ear up against the door and could barely hear the sound of her breathing. I found myself overwhelmed with the desire to go in and just watch her sleep. It sounded like such a peaceful thing to do. Instead, I went to my room, got undressed, and was soon asleep.

I was having a late breakfast at eleven the next morning when my phone rang. It was Theresa and she sounded pretty bad.

"Thomas," she said. "Can you come and get me tonight and drive me to the theater? I'm afraid that someone has stolen my car. I just got through talking to the police."

"You'd better call them back," I said as I tried not to laugh. "Your car is over at Steven's house. I drove you home."

"Oh," she murmured.

"Listen, why don't I pick you up anyway? I'll drive you over to his house and you can get your car."

"All right," she said. "Come around six-thirty."

"Good. I'll see you then."

I hung up the phone and then laughed out loud. She remembered none of it. My beautiful line about making love to her when I was sure she wanted me to was completely wasted. Still, all in all, it had been a very good night. I was well on my way.

Chapter Eighteen

Theresa didn't have much to say when I picked her up on Saturday night. We did our jobs backstage and the show was once again well received. I spent a good deal of time studying my coin book. After we locked up, I walked her to her car. When we got there, she turned and looked at me.

"I want to apologize for last night," she said.

"What's to apologize for?" I asked. "We worked hard on the play and last night was a chance to let loose. So you drank a little too much. Don't you think I've ever done that?"

"The trouble is, I do it too often. People say I have a problem."

"Do you?"

"I prefer to think of it as a bad habit."

"Have you tried to do anything about it?"

"My parents sent me up to a place in Hamilton for a couple of months. I did pretty good while I was there."

"What started you in again?"

"Hard to say. I think maybe I'm just weak."

"You're not weak when you're in that theater."

"That's different."

"Really? Why is it different?"

"I don't know," she said angrily. "It just is."

"Look, Theresa, I don't know what to say. I'm not a professional when it comes to these things. Hell, I'm still trying to figure myself out. One thing I do know is that it's better not to be alone. I like you. I enjoy your company. Let's do things together. That's really the only help I have to offer."

"That's a lot," she said quietly.

"We're going out Wednesday night, remember?"

"That I remember."

"Good. We'll have dinner somewhere. Just relax and have a good time."

"Sounds nice."

"I'll pick you up at seven."

"I guess you know where I live," she said shyly.

"That I do," I said as I bent down to give her a kiss.

I drove home with a big smile on my face. I couldn't believe how well this project was going.

Maggie had given me the fourth installment of my ten thousand dollars, right on schedule. But when it had come time for the last two thousand, she had put me off. She said she didn't have enough cash on hand and that she needed some time. I didn't like it, but she had been true to her word so far, so I decided to trust her and not make a fuss. With the rehearsals every night and working at the club during the day, I had completely forgotten about the last of the money. Maybe she had been counting on that. As I was driving home from the theater, I suddenly remembered and decided to call Maggie as soon as I got home. When I got in I tried her right away but didn't get an answer. I lay down on my mattress, determined to call every fifteen minutes until I got her. Instead, I fell asleep and was awoken an hour later by the sound of music coming from down the hall. Edith was playing her Perfume Highway piece. When she finished it, I heard several female voices scream with delight. I was tempted to go down there and see what was going on, but Edith started playing the piece over again and I drifted off to the sounds of my own sexual adventure.

I called Maggie Sunday morning and filled her in on the good news about Theresa. She gave me a few seduction hints and encouraged me to somehow get the conversation around to my interest in coins. We agreed that I would give it a try during my Wednesday date with Theresa. After that, I brought up the topic of my last two thousand dollars. She said she now had the cash and would get it to me during the coming week. I suggested that we meet on Monday night.

"I'm busy that night," she said.

"Your friend at the bank?" I asked.

"Warren, don't worry about it. I'm doing that for both of us."

"Oh, really?"

"The bank I'm working in is where the prime minister's family does all their banking."

"That's interesting," I said.

"They have a safety deposit box, and the coins may be in it."

"What makes you think that?"

"Because they are too valuable to keep around the house. It was Stuart's idea and, I think, a good one."

"You two must talk a lot."

"We do. If the coins are in the safety deposit box, it may mean that all you have to do is get a key. You get her key, I get the master key, and we're on a plane out of here. It might be months before they realize the coins are missing. It would be perfect."

"Are you trying to tell me there just happened to be an opening at the bank where the Newtons have their safety deposit box?"

"Of course not. One of the women who worked in the safety deposit box area had an accident."

"What!"

"Don't worry, she'll be fine in a few months."

"Jesus Christ. How did you manage that?"

"I was able to hire someone. It's why I was short of cash."

"My God, you people are serious," I said.

"Did you think we weren't?" Maggie asked.

"So you just marched in there the next day and applied for the job?"

"No, I'd been dating the bank manager before the accident. He was well aware of how badly I needed a job."

"Amazing."

"Thanks, but it's really just business as usual."

"You have been one busy lady."

"So have you. We're both earning our money."

"So what about Tuesday?" I asked. "Can I get my money on Tuesday?"

"Tuesday is fine. Meet at The Greek?"

"Sure. How about seven?"

"Perfect. See you then," she said, and she hung up.

I sat back against the wall and took a deep breath. I wondered if I wasn't in way over my head with these people. I was going to have to watch my ass. They obviously had no trouble playing rough if they had to.

We did the play again on Sunday night, so I saw Theresa once more before our date. She gave me a big smile when she first saw me and again squeezed my hand. During my slow time backstage, I got the coin book out and studied the pages as if they contained the most important information I had ever seen. There actually were pictures of the coins I was supposed to be after, but I made sure I stayed away from those pages. As I was reading the book, Theresa took her headset off, tiptoed over to me, and began rubbing my shoulders.

"Don't you have a cue coming up?" I whispered.

"Next one isn't for eight minutes," she whispered back.

I put the book down on my lap with the cover facing up and lowered my head as she massaged my neck.

"Are you interested in coins?" she asked.

"I've always been fascinated by them," I said casually.

"Me too."

"Really?"

"Sure. My grandfather had one of the world's foremost coin collections. It's mine now, only it isn't as foremost as it used to be."

"Did he leave it to you?"

"Yes. I was the only one in the family who shared his interest. When I was a little girl, he and I would spend hours going over them. He taught me a lot."

"Is it still a good collection?" I asked.

"Oh, yeah, I still have some very valuable coins. A few that are quite famous. I'll have to show them to you sometime."

"I'd like that," I said.

With that she patted me on top of the head and went back to her post. "Bingo," I thought to myself. I got such a big smile on my face that I had to turn away. We had ended up targeting the right Newton after all. It was a beautiful thing when it was working—absolutely beautiful.

I walked her to her car and we promised each other that we would have a good time on Wednesday night. I was very tempted to bring up the subject of the coin collection again but decided not to push it. Besides, I had to wait and talk to Maggie. If all I had to do was get the safety deposit box key, it might call for a whole different approach.

I drove home humming to myself. My ploy with the coin book had worked like a charm. I was convinced that I was one of the cleverest people on the face of the earth. Imagine: a brain like mine, stuffing envelopes for the phone company? I was sure that those days were over.

When I got home, I found Edith in the kitchen eating one of my meat pies. When I looked around the kitchen, the evidence led me to conclude that she was on her second one.

"Don't worry, I'll clean up the mess," she said as she saw me looking around.

"Can I get a bit of that?" I asked as I grabbed a plate and a spoon.

"Go ahead," she replied as she leaned back in her chair.

I scooped out half the pie and then went to the refrigerator for some wine. I poured us each a glass and then sat down opposite her. She took a long gulp of the wine and then went back to attacking the pie.

"Hungry woman," I said.

"Haven't had anything since those corn flakes this morning."

"I've got some eggs in there."

"Didn't have the time."

"You came in pretty late last night. Sounded like you had company."

"Had some friends over. I played 'Perfume Highway' for them. They loved it. Made me play it twice. Everyone said it was the best thing I've ever done."

"I'm proud to be a part of it," I said with a smile.

"I played it for the head of the music department today. Sort of an audition for the recital. He thinks it's some kind of breakthrough for me."

"Wow."

"He said I should continue down this road. See where it takes me."

"I'm all for that," I said with a sly smile.

"I've spent this evening working on something new."

"Don't you have to have another sexual experience with me before you can do that?" I asked innocently.

"I wasn't exactly thinking along those lines."

"Oh?"

"It's not the sex this time. It's who you are. What you're up to. All the mystery. I just know I'm going to come home someday and you'll be gone. You'll pull off whatever it is you're up to and then get the hell out of here."

"That's possible."

"What I want to do is write a suite. A long piece about this experience with you. 'Perfume Highway' would be part of it."

"Fine with me," I said.

"I was trying tonight. I came up with some good stuff, but I need to know more."

"About what?"

"About you. What you're doing."

"You've got to be kidding."

"Look, Thomas, I just want it for the music. You've got to believe that. I can feel this thing inside me. I need you to feed me more images. Please believe me, I won't say a word to anybody."

"Edith, I don't mind paying most of the rent and keeping you in food. That doesn't matter to me. But I can't spill my guts to you. That would be ridiculous. Surely you can see that."

"You don't trust me," she said with a pout.

"It's not a question of trust. It's a question of common sense."

"Then just tell me about the people involved. The woman in the booth. Tell me what happened before I met you. Tell me how you got into it and how it was planned. Change the names. Change the places. Just give me something that I can sink my teeth into."

She reached over for the wine and refilled my glass, as if to assist in loosening my tongue. I obliged by taking a sip, but instead of giving her the story she wanted, I repeated my objections. We went back and forth for a while until it seemed she was almost ready to cry.

"I need this," she said seriously. "The music has to come

out of me or I start to get crazy. It's like my brain gets clogged up. You've got to believe me, I won't tell a soul.''

I finally agreed to tell her what had happened, up to my arrival in New Zealand. I started with my night job and the phone calls from Australia. From there I went on to the arrival of Willem. I told her about tracking down Maggie and going to see her. Of course I changed all the names and didn't mention any exact locations. Edith kept pressing me for details and I had trouble not telling her everything she wanted to know. Her passion was overwhelming. I told her about the company we worked for, and she sat there with her mouth hanging open. When I told her about the return of Willem and our escape, she gasped.

After I was finished, she insisted that I had left out the most important part. She wanted the details of my personal relationship with the woman I was working with. I filled her in on my history with Maggie and even got into some of our sexual adventures. My better judgment told me not to do it, but I couldn't resist telling her about the sunset sex on the hill in Iowa. About halfway through with it, I realized that I was getting an erection and that Edith's breathing had changed. When I realized what was happening, I slowed the story down and told her every detail I could think of. When I was done, we both took sips of our wine at the same moment. We sat there staring at each other.

"My God," she said after a few seconds. "Do you realize what I can do with something like that?"

"Whole symphonies, I imagine," I said.

"It's so rich. There's so much to it."

"I don't know why I'm doing this," I said doubtfully.

"Because you trust me. I swear, it will become music and that is all."

"It better."

Again we stared at each other. I didn't know if I'd ever get another chance like this with her, so I decided to do something. My wineglass was empty, so I got up and put it into the sink. When I got behind her, I turned back and got down on my knees. When I did that, she froze in the chair, but didn't make a move to stop me. I pushed her hair to one side and began kissing the back of her neck. She reached up and put her hand on my head. I then reached my left hand around and started caressing her stomach. I slowly worked my way up to her breasts. She suddenly pushed my hand away and stood up. She stepped away from the chair and looked down at me.

"If I go to bed with you, what will it mean?" she asked.

"It will mean I find you very desirable," I replied quickly.

"Besides that. What will it mean about our living together? Am I to become your regular thing? Are you going to want to get laid all the time? Are you going to start making demands?"

"Edith, think of the other night on the piano bench. Have I changed since then? Have I been making demands? I gave to you because you wanted me to."

After I said that, she reached down and took my hand. I got up off my knees and she led me into her bedroom. We undressed each other, and when we were nude, she handed me a pack of matches and told me to light every candle in the room. When I was done, she raised her hand and invited me into her bed.

"Enough with the foreplay," she said. "Make me scream again."

So I did.

When it was over, I was delighted to find several of Edith's dark-purple hairs sticking to my chest. I grabbed one of them and wrapped it around my little finger. I decided it was something I wanted to have. I promised myself that I would carefully pack it away and take it back to America with me.

Edith hopped out of bed and brought back a glass of cold water that we shared. After we had both taken long drinks, she propped herself up on the pillow and looked over at me.

"A corporation for stealing," she said. "I would never have imagined such a thing."

"Me neither."

"You trust these people?"

"Up to a point."

"I hate to say this, Thomas, but the idea keeps popping up in my head that you're the one who's getting conned."

"What do you mean?" I said with a laugh.

"It's all just a little too fantastic. These calls from Australia. Her using your name by mistake. The guy showing up at her house. The narrow escape."

"It really happened," I said defensively.

"I don't doubt that," she said as she took another sip of water. "I just can't help but wonder about it."

"Wonder about what?"

"You see? The music is already starting to play in my head. I can hear it."

"That's what you wanted, isn't it?"

"Yes, but it doesn't sound right to me. It doesn't flow. It sounds like you're the fall guy. Like these people have done a very splendid job of setting you up. It plays like you're the pawn."

"Look," I said. "It's your music. You can play it any way you want. I assure you that I'm nobody's pawn. I'm going to make a lot of money on this thing."

"Fine," she said. "I just think you should be careful."

"Don't worry," I said. "I could never get suckered in this deep."

"You're probably right," she said calmly.

"Of course I am."

We sat there quietly while my mind raced through the details of the past month. I reassured myself that Edith didn't know what she was talking about. It was music in her head. It had nothing to do with what was really going on. The whole idea was absurd.

"The sex was wonderful," she said as she leaned over and kissed me.

"My pleasure," I replied.

"It energized me. I want to play for a while."

"Going to play my story?"

"I don't like to wait. The feeling is so strong right now. It would be a mistake not to get on with it."

She got up and slipped into her nightgown. She then came over and grabbed my hand and tugged me up off the bed.

"Go to sleep, Thomas," she said. "Go crawl into your sleeping bag. I have work to do."

"All right," I muttered as we walked out into the hall.

She walked down toward her piano and I started in the direction of my room.

"Hey," she called out as I was about to close my door. "Is it really Thomas?"

"No," I said.

I looked down the hall at her and she just nodded. I closed the door and got into my sleeping bag. Shortly after that, the music started. She began with my job at the phone company. I could hear the monotony of the machines. I could hear the graveyard-shift sorrows. Then the music changed. It became very spooky. As I was drifting off to sleep, I found myself wishing that there weren't this one thing I was sure of. I wished I weren't so sure that Edith was a genius.

When I woke up the next morning, the first thing I saw was a blurred vision of deep purple in front of my left eye. The strand of Edith's hair that I had wrapped around my finger had come off and was lying on the pillow next to my head. As soon as I realized what it was, I began to think about the conversation from last night. I got up and placed the purple hair on a piece of newspaper and folded the paper up. I then put it in one of the side pockets in my suitcase. While I did this, I vowed to spend the day in deep concentration. I needed to see if there were any flaws that would support Edith's conclusions.

There had been a dinner the night before at the cricket club. I came in to work and found a mountain of dirty pots waiting for me. They had been there all night and the food had crusted and dried onto them. I filled the sinks with steaming-hot water and scrubbed like a man possessed. By lunchtime I had the counter covered with gleaming pots. Even cynical Charlie was impressed.

I had also made a couple of decisions, the first being that I couldn't just dismiss Edith's conclusions. The idea of Maggie using my name for a phony grandfather suddenly didn't ring true. It just didn't seem like Maggie to mess up like that. The other thing that really started to bother me was her job at the bank. I couldn't put my finger on it, but it was just too damn pat. While I was scraping burnt cherry cobbler out of a pan, I remembered about Maggie's refusal to meet with me that night. She implied that she was seeing her squeeze from the bank, and maybe she was. There wasn't anything in particular I had to do that evening, so I decided to tail her. I hadn't seen or talked to her that much in the past two weeks, and it seemed like a good idea to find out how she spent her time.

After work I went home, got cleaned up, and then drove over to Maggie's street. I parked a block down the street and had the car facing away from the door I knew she would come out of. I moved the rearview mirror around until it was on the door and then settled in to wait. I'd been there just under an hour when the door opened and out she came. When she got to the sidewalk, she turned to her right and started walking away from me. I quickly got out of the car and followed her from the opposite side of the street. After we had walked five blocks, she came to a place called the Green Dragon Pub and Grill. She went into the front door and I settled in with a cup of coffee in the café across the street. I had a second cup and a hamburger as I waited for her to come out again.

I was just finishing a piece of cake when Maggie finally

reappeared. She came out by herself and headed back in the direction of her apartment. This seemed like very strange behavior for someone who was supposed to be on a date. My first thought was to get up and follow her, to make sure that she was going home. I decided to hang back for a minute or two and have a look at the faces of the people who came out after her. During the next couple of minutes, several people entered, but no one came out. I was just getting up to leave the café when the door to the pub opened and two men came out. They walked up the street, got into a car, and drove away. The two men were Stuart and Willem.

Chapter Nineteen

I sank back down onto my chair. A muscle near the bottom right rib started tightening up. It felt like a piece of rope that was being twisted around and around. I lifted my shirt and tried to massage away the pain, but it was too deep. My fingers couldn't reach into the afflicted area. I tried poking into myself, to get at the now steel-hard muscle, but only succeeded in causing myself more pain. An idea shot through my head that twisted the rope even more: Willem was the partner. When he had called me and taken me out to dinner, he was partnering. When we found him sitting in Maggie's living room, he was partnering. I began to wonder what Maggie had sprayed him with that day. Of course, now that I thought about it, I had smelled nothing. I remembered Maggie telling me that the con wouldn't work unless I trusted her. The irony of that statement was almost unbearable. I was involved in a very elaborate con that had a couple of marks, one of whom was me.

They had known all along that Peter Newton was gay. They knew all along that the sister with the drinking problem was the real target—that *she* had inherited her grandfather's coin collection. Maggie had played me perfectly. I could just see them all sitting around a table in Des Moines, trying to figure out how to go after the coins. I could just hear Maggie saying, "I know a guy who would be perfect." I even began to wonder about the office in Des Moines.

There was a movie house just up the street, and as I was sitting there, the doors opened and people came pouring onto the sidewalk. A crowd gathered at the corner across the street from where I was sitting. I sat there and looked out at the faces. They were all such healthy-looking people. It must have been a good movie; many of them had smiles on their faces. I watched them cross the street. I moved my eyes from face to face. I didn't know a one of them. I never would. Suddenly I felt like the loneliest person in the world.

I got the idea that I should walk, that maybe I would be able to think clearer if I was moving. I also hoped that walking would loosen the aching muscle in my gut. After I paid my bill, I started down the street at a near trot.

When I got down to where my car was, I decided to jump in and drive for a while. What was needed was a little slipping into neutral. I needed to calm my screaming brain. As I waited at a red light, I saw a liquor store in the next block. I pulled into a spot in front of the liquor store, went in, and stared at the rows of bottles. Then I thought, if vodka was good enough for Theresa, it was good enough for me. I grabbed a one-liter bottle, paid for it, and was soon driving out toward the ocean.

I found a bluff overlooking the sea and got out of the car. I sat down in the grass and started drinking. I gulped the vodka down, coughed and gagged, then swallowed some more. After drinking half the bottle, I sat there waiting for the numbness to arrive. It didn't. It was as if my body absorbed the alcohol and just shot it out through my pores. I looked down at the crashing waves and cursed my stupidity.

I cursed myself because once again it looked like I had been led around by my dick.

After drinking the rest of the vodka, I heaved the bottle over the cliff. I sat there as sober as I was when Willem and Stuart walked out of that pub. For some reason, I suddenly remembered all that business about my being followed on the trip from Los Angeles to Omaha. Renting the car in Denver and driving around. It looked as if I had been a puppet. I laughed a sick laugh at my own foolishness. Then I thought a lot of vengeful thoughts. I imagined dozens of things I could do to those three to make them suffer. As the muscle in my stomach began to slowly unwind, I thanked the stars that I had moved in with a purple-haired genius.

I was hoping that Edith would be up when I got home. I longed to sit on the window seat and listen to her play her wonderful music. Before I unlocked the door, I stood there and listened for the piano but heard nothing. When I walked down the hall to my room, I once again stood outside her door and waited until my ears were able to pick up the sound of her breathing. The moment I heard it, I became very still. It was so nice to let the rhythm of her life relax me. Just as I was taking the first steps toward my room, she sang in her sleep. Just a few notes, but it sounded like sweet candy slipping under her door and into my ears. I would have given anything to know what dream had caused it.

I zipped up my sleeping bag and tried to sleep, but couldn't. I played the information over and over again in my head. Trying to figure out what to do. My first thought was to get up in the morning, drive out to the airport, and get the first plane for America. Then I remembered that Maggie was going to hand over another two thousand dollars to me the next day. I decided to stay around for that. Why not fake it through the meeting with her and then run like hell? That thought relaxed me slightly and I fell off into a restless sleep. I had a very vivid dream. In it I was cutting Maggie's face with a knife. When I woke up in the morning,

I was swimming in my own sweat. As I walked down to the shower, I found myself wishing for another big stack of blackened pots. I needed once again to scrub and think.

No black pots awaited me. Only a few dishes and glasses from the night before. When I finished them, I got the mop out and did the kitchen floor. I worked up such a sweat that I had to take my shirt off. Charlie brought me in a Coke from the bar and told me to slow down. When I finished, I stuck my head under the faucet and let the cold water run over my neck. I stayed under the water for a long time, shaking my head back and forth.

Edith wasn't there when I got home. I wanted so badly to sit down with her and tell her that she was right, that everything had fallen apart. I was thinking I would leave her five hundred of my last two thousand dollars to make up for skipping out on her. I waited until a quarter to seven, but she never came home. I walked down to The Greek, got a booth, and waited for Maggie to arrive. When I looked around, I saw her sitting in a booth on the other side of the room. She smiled and waved to me. I got up and walked over to her table and sat down.

"You're early," she said.

"So are you," I replied. "I guess we just can't wait to see each other."

"Can't wait to see your two thousand dollars is more like it."

"That too, of course," I said with a smile. "Have you got it?"

"Don't I always keep my word?" she asked coyly.

She reached into her purse, pulled out an envelope, and slid it across the table to me. Once again, I was looking at twenty nice, new Ben Franklins. I folded the envelope in half and put it in my back pocket.

"Do you have some New Zealand money on you?" Maggie asked.

"Sure."

"Good, because you're buying dinner."

The waiter came and took our orders. We chatted for a while about her job at the bank and my coming date with Theresa. When the food came, we ate in silence for a minute, and then Maggie put her fork down and looked at me.

"Stuart is here," she said.

"Is that good or bad?" I asked.

"Good, because it means he cares about this project. Bad, because he may meddle more than he should. We have to humor him."

"All right," I said.

"He wants the three of us to have dinner on Thursday night. There's a pub down the street from me called the Green Dragon. Can you be there around six?"

"Sure."

"He'll want to hear all about your date with Theresa. Also, he wanted me to tell you to start paying particular attention to her keys. Look at them if you get the chance and see if any of them look like safety deposit box keys. It will look something like this."

Maggie reached into her purse and pulled out a large brass key. She handed it to me. I looked it over carefully and then handed it back to her.

"Notice where she keeps her keys. What she does with them after she gets into her house. Does she put them back in her purse or lay them on a table somewhere? Also, notice if her key chain has a lot of keys on it. Would she miss one of them right away?"

"She has a lot of keys," I said. "I can tell you that, right now. She locks and unlocks everything at the theater."

"Good. Warren, this may be the easiest money we ever made. You steal one little key. I open the safety deposit box, and we walk away with five coins worth a ton of money."

"Sounds too good to be true."

"Doesn't it?" Maggie said. "We're trying to find out if

the coins are in a safe at home or in the safety deposit box. If you can figure that out or get her to tell you, it would make everything a lot easier.''

''I'll try. She already knows I like coins. She's promised me a look at some of them.''

''Great. I have to say that your coin book idea was nothing short of brilliant.''

''Thanks,'' I said with a fake smile.

Her compliments twisted my gut muscle once again. I wanted to pick up my fork and stick it in her face. I wanted to make my dream come true. Instead, I sat there like an employee receiving praise from his boss. Maggie picked at her food for a moment and then got very serious.

''Warren, I know you're really not cut out for this kind of life. I know you want to change things. That you want to go to college and study your bugs. Five years from now, you'll probably be settled in somewhere. You'll have a wife and a couple of kids. I imagine that this will be the last scam you'll ever do. We both know this is the one that will get you what you want. So now you need to be ruthless. I need you to go into neutral like you've never done before. After Stuart met you, he told me he was afraid you might be too soft. That you might chicken out when the time came to really burn somebody. I told him he was wrong. I told him that you'd be a great partner. When things got flipped around and you had to become the point man, he again expressed serious doubts. He wanted me to send you home. To bring in someone else. Again I told him no. I've stuck my neck way out for you because I know you can do it. Please don't make me look like a jerk. I want you to be very focused. You need to not give a damn about this woman. Whatever you do, don't start worrying about her feelings. When we get on that plane, she will be out of your life forever. She'll be gone and you'll have what you want. That's the most important thing, isn't it?''

''Yes,'' I said very quietly.

"Good," she said as she nodded her head. "I know you can do it."

"Now I know I have to."

"That's even better," she said with a sneaky smile.

At that moment I hated Maggie. Her little pep talk had worked very well. What I now knew I had to do was make her pay for trying to make a fool out of me. I had to scam the scammer. Getting on a plane and flying out of here was too damn easy. She wanted ruthless. She wanted neutral. I was going to see that she got them.

As I sat there, I imagined the three of them talking about me at their meeting the night before. I imagined Stuart telling Maggie to give me this serious talk that I had just received. I pictured Willem sitting there, chuckling at the beauty of the setup. My gut twisted again until it became a labor to hide the pain.

"Are you all right?" Maggie asked.

"Yeah, I'm fine," I replied. "I think maybe this food doesn't agree with me tonight."

"Well, you stick with me, kid, and you'll be eating nothing but the best," she said as she reached over and took my hand.

I looked her in the eye and then slowly started to smile. She smiled back at me and we both started to laugh.

We finished our meal, and after some small talk about my date the following evening, we wrapped it up. She left first, and I got up and walked out a few minutes later. Instead of going home, I walked over to the university campus. I circled the quad several times as I thought hard about what to do. After a while, I came up with a plan. It wasn't all that original, but I thought it might work for only one reason. They had no idea I was on to them. So far I had been the perfect sucker, and I would continue to do so. Maggie's pep talk had worked very well, but not in the way she intended. I was going to be ruthless. I was going into neutral like I had never done before. I was also going to try to get the coins for myself.

The trouble was, I needed help. Someone with connections in the artistic community. I immediately knew who that person might be.

When I got a block away from the apartment, I stopped and looked up, hoping to see a light on in the living room. Unfortunately, everything was dark. As I started to look away, I saw a light come on in the kitchen. Edith's silhouette opened the refrigerator door and bent over, peering inside. I had bought a big chunk of ham that afternoon and I was witnessing her discovery of it. Despite my serious state of mind, I couldn't help but laugh. I was sure she'd be working away on the ham by the time I got up there.

When I walked into the kitchen, she was sitting there slicing up the ham. She took a piece of the ham and put it on a cracker. She then dabbed a spoonful of mayonnaise on top of the ham and popped the whole thing into her mouth. I leaned on the door frame and watched her go through the ritual a couple of times. She didn't say a word—just looked up at me and smiled. After her second mouthful, she reached for a glass of my wine and took a good, long drink.

"Want some ham?" she asked after she had swallowed the wine.

"Sure." I sat down across from her.

"Get yourself some wine," she suggested. "This stuff needs to be washed down."

I got a glass and then went to the refrigerator and poured myself some wine. When I got back to my seat, she handed me a cracker with some ham on it.

"Do your own mayonnaise," she said.

"So, how's the new suite coming along?" I asked as I dipped into the mayonnaise jar.

"Pretty good. I'm still working a lot of it out in my head. Trying to get everything in order. I got the beginning right away."

"Good. Got a name for it yet?"

"No. Titles just sort of come. One day, there it is. Of course, some more information from the source would be nice. Don't suppose you've thought of any more details that you could share?"

"Maybe I have."

"Really? So feed me, feed me."

"Actually, I have some new information that might be critical to the piece."

"Don't tell me I was right."

"Yes, you were," I said quietly.

"I knew it wasn't playing right," she said.

"You were more than right. You hit the nail smack on the head. I can't believe I didn't see it myself. They've played me like you play the piano."

"I'll be damned. How did you figure it out?"

"I followed my supposed partner. She had a meeting with one of the bad guys."

"Forgive me if I'm not too clear on who the bad guys are," Edith said with a laugh.

"Depends on your point of view," I said as I reached for the wine.

"What are you going to do?"

"I was going to run. Get on the first plane out of here."

"There goes the rent."

"But I've changed my mind."

"Good."

"They have no idea that I know. If I play this thing right, I could turn everything around on them."

"So do it. Outsmart them."

"I want to, but I need some help," I said as I looked her right in the eye.

"Forget it," she said after a second. "This is way too weird for me."

"You don't actually have to participate. I just need you to help me find some things."

"Like what?"

"Well, for instance, someone who works with metals. One of your friends in the arts. Maybe someone who does sculpture, that kind of thing."

"What would you want them to do?"

"Melt down some gold and shape it a certain way. Make blank coins of a specific size."

"That's not very hard to do," she said.

"I'm glad to hear that," I replied.

I reached into my back pocket and pulled out the envelope that Maggie had given me earlier in the evening. I laid twelve hundred-dollar bills, out on the table. Edith's eyes got very big.

"That's twelve hundred American dollars. You can get them exchanged at any bank. I need five gold coins that are half an ounce each. That's two and a half ounces of gold. Go buy the gold. Then find somebody to melt it down and shape it to the dimensions I give you. You get to keep whatever money is left over."

"How much is gold?"

"About three hundred and fifty dollars an ounce."

Edith sat there quietly and went through the figures in her head. I could see her lips move slightly as she added things up.

"So, after I bought the gold, I'd have a little over three hundred dollars."

"You'd still have to pay the person who melts and shapes it."

"True. It would probably only take a couple of hours."

"If you give them a hundred, you've made an easy two-hundred-dollar profit."

"But I could get into trouble," she said slowly.

"You won't be breaking any laws."

"I don't know," she mumbled as she shook her head.

"Easy money," I taunted.

"Why don't you go buy the gold and then I'll get it shaped?"

"We could do it that way," I agreed.

"How much do I get?"

"I'll tell you what. I'll give you the three hundred, but whoever you get had better do a first-rate job."

"It's a deal," she said.

I scooped up the money and put it back in the envelope. I then finished off my glass of wine and stood up.

"I'm going to call in sick tomorrow and go buy the gold. Why don't you see if you can arrange your part of it? If everything goes as planned, I'll give you the gold and the three hundred dollars tomorrow night."

"Don't forget, I'll need the dimensions of the coins."

"Of course."

"Thomas," she said as I started to leave.

"Yeah?"

"This is just a suggestion, of course, but why don't you drive down to Dunedin to buy the gold. It's a few hours south of here, and it might be, you know, better that way."

"That's a good idea," I agreed. "I'll get up early. Call work from a phone booth. I have to be somewhere tomorrow night. I can get down there and back in a day, can't I?"

"With time left over."

"Good. I'll see you here late tomorrow afternoon and we'll get this thing going."

"Sure," she said as she went back to the ham.

Chapter Twenty

I got up early the next morning and started driving south. At nine o'clock, I stopped at a phone booth and called the cricket club. I told Charlie that I had a bad cold and needed the day off. He gave me a short lecture about taking better care of myself and instructed me to drink a lot of grapefruit juice. I told him I would and that I would be there tomorrow.

It was just going on eleven when I came down the long hill that leads into Dunedin. After a meal at a Chinese restaurant, I went to a phone booth and started looking up jewelry stores. I called around to a few of them. They all had plenty of gold jewelry to sell, but not any raw gold. When I told one of them that I just wanted some gold to melt down, he suggested I try a coin shop. He said I could buy some gold coins and melt them down. It would be a lot cheaper than buying jewelry. It sounded like a good idea, so I got the addresses of three coin shops from the phone book and went looking for them.

The first two were on the main drag—bright, cheery places with big signs out front. I decided to have a look at the other one before I did anything. The third coin shop was on a side street next to a hotel. It was smaller than the other two and looked like it had been there for a long time. I parked the car and went in the front door.

"I need two and a half ounces of gold to melt down for an art project," I told the guy behind the counter.

"No raw gold, mate," he said. "But I can sell you some South African gold coins. You can do with them what you like."

"Can I get a break on the price if I pay American dollars?" I asked.

"Yank, are ya?"

"Canadian, actually, but I have some American money."

"I'll let you have two and a half ounces of gold coins for eight hundred and fifty Yankee dollars," he said after a moment.

"Let's have a look at them."

He went into the back room and came out a minute later with three coins: two large ones and another about half their size. He put them on a scale and showed me that they weighed exactly two and a half ounces. I gave him nine hundred-dollar bills. We then discovered we had a problem figuring out how to make the change. He was looking up the exchange rate when I got an idea.

"You don't do any engraving do you? I want to melt these down and then make them up to look like coins from ancient history."

"Not me, mate. I just sell the stuff. You need a trophy shop for something like that."

"A trophy shop. See, I would have never thought of that. Do you know any trophy men who might be real good at this type of thing?"

"There's a couple of shops in town."

"Do you know the owners?"

"Sure."

"If you'll give me the name and address of the best engraver you know, I'll let you keep that extra fifty dollars."

He looked at me for a moment and then reached under the counter and got out a piece of paper. He grabbed the pencil from behind his ear and wrote down a name and an address.

"His name is Bill Swift. He's a bit of a character, but he's been engraving for forty years."

"Sounds good," I said.

"He's six blocks east and down a bit. His shop is on the right. You flash those Yankee dollars down there and he'll probably do whatever you want."

"Thanks," I said as I took the address and the coins and walked out of the shop.

I pulled up in front of Bill Swift's engraving shop and parked the car. I peered into the windows at a counter and display case filled with dusty trophies. There was a man behind the counter with a leather apron on. He was eating a sandwich and drinking a cup of tea. I got out of the car and walked in the front door.

"Good day," he said with a thick Scottish accent.

"Bill Swift?" I asked.

"The one and only," he replied as he put down his sandwich.

"A fella I know just told me that you might be able to do some work for me."

"Yeah," Bill said slowly. "He just called me. Are you the Canadian with the Yankee money?"

"Word travels fast in Dunedin."

"Not always," Bill said with a sly smile. "So what's this wee labor you've got?"

"It's a very elaborate art project. I want to create some gold coins. They need to look exactly like some that existed a long time ago. I have pictures of them."

"I see," Bill mumbled as he rubbed his chin.

"Can you do that kind of thing?"

"What's on the coins besides writing?"

"On one side is a picture of the old Globe Theatre. The other side has a picture of Queen Elizabeth the First."

"That bloody bitch! She killed our Mary."

"Hold a grudge, do you?" I asked with a smile.

"Damn right," Bill said, smiling back at me. "It sounds like you're talking about some real fine engraving work. Could get expensive."

"How much would you guess?" I asked.

"How many coins would you be wanting?"

"Five."

"No sense punching that many out. I'd have to make myself a couple of wee dies. That's not easy work."

"Just give me an estimate."

"Well, it will probably take a day or maybe two to make each die. There's cleanup work on each coin that will take a couple of hours. Plus, the lettering of course. I'd say about one hundred and twenty dollars per coin. So, six hundred for the lot. I'm talking Yankee dollars, of course."

"Of course. Actually, that's just about right for my budget. I don't suppose you can melt down and shape the gold?"

"Not me, mate. You bring me the blank coins and I'll make 'em look like the pictures."

"It's a deal," I said as I got ready to leave. "I'll be back with the blank coins and the pictures in a couple of days."

"I'll be needing some money now," Bill said casually.

"What for?"

"I've got preparations to make. How do I know I'll ever see your face again?"

"I'll give you a hundred," I said. "But I want a receipt."

"That'll do her," Bill said as he stretched out his hand. I fished out the envelope and let good old Bill see my wad of money. I drew out a hundred-dollar bill and placed it in his hand. He held it up to the light and looked it over.

"One hundred, American," he said. "Never seen one of these before."

"Do a good job and you'll see five more of them," I said as I put the envelope back in my pocket.

"No worries, mate. I've been engraving longer than you've been breathing."

Fifteen minutes later I was on the highway back toward Christchurch. The two thousand dollars that Maggie had given me the night before was going fast. I hated spending it so quickly. Then I had a vision that made me think that it was all worthwhile. That vision was a scene in which Maggie, Stuart, and Willem are all being told that the coins they have are phonies. I pictured their faces and it made me laugh out loud.

Edith was sitting in the living room reading when I walked into the apartment. She put the book down and looked up at me.

"Well?" she asked.

"Amazing day," I responded.

"You got the gold?"

"Yup."

"Let's have a look."

I got the three coins out of my pocket and dropped them into her waiting hand.

"Going to be a hot day tomorrow for these fellows," she said.

"You've arranged it?" I asked excitedly.

"Found the perfect person for the job."

"I guess you'd better keep them," I said with a shrug.

"Fine," she said as she closed her fist. "I'm starved. Want to finish off that ham?"

"No, you go ahead. I've got to get cleaned up."

"Plans for the evening?" she asked.

"Edith, I've got plans coming out my ears," I said as I headed down the hall.

I took a shower, got dressed, and then drove over to Theresa's. The white-haired caretaker was washing her car when I pulled into the driveway. He had the car right by the street, so I backed out and parked in front of the big bushes that surrounded the house. When I came around the corner, he motioned for me to come over to him. As I approached, he turned the hose off and gave me the once-over.

"Thomas, right?" he asked as he held out his hand.

"Yes," I replied. "And you're Douglas."

"You got it," he said with a quick nod.

"Nice to see you again."

"I take it you and Miss Theresa have some plans for the evening."

"Yes. We're going to dinner."

"Good. I'm glad to see her making new friends. Yank, are ya?"

"That's right."

"I want to thank you for helping her out the other night. In the future, if you find yourself in similar circumstances, just blow the horn when you pull into the driveway. I'll come out and see that she gets into the house."

"Tonight is just a quiet dinner. I doubt there'll be a problem."

"Good. Encourage her not to drink, if you can. We're kind of worried about her."

"I will," I said very seriously.

I walked up to the house and rang the doorbell. As I stood there waiting for the door to open, I couldn't help but think that Douglas had a very intelligent air about him. It didn't fit with his washing other people's cars.

After a few seconds, Theresa answered the door. She was ready to go, so we walked out to my car and got in.

"What are you hungry for?" I asked.

"I haven't had any seafood for a while," she replied. "Would you mind that?"

"Sounds good. Got any particular place in mind?"

"Yes, if you don't mind driving for forty-five minutes. There's a wonderful restaurant out by the ocean. It's at the end of a long pier. You feel like you're eating out on the sea.''

"Let's go," I said as I started the car.

Theresa gave me directions, and I found myself driving over the same roads that I had traveled two nights earlier. We got to the ocean and then turned south. After another five minutes, we drove past the bluff where I had tried to get drunk. I wondered if my empty vodka bottle was still lying on the beach below.

"My father owns a lot of the land along here," Theresa said. "Seven kilometers of this beachfront is his."

"Wow. That's a lot."

"Yeah, it starts right about here and goes to the north. It's completely undeveloped."

"Is he going to keep it that way?"

"He wants to, but my brother and I want to build retirement homes out here when it comes to us."

"That'll be nice."

"Some of the ecology nuts wanted him to donate it for a national park. The people in his political party thought that would be a very smart move," Theresa said with a smirk.

"You didn't?"

"Hell no! He said he would leave a kilometer to each of us, and the other five for the park. My brother talked him out of it, and I'm glad he did. We'd never have any peace and quiet with all those people coming out here and using the beach. You know they'd trespass down onto our beach. They'd leave their beer cans all over. The place would be ruined."

"I see what you mean," I said quietly.

Soon we came to a parking lot at the foot of a long wooden pier. At the end of the pier was a big blue building with "Land's End" written in neon on the roof. The words flashed on and off and lit up the rolling sea around the base of the restaurant. It was a good two hundred feet out to the building, and I could see several couples walking to and from the restaurant.

"Very romantic," I whispered as I parked the car.

"I think so," Theresa said. She looked over at me and smiled.

We walked out slowly and stopped once to look down at the water. There were a couple of kids fishing off to one side and we asked them if they had caught anything. One of the boys pulled a rope out of the water, and we saw two large fish hanging from it. We congratulated them and walked on.

"Hate to be eating out here when a sudden storm comes up," I said as we got close.

"Every few years this place gets damaged by a storm," Theresa said. "But they always build it right back up again. Must be a good business."

We had to wait a few minutes for a table and eventually got one looking back down the pier. She had a screwdriver in her hand before I even opened my menu. When I got my beer, I proposed a toast to George Bernard Shaw, the man who had brought us together. Theresa gave me a big smile, and I knew I had said just the right thing. We then ordered our meals and were soon working away at our salads. As we ate, we chitchatted about the play and the people at the theater.

Theresa was on her fourth screwdriver by the time the fish came. We were talking nicely, and I was trying very hard to think of a way to bring up the subject of coin collecting. I was about to try when the man at the next table stood up so quickly that he knocked his chair over.

"Bloody hell!" he said as he looked down the pier.

I followed his eyes and immediately saw what had alarmed him. Down where the young boys had been fishing, there were flames shooting up into the air. The kids were running around, trying to stamp it out, but the fire was already too big for them. I watched as they ran around the fire and down the pier toward the shore. By this time Theresa and everybody else in the restaurant were looking out the window. There was still a gap on the right side of the pier. About a hundred people all realized at once that they had to make a dash for the gap or risk being cut off from the shore. Everyone poured out of the restaurant at once. I grabbed Theresa's hand as we ran along with the crowd. She was not a good runner, and the four screwdrivers didn't help. We soon fell behind and were among the last to arrive at the fire. Most of the people made it through the gap, but now it was too late. There was a solid wall of flames, and about a dozen of us stood on the wrong side of it.

"I slowed you down," Theresa said.

"Don't worry," I replied. "They'll call the fire department. They'll be here in no time."

"Thomas, we are at least thirty miles from the nearest fire department."

"We'll be fine," I said as our little group started walking back toward the restaurant.

We didn't know what else to do, so we went back to our table and sat down again. I finished off my fish while Theresa downed her screwdriver and then went looking for another one.

"Why don't you make that your last one?" I suggested when she sat back down. "We may need to have our wits about us."

"All right," she said in a whisper.

The manager came into the room and told us that he had not been able to call out, that the phone lines ran under the pier and had probably been burned through. He said he was positive that the people on the shore would notify the fire brigade. As he was finishing his speech, there was a blast from a boat's horn off to our left. We looked out the window and saw a good-sized fishing boat making its way around to the back of the restaurant.

"Thank God for Ivan Evans," the manager said. "All

right, everybody, let's go through the kitchen and out to the back. There's a ladder that we'll have to climb down. It's perfectly safe, but please be careful and take your time.''

We followed him out to the back and watched as the boat maneuvered to get into position under the ladder. It was a thirty-foot drop to the boat deck, and the ladder looked old and worn.

"Can you do this all right?" I asked Theresa.

"I think so," she said quietly as she grabbed my hand.

"I'll go first and then help guide your feet. Take all the time you need and don't look down.''

When everything was lined up, the other people started going down the ladder. The bobbing ship and the ladder didn't quite meet, and the men down on the deck had to reach up and lower each person by hand. Theresa and I were toward the end. I got on the ladder first, went down a few steps, and waited for her to appear overhead. Soon one of her feet came over, and then the other. I started talking to her, encouraging her and telling her she could do it. Her moves were very shaky and she gave out lots of little moans and groans. About halfway down, she pulled herself up against the ladder and froze. I tried to coax her down to the next step, but she wouldn't move.

I stroked her ankle and she just started to move her foot again when a gust of wind came ripping through and blew her dress up around her head. Again she froze.

"Nice panties," I shouted up to her. "May I see them again later?''

"Don't make me laugh," she shouted down to me.

After a moment, the wind died and we started on our way again. After another minute, we were on the deck, hugging each other. Soon, everyone was on the boat and we pulled away. When we were almost to the dock, a helicopter came over the bluffs, hovered over the pier for a moment, and then dropped a huge amount of water on the flames. The fire sputtered for a second and then died. Everyone on the boat cheered. After Theresa and I had joined the cheering, we had a nice, long kiss.

"We call them knickers," she whispered in my ear.

"I like panties better," I said.

"Well, either way, your request just might be granted."

"Lovely," I replied.

When the boat docked, we all shook hands with Ivan Evans and then were helped down to the dock. Theresa put her arm through mine as we strolled toward the parking lot. Just as we got into the car, a fire truck came screaming down the hill and pulled up to the end of the pier. We sat and watched as the firemen hosed down the burned area. While we watched them work, Theresa reached over and stroked the back of my neck.

"Thanks," she said.

"No problem," I replied as I started the car.

"Some first date."

"Hey, so far it hasn't cost me a cent."

"That's right! We never paid."

"I don't know about you, but I ate all of my fish."

"And I drank five screwdrivers," she said quietly. "Thomas, you don't think I'm hopeless, do you?"

"I think you drink too much," I said. "But you're human; you've got some serious worries about your future and so you drink a lot. It's not unheard-of."

When I said that, she sighed and leaned back in her seat. She closed her eyes, and it was good that she did, because I had a big smile on my face. I had to admit, I was getting pretty good at this game. Not only that, it was a double game now. I had two neutrals to slip into. One for Theresa and one for Maggie. Taking from Theresa helped me stab at the heart of Maggie. Knowing that made me feel very motivated.

We stopped at another restaurant and I had a salad while Theresa ate a full dinner. This time she had orange juice without the vodka. I told her I was proud of her. Inside I was wondering if maybe I wasn't overdoing it. The last thing I really wanted was for her to start cohering up. It worried me for a few minutes, but then I began to doubt that she could just turn it off like that. It had been a highly exciting evening, and she had probably just replaced the alcohol with adrenalin.

It was too late for a movie, so we went for a walk and then got back into the car and drove to her house. When we pulled into the driveway, I noticed that there were lights on in the back cottage. When we got to the porch, Theresa had to spend a few seconds fishing through her purse for her keys. I was getting ready to pay particular attention to the keys when Douglas popped around the corner.

"Have a nice evening?" he asked.

"You'll read about it in tomorrow's paper," Theresa said as she pulled out her key chain.

"Pardon?" Douglas asked.

"We were at Land's End and there was a fire," she said, unlocking the door.

"Everyone all right?"

"Yes," Theresa said as she pushed the door open. "Thomas and I are going to go in and talk for a while. Everything is fine, Douglas. You may go back to your biographies."

Douglas looked at me and I just shrugged. He then turned and walked back down the driveway. Again I turned my focus to the keys. Theresa put them in her purse and then walked into the living room. She set her purse on the coffee table and turned to look at me.

"Please sit down and make yourself comfortable," she said. "I need to use the ladies' room."

As soon as she left the room, I reached into her purse and pulled out the key chain. There were about fifteen keys on it, but I soon saw one that looked very much like the key Maggie had shown me. The number 5596 had been etched into it. I put the keys back in the purse and sat down on the sofa. Theresa came back into the room a minute later and sat down very close to me. We chatted for a bit, and then I leaned over and kissed her. She immediately turned to me and returned my kiss passionately. When we broke the kiss, I bent down and kissed her breasts through her clothes. She unfastened her blouse for me and I carefully slid my hand around her back and unhooked her bra. She had large, warm breasts, and I have to say, kissing them was very pleasant. When I came back up and kissed her neck, I slipped my hand up her dress and stroked her stomach. Her breathing increased as my hand went lower. Suddenly, she grabbed my hand and pulled it away.

"Thomas," she said. "I want you, believe me I do. I really like you. I want to be with you. Just not yet."

"Sure," I said. "I was going too fast. I'm sorry."

"No, please, don't be sorry. I'm very happy that you want me."

"Well, once I saw those yellow knickers, I was a goner," I said with as big a smile as I could muster.

"You're terrible," she said with a laugh as she gave me a phony punch in the stomach.

We talked awhile longer. We agreed to go out for a late dinner after the show on Saturday night. I drove home humming to myself.

Chapter Twenty-one

I walked into the Green Dragon the next night and went straight to the bar. I ordered a screwdriver and carried it with me over to the restaurant side of the pub. I saw Maggie and Stuart sitting in a booth by the back door. I slid in next to Maggie before they even noticed that I was in the room.

"Thomas!" Maggie said with a big smile. "What a nice surprise!"

We all laughed at that, and then Stuart reached his hand across the table and we had a nice, sincere handshake.

"I've been told that you're doing excellent work," he said.

"Not exactly the job I applied for," I replied.

"Yes, I must apologize for not knowing about Peter's sexual orientation. That oversight made me feel very embarrassed."

"Turned out all right. Wouldn't you say, Thomas?" Maggie chimed in.

"That depends," I said with a shrug. "If we fly out of

here with the coins, then yes. If not, this will have been a colossal waste of time.''

"We have no intention of letting that happen," Stuart said seriously.

"Of course not," Maggie added. "So, tell us about your date last night. Did little Miss Mark manage to get tipsy?"

"She was on her way, but it didn't quite work out."

I proceeded to tell them the story of the fire and our rescue by boat. Stuart shook his head as if he couldn't quite believe what rotten luck it had been.

"There's always next time," he said when I was finished.

"Are you kidding!" Maggie said. "This is terrific. You've been through something together. You got to play protector and hero. I bet there was some hugging and kissing when it was over."

"That and a bit more," I said with a grin.

"Wonderful," Stuart said as he broke into a big smile.

"Anything about the key?" Maggie asked.

"I saw the one you're talking about. It has the number five thousand five hundred ninety-six scratched into it."

"That's their box," Maggie said as she looked at Stuart. "Could you get that key if you had to?"

"I don't think it would be a problem," I replied. "She has so many keys on that key chain, I doubt she would miss it until she needed it again."

"Good," Maggie said. "Don't do anything yet. It's very risky for me to go into that box, and I don't want to do it unless we're positive that the coins are in there. That's your next job. Find out exactly where they are. If she has them at home, it becomes a whole different problem."

"You mean it becomes my problem," I suggested.

"It's very unlikely that she keeps the coins at home," Stuart said. "They are very valuable and it makes sense for them to be at the bank. We just need to know for sure."

"All right," I agreed.

"By the way, I've been told about your reading the coin

COMPANY OF THIEVES   245

book around the mark. I think that was very clever. Did it
work? Have you been talking about collecting coins?"

"Just once. I was going to bring it up again last night,
but as you can imagine, it didn't work out."

"Of course," Stuart said quietly. "But you will be seeing
her at the theater several nights a week."

"Not only that, she and I are going out after the play on
Saturday."

"Excellent," Stuart said, nodding his approval. "See if
you can get her drinking and then bring up the subject of
coins. Let's make it our goal for this week to find out if
they're in the bank or at home."

"I'll do my best," I said as I took a drink of my screwdriver. "Speaking of her home, there's a man named Douglas who lives in the back. He's sort of a caretaker. I get the
feeling he's more like a security person. His job may be to
keep an eye on Theresa while the parents are away. If the
coins are in the house, we'll have to figure him into our
plans."

"Could be a problem," Stuart said seriously. "I'll look
into it."

"See?" Maggie said proudly. "I told you Thomas was
the right man for the job."

"Yes," Stuart agreed. "You were right once again."

I wanted to take my fist and shove it into Stuart's face.
I sat there thinking how nice he would look with all his
teeth missing. My gut was twisting again. I ordered a second
screwdriver in the hope that it would help me not give away
my true feelings for this pair of backstabbers. I couldn't
help but wonder what they had planned for me; how they
were going to shove me aside at the last moment.

We talked quietly about all the little details of the operation. Maggie said her relationship with the man at the bank
was working out fine. I asked Stuart if it would be all right
for me to quit my job at the cricket club, but he said he
liked it as a cover. They kidded me about washing pots and

I kidded Maggie about being around all that money. We got along just fine. I was sure they had no idea that I was onto them. During dessert, Stuart looked over at me very seriously for a moment. Then he looked at Maggie and nodded.

"Tell him," he said.

"Well," Maggie said softly. "There is one little problem. I've had to tell Stuart about Willem."

"Why?" I asked.

"Because I always do some follow-up on our cases," Stuart said. "Just to make sure nobody is trying to track us down. I was able to find out that Willem had been issued a visa for the United States. That worried me. When I saw that a few weeks later he was issued one for New Zealand, I got very nervous and called down here. That's when I was brought up-to-date."

"I should have known better than to think Stuart wouldn't find out," Maggie said.

"But why New Zealand?" I asked. "How did he know that?"

"Who knows?" Maggie said. "Plane tickets, that newspaper in my car. Maybe he was able to find out about our visas."

"There's another part that's also rather scary," Stuart added. "We can't be completely sure, but there may have been a break-in at our office."

"Shit," I said as I took a long drink. "This is all I need."

"Remember," Maggie said. "He's not looking for you. I'm the one who has to be careful. Just go about your business and let me worry about Willem."

"I'm going to stay for a while and see if there's anything I can do about it," Stuart said.

The whole thing fell into place. I knew exactly what was going to happen. We would get the coins, and sometime shortly after that, Willem would explode into the picture. There would be some kind of ugly scene, during which I would get separated from Maggie and the coins. I would be made to feel lucky to have escaped with my life. That had to be it. Why else the warning about Willem? After it was all over, Maggie would disappear from Iowa forever and I would never see her again. It was going to be a great performance to watch—especially if I was standing there with the real coins in my pocket.

The three of us talked strategy for a while longer and then joked about how merry we would be when we pulled this off. We congratulated ourselves on our cleverness and called our victims fools. The ironies of the situation flowed out one right after the other. I could only imagine what ironies they were enjoying for themselves. Only mine were better. I was the only one with complete information.

We finished our meals and walked out separately. It was almost like two nights before, except now *I* was part of the group coming out of the Green Dragon. I couldn't help but wonder if Willem had my seat across the way. My eyes wanted to search around for him, but I resisted the urge. I got into my car and drove home. I wanted very much to curl up in my sleeping bag and take a step-by-step review of what I knew. I had to make sure I had a clear understanding of my situation. I also wanted to lie there and giggle at the disaster I was about to drop on my comrades-in-con.

As I walked up the stairs, I heard Edith at the piano. She was playing some music with a wonderful flowing feeling to it. I stood outside the door and listened for a few minutes. It was like listening to a musical river. I could see the notes floating by on a big, beautiful Mississippi.

I walked in and went directly to my place in the window seat. Edith smiled at me briefly and then lowered her head and went back to the music. She played for another ten minutes, stopping here and there to go back and try different things. When she finished, she reached up and wrote the music on the papers that were scattered over the top of the piano. I started to say something, but she held up her hand to stop me. She shuffled the papers around, wrote for another couple of minutes, and then put the pencil down. After that, she stood up, stretched her body as high as it would go, and then sat back down again.

"I'm there," she said.

"Where's that?" I asked.

"Where it just comes. The music pours out of me. It's almost like cheating. Like the music is writing itself. This is what I live for. Brian used to say I became a musical faucet."

"It sounded great. The piece was like flowing water. I pictured a beautiful river."

"Really?" she said with a surprised look. "That's close, but not exactly what I was going for."

"What was it meant to be?" I asked.

"Something heavier. Not flowing water. Flowing hot metal."

I stared at her for a few seconds and then slowly started to smile.

"You've got the coins," I said.

"Aren't you the smart one," she said with a devilish grin.

"Did you watch him do it?"

"Sexist!" she yelled. "It wasn't a him, it was a her."

"Well, did you watch her do it?"

"No."

"Shame on you. Writing music about something you didn't experience."

"I didn't have to watch because I was the 'her' doing it."

"What?"

"I did the coins myself. Thomas, I've taken four courses in the physical arts. Melting down metal and pouring it into different shapes was in the first course. It's really easy, once you know what you're doing. I just told my old teacher I needed to make some awards medals for a music competition. He gave me the run of the place."

"I'll be a son of a bitch," I mumbled.

"Now, you get out your money and I'll go get the coins."

I went down to my room and got out three hundreds. I went back to the living room and found Edith there waiting for me. When I walked up to her, she opened her hand and showed me five beautiful gold coins. She placed them in my hand as I held out the three bills.

"This will buy a lot of food," she said as she put the money in her pocket.

"Save it," I said as I looked at the coins. "Let me buy the food. You'll need it after I'm gone."

"Deal," she answered.

I walked over to the light by the piano and studied the coins. They looked perfect. They were all the same size and were wonderfully smooth and cool.

"Your job is to add the heads and the tails," Edith said as she sat down on the piano bench.

"I think I've found just the guy to do it."

"In Dunedin?"

"Yeah."

"All this is going to be happening very soon, isn't it?"

"Maybe."

"Someday I'll come home from class and you'll be gone."

"It won't be tomorrow or the next day, if that's what you're thinking. I still have a lot to do."

"Sleep with me tonight," she said after a few seconds. "I'm going to play awhile longer. When I stop, give me a few minutes and then come to my room."

"Sure," I said.

"Do you mind if we try a little game?" she asked. "A fantasy."

"Sounds delightful. Don't spend all night at the piano," I said as I walked out of the room.

When the music stopped, I gave her some time and then took my clothes off and went to her room. When I opened the door, her voice came out of the pitch black.

"Don't turn the light on," she said.

"All right," I answered as I closed the door.

"Can you pretend that you're Brian tonight? Would that bother you?"

"I'll get over it," I said.

"He used to massage my hands after I'd been playing. Could you do that for me?"

"Sure, Edith," I said. I got down on the bed.

"Call me Edie," she said as I picked up her left hand.

Chapter Twenty-two

The five blank coins were in my pocket while I was washing dishes the next morning. My plan was to have a relapse of the flu around nine-thirty. After that, I'd go get some photocopies made from my coin book. I wanted to get nice blown-up pictures of the coins and then trim away all the information about them. I didn't need old Bill Swift knowing any more than was necessary. Then I would hit the highway for Dunedin and be back in time to do the play that night.

Everything went according to plan, but I got a late start because Charlie insisted that I drink his antiflu concoction. It consisted of tea, lemon juice, a touch of cinnamon, and two shots of Scotch whiskey. I don't know if it would have helped with the flu, but it sure settled my nerves.

I pulled up in front of Bill Swift's trophy shop at two-fifteen. I could see from my car that no one was behind the counter. When I walked in the front door, I could hear a teapot whistling in the back room. I shouted a couple of

hellos but got no response. I then went around the counter
and peered through the curtain into the back room. The
whistling teapot was sitting on a hot plate on one side of
the room. On the other side of the room, Bill Swift was
sprawled out on a very old couch. His teacup dangled from
his fingers as he lay there snoring softly. Every few seconds
he would grunt and jerk in his sleep. When he did that, the
teacup would chink against the floor. I watched the scene
for a moment and then went over and took the teapot off
the hot plate. The whistle faded away and Bill popped up
his head and looked over at me.

"Tea's on," he said in a sleepy voice.

"I'm afraid not," I said as I held up the teapot. "Most
of it has boiled away."

"Ah, yeah. Put some more water in it, would ya?"

I walked over to the dirty sink and filled the pot with
water. As I did that, Bill sat up on the couch and had a good
yawn. He then shuffled over to a cabinet and got out a
second cup.

"Have a cupper?" he asked.

"Sure," I said as I put the pot back on the hot plate.

"You're the Canadian with the coins, right?"

"That's me."

"Have you got the blanks?"

"You bet. Plus, nice big photocopies of what I want them
to look like."

"Lay it all out on the bench there," he said as he put
some sugar in his cup.

I placed the photocopies and the five coins on top of the
workbench. When I turned around again, Bill was no longer
in the room. A short while later a door opened and Bill
came out of the bathroom pulling up his zipper.

"In with the new and out with the old," he said with a
smile as he checked the teapot.

He ambled over to the workbench to have a look at the pictures and the coins. I don't think I've ever seen a man move slower in my life. He was the New Zealand equivalent of some of the good old boys I knew back home. Except, I'd have to say, he moved even slower. He picked up each of the coins and looked them over for a long time. He then got an old pair of glasses out of his shirt pocket and studied the photocopies for what seemed like forever. When the teapot sounded off again, I quickly went over, poured the water, and brought him his cup. He sipped at his tea, looked at the pictures some more, and then went back to the coins.

I was getting frustrated, but I decided to keep my mouth shut. I needed him too badly to take any chances. Plus, this kind of slow, deliberate personality might be exactly what was needed for the job. So I sipped my tea and watched him study the situation. I laughed to myself when I thought of this slow-moving man having the name Swift.

"How much did we agree on?" he asked after a while.

"Six hundred American dollars. I already gave you one hundred."

"Ah, yeah. That you did."

"You're not going to raise the price, are you?" I asked.

"Oh, no. That'll do her."

"Bill, I want you to take your time and do them right, but I need at least a guess of when they'll be done."

"Got to make a couple of wee dies. That's a lot of work in itself."

"Just give me a rough estimate."

"There's about twenty hours of work here. But I haven't got much else to do, so I'll work on them this weekend. Give me a call early next week."

"Fine."

"I'll need another hundred now."

"Give me a receipt and you can have it," I said.

He went out to the front counter and brought back a pad. He wrote out the receipt and then handed me the paper.

"Phone number is on the top there," he said, pointing at it with the end of his pencil.

"Anything else you need to know?" I asked as I gave him the money.

"No, I see what needs to be done. It ain't easy work, but you're paying well, so I'll get her."

"Good. I'll call you next week."

"I'll be here," he said as he winked his left eye.

He sat down at the bench, opened a drawer, and got out a magnifying glass. He put his tea down and started studying the photocopies through the glass. He didn't say anything more, so I turned and walked out of the shop.

I decided to stop at that Chinese restaurant again and have a fast lunch before driving back to Christchurch. I bought a local paper to read while I was eating, but had trouble concentrating. It was a battle for me to think of things other than my present situation. My brain just wouldn't be satisfied, no matter how many times I reviewed the facts and the plans. I had to switch the coins but didn't know yet how I would do it. If that worked, then the phony coins had to be convincing enough not to be questioned right away. I would depend on my own wits for the first part. For the second part, I was dependent on a very slow-moving trophy maker whom I knew nothing about. That was the part that worried me.

The afternoon was sunny and clear as I drove up the hill out of Dunedin. The sky was a rich deep blue, and there was a nice, warm breeze coming through the car window. For the first time, I began to notice the beauty of the country I was passing through. I studied the emerald green hills off to my left. When I got to an overlook, I stopped the car for a minute and looked out over the sea. Everything looked so peaceful and safe. In my case, though, you didn't have to scratch very deep to get to the chaos.

I got back to Christchurch later than I expected and had to drive straight to the theater. I was only a few minutes late and Theresa didn't even seem to notice. She gave me a back rub again during the first act, and this time I really needed it. I read my coin book for a while during the second act and was sure that she saw me doing it. We walked out to our cars together and had a nice, long kiss before we parted. We were supposed to have a late supper together the following night, and I was determined to work the subject of coin collecting into the conversation.

When I got home, I found a small party going on in the apartment. Edith and several of her artistic friends were dancing in the living room. There was another group in the kitchen having a heated discussion about literature. The refrigerator had several new wine bottles in it, so I poured a glass for myself and settled in to listen to the college crowd battle it out over Thomas Hardy. One faction thought he was the best English novelist of all time, and the others thought he was a country gentleman who dabbled where he shouldn't have. They were quite drunk and very passionate. After a time, Edith came in and joined in with the pro-Hardy forces. I had never read a book by the man, so I sat there very amused and prayed that my opinion wouldn't be requested. Edith became so disgusted with the opposition that she jumped up and stomped off to do some more dancing. Her head soon reappeared around the corner to tell me that my phone was ringing. I ran down the hall, lifted the receiver, and found myself talking to Theresa.

"We have a favor to ask," she said.

"What is it?"

"Walter's grandmother has died. He's got to drive up to Napier for the funeral. He's leaving tomorrow morning and won't be able to do the play Saturday or Sunday. It's only two lines and Steven wanted me to ask if you would do it."

"Why me?" I asked with a chill of fear.

"Because you're about the same size. You'll fit the costume. It's very easy, Thomas. You come in, say one line, look around the room, say one more line, and then leave. You're smart enough to handle that."

"I've never been in a play in my life, Theresa."

"Don't be a ninny," she said. "Steven is going out of town tomorrow and I can't have my nightly screwdriver until I get this solved. Say you'll do it and I'll buy the supper tomorrow night."

"You don't have to do that," I replied.

"Come on, Thomas. I'll get you through it just like you got me down that ladder."

"All right," I said. "I don't like it, but I'll do it."

"Great. Come at six and we'll go over it a few times. Don't worry, you'll do fine."

After she hung up, I got the script out of my book bag. I discovered that because I had heard the play so many times, I already knew the two lines. As I was putting the script away, I heard the piano. There could be no doubt that it was Edith and she was playing some new music. I walked down the hall and found everyone in the living room, listening to Edith play. My seat by the window was taken, so I sat on the floor and leaned back against the wall. Everyone was completely silent and some even had their eyes closed as they listened. The stillness in the air told me that these people really respected Edith, that her music deserved their full attention. Edith responded to her audience. She pounded out something that might have been music for the ocean. She played light, sweet notes that reminded me of the mornings in Christchurch. For about a minute it seemed as if her right hand and her left hand were having an argument. Then suddenly it stopped. Everyone sat still for a moment, and then Edith looked up from the keyboard.

"That's as far as I've gotten," she said softly.

There was loud applause, and when it died down, the woman in my window seat spoke up.

"What's it about?" she asked.

"Him," Edith said as she pointed at me.

All the faces turned in my direction. I smiled and shrugged my shoulders.

"Just roommates, huh?" one of the guys said.

Everyone laughed and I turned very red.

Chapter Twenty-three

I did the part the next night and it turned out to be quite easy. I loved looking at myself in that dashing red uniform. Theresa caught me admiring myself in the mirror and kidded me about it endlessly. Everyone in the cast acted as if my appearance in the part was some sort of major triumph. The actors insisted that we all go out afterward and toast my successful debut. That, of course, put an end to my late supper with Theresa. We all headed for a nearby pub and took over one of the corners of the room. We bought half a dozen pitchers of beer, which were soon emptied. Theresa ordered screwdriver after screwdriver and told everyone she was doing it for the vitamin C. They all laughed, but I got the feeling they'd heard that line before. Someone who was in the pub had seen the show that night and came over and toasted the group. Everyone cheered and the theater patron insisted on buying another round of pitchers. Naturally, he was cheered again.

When the party finally started to break up, Theresa turned to me with a drunken smile.

"Want to follow me home, soldier boy?"

"Maybe I should drive you," I suggested.

"Oh, I'm not that bad," she said with a wave of her hand. "Just stick close behind me."

She drove home at about twenty miles an hour and did fairly well at staying between the white lines. When we got to her house, I pulled in behind her. Before I even locked my door, Douglas was there with his flashlight.

"Everything all right, Miss?" he asked into Theresa's window.

"Yes, Douglas, I'm fine. Thomas and I are going to go into the house and do some necking. Is that all right with you?"

Theresa laughed. Douglas stepped back from the car and turned to me with a very sour look on his face.

"He's a great kisser," Theresa yelled from inside the car.

"I am," I agreed.

Douglas turned quickly and walked back down the driveway toward his cottage.

"That man needs to get laid," Theresa said as she got out of the car.

"Could be." I took her arm.

"As a matter of fact, so do I," she said, and we started toward the front door. "I wish we could go back to the theater and get that red uniform. I'd love to slowly undo all those buttons."

"We can always pretend," I said as we entered the house.

She didn't stop in the living room. We went right over to the stairs and started up to her bedroom. I marched along behind her like the red-coated soldier she wanted me to be. When we got to her room, she turned around and immediately started unbuttoning my shirt.

"Are you going to be a good soldier and do as you are instructed?" she asked.

"Yes, sir!" I said as I saluted.

"I'm not a sir," she said as she pulled down my zipper.

"Yes, ma'am," I said as I saluted again.

"Right here is why you're the sir and I'm the ma'am," she said as she reached inside my pants.

She was quite drunk and it was a silly game, but I was enjoying myself, so I went along with it. She completely undressed me and then commanded me to unzip her dress and hang it in the closet. I was then ordered to unfasten her bra and march naked through the hall and throw it in the hamper in the bathroom. When I came back into the room, she was lying naked on the bed. I stopped in the doorway and looked at her for a few seconds.

"Don't just stand there," she said. "Do me."

In the end I wasn't sure who did who. She had the hunger of someone who hadn't had sex for a long time. She was very aggressive and pretty much took charge. She was not a quiet lover, and I couldn't help but wonder if Douglas had left his bedroom window open. If he had, he certainly would have known that we were doing more than necking. When it was over, she curled up next to me and was breathing softly a few minutes later. When I was sure that she was asleep, I got my underwear on and did some exploring around the house. I poked around into the other rooms and even got up the nerve to open a few drawers and closets. As I was walking back to her room, I went past a door in the hallway and decided to have a look behind it. The door was locked, and of course that made me want to look behind it all the more. I went back into the bedroom and found Theresa's keys inside her purse. After trying eight of the keys, I found the one that opened the hall closet. I turned the light on and immediately knew that I was in coin collector heaven. It was a big walk-in closet that had been converted into a windowless study. There was a wooden table with several coin books sitting on top of it. There were two large strongboxes under the table. Up against the wall, on the far side of the room, was a very large safe. I stood there frozen in my tracks. I then started to move toward the safe. As soon as I got to it, I realized there was nothing I could do. That I was taking a chance of getting caught when I had nothing to gain. I turned around and walked out of the closet. After locking the door, I went back down the hall and got into bed with Theresa.

When I woke up the next morning, Theresa was still dead to the world. I lay there for a while trying to figure out how to make the best of the situation. The temptation to get the keys and go rummaging around in the coin room was almost impossible to resist. That those five wonderful coins might be just down the hall was fascinating to me. All those thousands of miles, and now they might be only a few steps away.

To the right of Theresa's bed was a huge bookshelf. I got up without putting any clothes on and went over and had a look at the books. Most of them were play scripts. Many of the others were either on theater or economics. Down in the right-hand corner, not very far from Theresa's head, was a section of about a dozen books that were all on coins and coin collecting. I slipped the first one out and had a look at it. Inside the front cover was a lengthy inscription to Theresa from her grandfather. I started to slip it back into place, when I got an idea. I pulled the book back out, held it high over my head, and then let it drop to the floor. Theresa's whole body jerked and then she sat up and blinked her eyes. When she saw me standing there, she seemed surprised, but then she relaxed and gave me a sleepy smile.

"Sorry," I said sheepishly. "I was looking at your coin books and one of them fell."

"You're quite a sight to wake up to," she said as I turned around to replace the book on the shelf. "It's not every morning I find a naked man standing over me."

"Must mean it's going to be a good day." I turned back around.

"Certainly was a good night. You're quite a lover, Thomas."

"I enjoyed you very much," I replied. "I hope this becomes a habit of ours."

"You do say the right things," Theresa said.

"You don't have to get up," I said. "Sleep in for a while. These coin books are wonderful. You don't have to worry about me being bored with this kind of stuff to read."

"Would you like to see some of my coins?" she asked.

"Sure, but get some sleep. We can do it later."

"No, I'm awake now. Let's get dressed, go down and make some coffee and then I'll show you my secret room. We'll sip expensive coffee and finger rare coins. It's often what I do in the morning anyway."

After the coffee was made, we brought our cups up to the second floor. Theresa told me to wait while she went into her room to get her keys. I almost made the mistake of walking to the closet and waiting there. I caught myself in time and moved back to the head of the stairs. She came down the hall, went to the door, and unlocked it.

"This is great!" I exclaimed when we walked into the room. "I would never have guessed it was here."

"Used to be a walk-in closet," Theresa said as she reached for one of the strongboxes. "My grandfather changed it over. He and I used to spend hours in here."

"Now it's all yours?" I asked.

"It was supposed to be all mine. My father cashed in a large portion of the collection to start his car import business."

"You let him do that?"

"I was just a kid at the time. He got the lawyers to go along with it. He created a trust fund for me instead. I never have to worry about money, but I still think it was a rotten thing to do to a kid. I promised my grandfather that I would take care of his coins."

"That would make me want to leave home even more," I suggested.

"I know, I know," Theresa said. "I'll get out of here sooner or later. The problem is, it's so damn easy to stay."

"Think about how much more fun life will be without Douglas shining his flashlight in your eyes all the time."

"Yeah, it's like I have two dads," she said with a sad laugh.

There were two chairs in the room, but we sat on the floor and looked over the coins. I could just see Theresa and her grandfather doing the same thing. We went through the strongboxes and the books and I did my best to act like I knew what I was talking about. Fortunately, I had read quite a bit of my coin book and was able to say something intelligent now and then. After we had gone through the books and the strongboxes, Theresa asked me to turn around while she opened the safe. She pulled three more strongboxes out of the safe and we spent over an hour looking at the coins they contained. When we were done, she put the strongboxes back into the safe and came back and sat on the floor again.

"Have you ever heard of the Old Globe Sovereigns?" she asked.

"Are you kidding?" I replied. "Those are some of the most famous coins in the world. There's a set of seven. Separately they're valuable. The set of seven together would be worth a fortune. But I don't think anybody has the set."

"I have five of them," Theresa said with a big smile.

"What?" I almost shouted. "Do you have them here?"

"Of course not. I keep them in a safety deposit box. I go into the bank every few months just so I can fondle them."

"How much are they worth?" I asked.

"Several million. If I could get my hands on the other two, the value would probably double. We've been having a standoff with this man in Brazil for years. He wants my five. I want his two. We've been trading offers back and forth since I was twenty-one."

"God, if you sold them to him, you'd be rich."

"Thomas, I'm already rich," she said casually. "I want

the complete set. It was my grandfather's dream to own all seven, and I plan to make it come true.''

''Kind of make up for what your father took out of the collection,'' I suggested.

''That's why I like you, Thomas,'' she said as she leaned over and kissed me. ''You understand that kind of thing.''

''Let me know the next time you go in and fondle them. I'd love to tell my buddies back home that I touched five of the Old Globe Sovereigns.''

''Sure. I'm due to spend a little time with them any day now.''

''I'd consider it an honor,'' I said very seriously.

Theresa smiled and kissed me again. We talked for a while longer and then went downstairs and had a second cup of coffee. I left around noon and drove straight home. Edith was nowhere to be found and the apartment was nice and quiet. I decided to go into my room, turn out the lights and have a real good think. I had a lot of information to juggle and a lot of things to figure out.

One thing was now beyond all doubt. I wanted the Old Globe Sovereigns for myself. I could have worked it out so that Maggie got the phony ones and Theresa ended up getting the real ones back. That would have been real sweet of me, but I hadn't come all this way and dug in this deep to be sweet. What had really sealed it for me was Theresa's saying that she was rich already. Not only that, but the way she had said it. Like it was a given. Well, I wasn't rich already and probably never would be unless I grabbed these things when I had the chance. As for Theresa herself, her drinking problem disgusted me. I felt no pity for her and her stupid situation. The ''poor little rich girl'' routine made me want to puke.

More than ever, I was slipping into lovely neutral. I didn't give a damn about her or her grandfather. I wanted to do everything I could to put the screws to Maggie and her gang of clowns. I leaned back against my pillow and smiled. I knew I would be able to figure this thing out. I would get what I wanted.

I hadn't slept very well in Theresa's bed, and before too long I fell off into an afternoon nap. When the phone rang an hour later, I was startled awake. For a moment I thought I was back in Los Angeles and about to have one of those sleepy phone conversations. When I picked up the receiver and heard Maggie's voice, I instantly got my bearings.

"Been trying to get you all morning," she said. "I don't suppose it was one of those dates where you don't get home until the next day?"

"That it was," I replied with a yawn.

"She must have worn you out."

"Yeah. She's a bit of a screamer."

"I knew it," Maggie said. " Those types always are."

"Guess what she and I spent this morning doing?"

"I'm not sure I want to know."

"We spent over two hours looking at her coin collection."

"Oh, you beautiful man," Maggie said with a laugh. "I knew you'd be good at this. So, what did you find out?"

"She definitely has the five sovereigns. But she doesn't keep them at home. They're in the safety deposit box at the bank. You probably walk right by them every day."

"Did you get the key?"

"No, I didn't get the chance. I'm sure we'll be going out again next weekend after the play. I'll get her drunk and then get the key."

"Can't you get it sooner?" Maggie asked.

"I don't see how. I'll see her tonight, but generally people don't hang out after the show on Sunday night. My best chance will be on one of the upcoming Friday or Saturday nights."

"I guess that will have to do," she said. "I'm a little anxious now that Willem might be in the country."

"Is Stuart still here?" I asked.

"Yeah, but he's flying to South America tomorrow."

"Another scam?"

"I don't know, but that's a pretty good guess."

"Busy boy," I said.

"By the way, he found out that the Douglas guy at Theresa's is a retired cop."

"I knew it."

"Be careful around him."

"I will. The next move is for me to get the key. I'll call you when I've got it."

"Hope to be hearing from you soon, lover boy," Maggie said just before she hung up.

I put the receiver down and let out a long sigh. The real next move was for Bill Swift to get the damn coins made. After that, I had to pull the switch before I got Maggie the key. That would be the trickiest part of all. I had no idea how I was going to manage it.

When Monday morning came around, I got up to go to work as usual. On the way over to the cricket club, I decided it was stupid for me to keep working. I was soon going to have to come up with another excuse so I could go to Dunedin again. Plus, I was sick of washing those damn pots. When I got there, I told Charlie that I was going to be moving on. He made a few comments about undependable Yanks, but in the end he shook my hand and wished me luck. He followed me out of the kitchen and put the old "Help Wanted" sign back up. I said good-bye to the bartender and anyone else I could find. I then hopped into my car, drove home, and immediately called Bill Swift.

"Good day," he said when he picked up the phone.

"Hello, Bill," I replied. "This is the guy with the coins. Just wanted to call and see how it was coming along."

"Finished them up just before midnight last night," he said casually.

"You did?"

"You bet. Worked right through the weekend."

"How do they look?"

"Like the pictures, I'd say."

"Great! I'll drive down there today and pick them up."

"Right. One thing, though," Bill said slowly.

"What's that?"

"They're all bright and shiny. It's none of my business what you're doing with them, but I'm guessing you don't want them bright and shiny."

"You're right, I don't," I said quietly. "Can you dull them up?"

"Sure enough, but they'll need to soak overnight. Wouldn't be ready until this time tomorrow."

"That's fine," I said. "I'll be there tomorrow morning to pick them up."

"I'll have to go buy some chemicals. There'll be a wee soaking fee."

"How much?"

"Oh, fifty American dollars ought to do her."

"All right," I said with a sigh. "I'll see you tomorrow."

I sat there on my mattress and felt the adrenaline starting to flow. My toes and fingers were twitching. Suddenly, I felt like running a couple of miles. Instead, I decided to drive down to Dunedin today. I'd get a motel room and be at Bill Swift's shop when he opened on Tuesday. I grabbed my money and a few overnight things and was soon driving south along the coast.

I got down there in the early afternoon and found a motel. After a nap, I went out to an early dinner and then went to the movies. I was in bed by eleven, and sitting in my car outside the trophy shop when Bill Swift came walking along the sidewalk the next morning. After he unlocked the front door, I gave him ten minutes and then got out of the car and went into the shop. The teapot was whistling again, and when I looked through the curtains, I could see Bill in the back, studying the morning paper.

"Hello," I shouted.

"Is that my Canadian friend?" Bill asked as he looked up from the paper.

"Yes," I said after a second. I had completely forgotten that I was supposed to be from Canada.

"I didn't expect you so early. Come on back. I was just about to pull them out of the soak."

"I hope it works," I said as I walked into the back room.

"Not to worry. This is a goldsmith's trick from way back."

"What did you soak them in?" I asked.

"Hey," Bill said with a twinkle in his eye. "We all have our trade secrets, don't we?"

He took the teapot off the hot plate and then walked over to an old rusty can that was sitting on the workbench. He leaned over and looked inside. I joined him and did the same thing.

"Smells like vinegar," I said.

"That it does," Bill agreed. "But don't think that's all there is to it."

"Let's have a look at them," I said.

He pulled out a drawer from the workbench and got out a long pair of tweezers. He poked the tweezers into the cloudy liquid and pulled one of the coins out, wiped it on a rag, and then handed it to me. I stared at both sides of the coin and had to admit that it looked pretty good.

"At the risk of inspiring any new charges, I will have to say that you did a good job."

"No new charges," Bill said with a smile. "Just the wee soaking fee."

"All right," I said with a laugh. "Let's have a look at the other four."

He pulled the rest out and they all looked remarkably the same. He wiped each of them off and then handed them to me. After he pulled the last one out, he walked over to the teapot and poured himself a cup.

"Have a cupper?" he asked.

"Sure," I said. "Bill, these look great."

"They were a lot of work," he said as he got a cup for me. "Now, I just have one thing I'd like to ask you."

"What's that?"

"Sometime down the line, am I going to be reading my morning paper and see a story about some poor bloke whose coins have gone missing? Will I be reading about some fake coins that they found in their place?"

"I doubt it," I said.

"I'm being well paid, so I have no complaints. You see, I just don't want the Dunedin Police knocking on my door one of these days. I've had a problem or two with them in the past and I'd rather not have them coming around."

"You'll never be bothered. I guarantee it. I'm not even living in Dunedin. This is for someone in another city."

"Ah, well, that helps. I'll be retiring soon and I want everything to be nice and peaceful."

"You did a job for me. That's all it was. You have nothing to worry about."

"I guess that's right," he agreed. "Speaking of which, I'll take my money now."

While he sipped his tea, I got out my wallet and laid five hundred-dollar bills on the bench. He put his cup down and counted the money. When he was done he gave me a funny look.

"I guess you'll be wanting some change," he said.

"No," I replied. "The aging looks so good, I've decided to pay you a hundred for it."

"It's good pay," he said, nodding his head. "Good pay, indeed."

I had a flat tire on the way back and had to stop and change it in a narrow pull-off just above the ocean. When I was done, I turned around and looked at the view and was struck by the beauty of the place. It seemed that every time I turned around, this country served up a special piece of scenery. After I put the tools away, I sat in the grass and

looked out over the deep, blue ocean. I got the coins out of
my pocket and studied them closely. To me, they looked
perfect. But then, what did I know? I doubted that they
would fool Theresa, but they would probably be good enough
to make Maggie think she had the real thing. I was going
to have to pull the switch when I knew Theresa wouldn't
be looking at them again. Maybe if she took me to the safety
deposit box, I could manage to sneak the old ones out and
the new ones in. I shook my head as I thought of that. It
sounded like an impossible thing to do.

Maggie often talked about how much she wished she
could be there to see the realization on her victims' faces.
I understood that wish. In Theresa's case, I had no such
desire. I felt very sad for her and her silly life. That she was
rich and still trapped in other people's opinions was a mystery to me. What she wanted was fairly simple, but she
wouldn't do what she had to in order to get it. I had no
patience for that kind of thing. I was really beginning to
like the idea of ripping her off. It was going to be a pleasure
doing it. I didn't need to see her face.

After all this was over, I would have to disappear for a
while. Calling myself a Canadian had given me the idea that
I might go study in Canada. All I needed to do was peddle
one of these coins and I'd probably have enough money for
any university in the world. Who knows, maybe I could find
that man in Brazil who wanted them so badly. He probably
wouldn't care how he got them, as long as he got them.

I sat in the grass, thinking about everything. Thinking
while staring out at the ocean was becoming a habit. After
a while, I dozed off and was awakened by a policeman. He
was shaking my shoulder when I opened my eyes and looked
up into his face.

"Car trouble, mate?" he asked.

"No, just stopped to admire the view. Guess I fell asleep."

"Your car is quite close to the road. I suggest you find
a safer spot."

"Sure," I said. "It's time I got going anyway."

I stood up and stretched as the cop walked back to his car. I shoved my hand down into my pocket to make sure the coins were still there. I counted all five with my fingers and couldn't help but smile. I got back in the car and headed north again. After an hour, I stopped and had a nice, long meal while I read the newspaper. I got back to the apartment around six and found a note on the kitchen table from Edith. She was playing at a recital on campus that evening at seven o'clock and she wanted me to come. She told me what building it would be in and, in a postscript, mentioned that she would be playing "Perfume Highway." I had nothing pressing to do that evening, so I decided to go. It would be fun to hear my sexual experience played out before a room full of people. I took a quick shower and, at six-thirty, walked over to the college and got a good seat.

A few minutes after I was seated, a woman I had never seen before came over and looked down at me.

"Thomas?" she asked.

"Yes."

"Edith has sent me out here to request that you change your seat."

"Really?" I asked as I looked around for Edith.

"She saw you through the curtain," the woman confided.

"Where would she like me to sit?" I asked.

"In the front row. There's a seat on the very end that's reserved for you."

"All right," I said as I got up and walked to my assigned seat.

The seat on the far right side of the front row had a little piece of paper on it that said, "Reserved." I picked up the paper and noticed that the writing was in purple ink. After I sat down, it didn't take me long to realize why I had been asked to sit there. The little corner of the audience that I was part of was the only section that the person playing the piano could easily see. The person playing would be able to look across the top of the piano and directly at me. I smiled when I realized I was there for inspiration.

The first three pianists were very average in my opinion. I had gotten so used to Edith's passion that anything less than that felt very hollow. There was a short intermission, and then a young boy who looked to be about twelve came out and played twenty minutes of classical music. His youthful enthusiasm was very catching, and the audience applauded him loudly. When he left the stage, there was definitely a change in the room. There was an anticipation in the air preceding Edith's performance. When she walked out, everyone applauded. She looked beautiful. Her hair was a little different. It was a darker, richer purple. She wore a white dress trimmed with purple flowers. As soon as she sat down at the piano, the audience became perfectly still. She looked down at the piano keys and slowly lifted her head and looked me straight in the eyes. A second later, she began to play.

I had heard "Perfume Highway" before, so I knew what to expect. As the piece went on, I could feel the passion build, and also feel the people in the room get caught up in it. Edith looked at me quite often, and I could see little beads of sweat forming on her upper lip. She played out the sexuality of the piece as if she was having sex. The piano echoed her feelings and her excitement cut through the audience. When she pounded on the keys for the climax, the woman next to me drew in her breath as if she'd been punched in the stomach.

When she finished, the audience stood on their feet and cheered. Edith took several bows and then slipped behind the curtain. The applause carried on and she had to come out and bow once more. When she went behind the curtain again, the clapping finally died down. Even then, there was still a feeling of high energy in the room. Everyone was talking and smiling.

"My goodness, she is wonderful," the woman next to me said.

"Yes, she is," I agreed.

I hung around and waited for Edith to reappear. After a few minutes, all the performers came back out on stage. Champagne was poured and there were several toasts. I got a glass of champagne and stood in the back and watched. Edith was beaming. Many of the audience members had stayed around, and it seemed that every one of them wanted to shake her hand. At one point she looked around the room, and when she saw me she smiled. I raised my glass to her and she mouthed, "Wait." I nodded and she went back to accepting the many congratulations that were coming her way. A man wearing a tuxedo soon called for everyone's attention, and the room quieted down. He held up a felt pen and said that he had decided that Edith should join those excellent past performers who had signed the inside of the concert piano. Everyone gathered around as Edith added her name to those that were already written on the wooden shelf inside the piano. When she finished, everyone applauded and Edith took a bow.

The reception went on for another fifteen minutes. I ended up having three glasses of champagne and a lot of cheese and crackers. When the crowd had thinned out, Edith walked over to where I was sitting and sat down beside me.

"Quite a night," I said. She let out a sigh.

"I'll say."

"You were wonderful," I whispered, kissing her cheek. "I felt like I was getting laid in front of two hundred people."

"You were," she replied with a laugh.

"I'm honored," I said as I raised my empty glass.

"Will you walk me home?" Edith asked.

"Sure."

"Let me get out of this dress. I'll only be a few minutes."

She got up and walked back through the curtain. Five minutes later, she came back wearing jeans and a T-shirt.

She was carrying the dress over her arm, and her purple shoes hung from her fingertips.

"Let's go," she said when she got over to me.

A few people shouted good-byes as we left, and Edith rewarded them with a big smile. We walked out onto the campus and across the huge lawn toward our apartment.

"I hope you didn't mind coming," Edith said. "I wasn't sure if you'd want to be there."

"Are you kidding? I wouldn't have missed it for the world."

"Good. I'm glad you enjoyed it. Every time I see you now, I think it's going to be the last time. When you didn't come home last night, I thought maybe you had gone."

"Not yet," I said with a smile.

"But soon?"

"Probably."

"Guess I'd better start looking for a new roomie."

"Edith, let's stay together tonight," I said softly.

"No, I don't think so, Thomas," she replied. "I've decided I don't want to sleep with men that I know will be leaving soon. I need at least the illusion that we'll be together for a while."

"I can understand that," I said.

We walked along quietly through the wet grass. It was a little chilly and Edith wrapped the dress around her shoulders like a shawl. I ended up carrying her shoes.

"I got a letter from Brian today," she said. "He says he misses me. Wants me to come to England. I've been thinking about it all day."

"Are you going?" I asked.

"He says there are a lot of opportunities there for someone like me."

"That's probably true."

"Yes, but that's what constantly happens to New Zealand. Talented people are forever heading off to England or America to seek their fortunes. I don't know, maybe I'm feeling overly patriotic or something, but I'm a New Zealander. This is a wonderful country. This is where I want to make my music. I wouldn't mind touring and that kind of thing, but I don't want to live anywhere else. I want to be a musical voice for this country.''

"Then that's what you should be,'' I said.

"Yes,'' Edith agreed, nodding her head. "That's what I should be.''

Chapter Twenty-four

When we got back to the apartment, Edith went to her room and I went to mine. I was pulling my undershirt up over my head when the phone rang.

"Where have you been?" Maggie asked.

"Went to a concert," I replied.

"Guess who came into the bank today and got something out of her safety deposit box?"

"Theresa?"

"Yes, Theresa. I was the friendly little clerk who checked her in and settled her into a room with her goodies."

"Don't suppose you picked her pocket on the way out."

"God, I wish I could have. Warren, I held the box when I handed it down to her. My hand was within inches of the coins!"

"Do you know for sure that she took them with her?"

"I don't get to watch, but isn't that what it has to be? Didn't she promise you that she'd let you see them?"

"Yeah, she did. I thought I'd be going to the bank with her. I never thought she'd bring them home."

"This is it, Warren! She's going to call you up and invite you over to have a look at them. Get her drunk and steal them. Then call me and we'll get the hell out of here."

"That won't give us much lead time. As soon as she sobers up, she'll realize that they're gone."

"Pack your bags. Put whatever you can in the trunk of the car. I'll pack some of my stuff tonight. When you get the coins, we'll run up to Wellington and catch the first plane to anywhere."

"Jesus, this is scary."

"No, Warren, this is it. This is your moment. Don't go to any more concerts. You stay near that phone and wait for her to call. If she doesn't call you by Thursday, you call her."

"All right."

"Just keep thinking about the money."

"I will," I said.

"Good luck, partner."

I hung up the phone and sat there staring at the wall. I had been thinking that I might spend Wednesday in the local mountains. Have a nice quiet day before the madness began. It didn't look like I would get a chance to do that. The madness was already here.

Twenty minutes later, the phone rang again. This time it was Theresa. I could tell right away that she had been hitting the vodka.

"Hope I'm not calling too late," she said. "I've been trying to get you all evening."

"I went to a concert," I replied. "It's all right; I just got in."

"Oh, good. Guess what I've got?" she asked.

"Beautiful breasts?" I said quickly.

"Besides that," she said with a giggle.

"I don't know. What?"

"Five little coins that I think you'll want to see."

"You've got the sovereigns?" I asked excitedly.

"That's right."

"You took them out of the bank? Isn't that kind of risky?"

"You're the only one who knows; and I can trust you, can't I?"

"Of course you can." I said.

"You said you wanted to see them, so I got them out for you."

"This is great, Theresa. You're too good to me."

"Why don't we go out to dinner tomorrow night. Afterward, we can come back here and you can see my breasts and my coins."

"Sounds like a lot of fondling," I whispered.

"I hope so," she said, giggling again. "Come around seven."

"See you then," I said.

I put the phone down and thought for a moment. Should I call Maggie and tell her? It would seem to be to my advantage to keep her in the dark. Yet Maggie knew that Theresa had taken the coins home. She knew Theresa was going to show them to me. If Theresa went back to the bank in a few days and put the coins away without my having said anything, it would surely raise Maggie's suspicions. I had to tell her what was going on. I picked up the phone and dialed Maggie's number.

"It's me again," I said when Maggie answered.

"What's up?" she asked.

"Theresa just called me. She wants me to come over tomorrow night and look at the coins."

"Terrific. Pack your bags, Warren. Get everything ready for a quick run."

"All right."

"You know what you have to do. When you get the chance, don't hesitate. Grab the damn things and then call me. Get her drunk, give her some sleeping pills, knock her over the head. Whatever it takes. Don't blow it!"

"I won't."

"We're counting on you," Maggie said just before she hung up.

"I bet you are," I muttered to myself as I stared down at the phone.

On a hunch, I waited for a minute and then dialed Maggie's number again. As I suspected, her line was busy. I slipped just a little bit further into lovely neutral.

I didn't do much on Wednesday. I did do some packing, but just a few things. Maggie thought leaving time was imminent, but I knew it would be a few days yet. Calling her had been the right thing to do. While I was not about to knock Theresa over the head, Maggie's idea about the sleeping pills sounded like something I could use.

I went for a long walk in the afternoon and got back to the apartment around five-thirty. I took a shower, got dressed, and drove over to Theresa's. On the way, I stopped at a drugstore and bought some sleeping pills. I had wrapped the five phony coins in some aluminum foil. When I was dressing, I stuffed them down inside my underwear, but then I realized that Theresa would probably end up with her hands down there. In the end, I put my change and keys in one pocket and the magic coins in the other.

I got to Theresa's at seven, and good old Douglas was out front, trimming the hedges. He gave me a rather cold nod as I came walking by. I waved and smiled, hoping to win a few points with him, but he just went back to his work.

Theresa let me in and suggested that we have a drink before dinner, which we did.

"The play closes this Sunday," she said as she sat on the couch sipping her screwdriver.

"I know," I replied. "I think I'm going to miss it."

"There'll be a big party after the show that night. Have you ever been to a closing night party?"

"Can't say that I have."

"They can get pretty wild. Of course, at first, everybody

is very sentimental. The director burns a copy of the program and we all watch in silence. After that, the liquor flows and everybody dances like crazy.''

"Sounds great," I said.

"We can start going out on Saturday nights, like normal couples," Theresa whispered in my ear.

We finished our drinks and drove off toward an Italian restaurant that Theresa said was the best in town. Douglas was raking when we went out and got into the car.

"Don't wait up," Theresa said to him as we pulled away.

On the way to the restaurant, Theresa told me she knew a lot of the people who worked there and that she was taking the opportunity to show me off a little. The people she knew at the restaurant were aspiring opera singers who had to earn their living being singing waitresses and waiters. They were trying to start up their own opera company. Until that happened, they sang in this Italian restaurant and ran around with the pasta. Theresa said she had agreed to stage manage their first production if they ever got their opera company going. She assured me that we would get a lot of special attention and that at least an aria or two would be sung at our table. I wasn't too thrilled about getting any attention, let alone special attention. I had been hoping for a nice, quiet place where I could slowly get Theresa very drunk.

Things went pretty much as she had predicted. A great fuss was made when we came in, and several of the tenors came over and sang us a welcoming song as soon as we sat down. Theresa applauded wildly when they were done, and as I looked around, it was easy to see that every eye in the place was on us. Theresa then ordered a bottle of very expensive burgundy and drank all of it except for the one glass that I had. By the time we had our sherbet, she was back to the screwdrivers and again making jokes about drinking them for the vitamin C. Just about every waiter and waitress in the place stood around the piano and sang us a farewell song as we got up to leave. They all waved as we

went out the door, and Theresa blew the entire place a big
kiss. She was drunk on the booze and all the attention. When
we walked down the front steps of the restaurant, she started
to fall over and I had to grab her by the back of her dress
to hold her up. I was feeling rather disgusted by then and
couldn't wait to get the damn sleeping pills into her.

It was still pretty early, but I wanted to get her home
before she passed out on me. As sick as I was of her, I still
needed her to open that safe. I didn't ask her if she wanted
to do anything else. I just got in the car and started driving
back toward the house. She kept up a constant stream of
drunken chatter about how nice all those people were and
what a great opera company they were going to have. When
we got to her house, I shut off the headlights and coasted
into the driveway in the hope that Douglas would fail to
notice our arrival. When we got into the house, Theresa
turned around and gave me a long kiss and then leaned up
and whispered in my ear.

"I've got this all planned out," she said. "I'm going
upstairs. You wait here for five minutes and then come up
to the coin room."

"Are we going to look at the sovereigns?" I asked.

"Of course we are," she said as she turned to go.

"Should I make us each a screwdriver?" I asked as she
started up the stairs.

"Why not?" she replied. "You know where the vodka
is, and there's lots of orange juice in the kitchen."

I got the vodka from behind the bar and then went into
the kitchen and opened the refrigerator. There were four
bottles of orange juice sitting on the top shelf. I mixed a
couple of drinks and then found a big spoon and crushed
three of the sleeping pills into a powder. I put the powder
in one of the drinks and then walked to the foot of the stairs.

"Ready?" I called.

"One more minute," came the reply.

I took a sip out of my drink, then walked around to the

kitchen again and looked out the back window. No lights were on in the cottage. Either Douglas wasn't home, or my idea of coasting into the driveway had really worked. I breathed a sigh of relief, took another sip, and went up the stairs to the coin room. I walked down the hall and looked into the open door. Theresa was in there, wearing a very small, silky nightgown. She had brought a bunch of pillows into the room and was lying on them. I noticed there was a brown padded envelope on her stomach. She smiled at me and I smiled back. When I did that, I noticed that the safe door wasn't quite closed.

"Not the bedroom tonight, huh?" I said with a sexy whisper.

"This is my favorite room in the world," Theresa said with her slurred speech. "I've always wanted to make love in here, and tonight is the night. That is, if you don't mind?"

"No, not at all. I like this. You look very sexy lying there on those pillows. Should we look at the coins first or after?"

"First. I know they'll get your blood running," she said.

"You're right about that. I can't believe I am going to touch five of the Old Globe Sovereigns. I think I need a drink first."

I started to drink my screwdriver and then pretended to remember that I had one for her too. I took one gulp and then bent down and handed Theresa her drink. She sat up on the pillows and drank it straight down. I finished mine and then sat on the floor.

"You make a strong one," she said as she lay back down.

I picked up the padded envelope and unfastened the clip that held it closed. Inside the envelope was a small glass box. I pulled the box out and lifted the lid. There was a wad of cotton, which I carefully removed and placed on the floor. My first reaction was mild panic, because the coins were quite different from the ones Bill Swift had made. These had a green tint to them and the writing was much smaller. Not only was the writing smaller, so were the coins themselves. Smaller and thicker. Edith must have fudged a little on the dimensions. I lifted one of the coins out of the box and studied it up close.

"Beautiful, aren't they?" Theresa said.

"My God," I replied.

"If you really want to study it like that, take the cotton and lay the coin on top of it. You know, perspiration, skin oils, all that."

"Of course," I said quickly. "This is so amazing, I completely forgot."

I put the cotton in my hand and one by one studied the coins. I took as long as I possibly could with each one, in order to give the sleeping pills the time to do their job. When I was done with the last one, I looked down at Theresa and saw that she was looking up at me with a glassy-eyed stare. I reverently put the coins back in the glass box and slid the box down into the envelope. I placed the envelope on the floor near her head and then leaned over and kissed her. She returned my kiss and then I lay on top of her. As soon as I did that, she sighed and started kissing me very passionately. At the first opportunity, I lifted her nightgown up over her head and then got myself undressed. While I was undressing, I looked over at her face and saw that she was drifting away.

When we started having sex, she grabbed my head and pulled my ear down by her mouth as if to tell me a secret.

"Hurt me, Thomas," she whispered. "Hurt me, if you want to."

I had never had a woman say that to me before. I couldn't imagine what I was supposed to do. If anything, I wanted long, soft sex. I wanted the alcohol and the pills to have every chance to knock her out.

"No pain, baby," I murmured in her ear. "I just want to make you feel good."

"You're doing it," she mumbled. "You're doing it."

She acted as if she were trying to go wild, but just couldn't do it. There was another five minutes of moaning and then a very muted orgasm. When it was all over, I lay down next to her and stroked her hair as she fell asleep.

She called me "Pop-pop" as I picked her up and carried her to her bed. I tucked her in and then went back to the coin room. I took the coins out of the glass box and wrapped them in my piece of aluminum foil. I placed Bill Swift's coins under the cotton and put the glass box back into the envelope. After that, I put the brown envelope into the safe, closed the safe door, and turned the dial. As I was carrying the pillows back to Theresa's room, I marveled at how easy it had been. I locked the coin room and then went and got into bed with Theresa.

I lay there thinking about the next day. That was the part that really scared me. I had to get her to take that brown envelope back to the bank without looking inside it. It was important that I stick by her side until that was done. I fell asleep picturing the look on Maggie's face when Theresa and I walked into the bank the next morning.

Chapter Twenty-five

I woke up at eight, but Theresa slept until eleven. During the three hours in between, I drank a lot of orange juice and went through the books on the bookshelf. When she first started to stir, I went into the bathroom and got three aspirins and a glass of water. I put them on the night table next to her and waited for her to come around. She woke up with a groan fifteen minutes later. I was sitting in a chair reading a book when she opened her eyes and looked at me. She didn't look startled to see me. She just lay there, as if trying to get her bearings.

"God, you make a mean screwdriver," she said at last.

"There's aspirin on the table," I said.

"Thanks," she replied, and she sat up and swallowed them down. "My head is killing me."

"That's been known to happen," I joked.

"Aren't you supposed to be at work?" she asked.

"I called in sick. Decided I'd rather spend the day with you. That is, if you want me to."

"Sure, I don't have anything planned, except . . . Jesus, where are the sovereigns?"

"In the safe. You put them away before we went to bed."

"I did?"

"Of course. You think I would have let you leave those beauties sitting around?"

"I have to get them back to the bank today. The insurance people would scream bloody murder if they knew I had them out."

"That's something we can do. We'll go to the bank and then go have a nice lunch."

"Please, don't mention food right now," she said with a sour look on her face.

"Sure. Why don't you take a shower and I'll go downstairs and make you some coffee."

"No, don't," she said. "The housekeeper will be down there by now. I'll take a shower and we'll stop and get some coffee on the way to the bank."

"Fine with me," I said with a shrug.

"We made love last night, didn't we?" she asked.

"Sure, it was very nice."

"I think I only remember the beginning."

"You had a wonderful time. I was there and I can swear to it."

"Good," she said as she got out of the bed and walked to the bathroom.

She showered and got dressed and seemed to be feeling better by the time she went down to the safe to get the coins. She brought the brown envelope back into the bedroom and immediately handed it to me.

"I bet you'd like one last look at them," she said.

"No," I said as I held the envelope. "It will just make me terribly jealous all over again. Let me hold them for a while. It's comforting just to know I have them in my hands."

"All right. Now, let's walk straight down the stairs and

out to my car. If we get lucky, the housekeeper won't even see us."

We walked out of the house and didn't see anyone. Theresa drove directly to the bank and we got there just in time to see Maggie letting a customer out of the safety deposit box area. Maggie got an angry look on her face when she saw me. She quickly wiped it off. She knew that if I was there with Theresa, I obviously hadn't gotten the coins.

Theresa filled out the card and told Maggie that I would be going with her into the back room. Maggie got a card out of the file drawer and studied Theresa's signature for a few seconds. Then Maggie, Theresa, and I went into the room with all the safety deposit boxes. Each of the women provided one of the keys needed to open the lock, and then Theresa and I were guided to a little room. When we were alone, I kissed the brown envelope and then handed it to her. She laughed when I did that and then slipped the envelope into the box. My heart, which had been pounding like a steam engine, returned to its normal rate. After the box had been slid back into its place in the wall, we walked out the front door of the bank. I could feel Maggie's eyes burning into my back as I left.

Theresa and I then went and had lunch together. I had a full meal and Theresa just had coffee and toast. Her hangover kept her quiet, and my adrenaline rush at the bank made me the chatty one. During the drive back to her house, she hardly said a word. When we got there, she told me that she needed to go in and lie down for a while. I said that was fine and that I would see her at the theater on Friday. I kissed her good-bye and drove home humming a happy tune.

I could have easily taken off with the coins that afternoon. They were in my pocket, and at this point, no one knew I had them. The trouble with that idea was that my disappearing would tip off Maggie. They would be after me in a flash. It seemed to me that the wise thing to do was to play it out according to their plan. Let them get the phony coins and then cut me out of the picture. That's what they were surely planning to do, and I should let them do it. They would fly off to America with Bill Swift's coins, and I could take my time and cover my tracks. There was always the chance that the way they had chosen to cut me out might include some pain on my part. Whatever that might be, I didn't think it would be fatal. Even a broken bone or two would be worth it if I got the time to make sure I couldn't be found.

I got home around two-thirty and was changing my clothes when the phone rang. Of course it was Maggie.

"What the hell happened?" she asked angrily.

"I couldn't get them," I said.

"Damn it, Warren, you're not going to get another opportunity like that."

"It was impossible. There was nothing I could do about it. She kept them in the safe, and when she got them out, that ex-cop, Douglas, was sitting at the kitchen table with us. She said she had to have him there as a precaution. Some stipulation with the insurance company. What was I supposed to do? Try to knock them both out and then run off with the coins?"

"You were alone with her today."

"Just for the ride to the bank. I went with her as protection because Douglas was at the doctors. I couldn't just push her out of the car. Any opportunity I had in the last twelve hours would have immediately landed me in jail. We need to do this so we have enough lead time to get away. I did the right thing, Maggie. I want the coins as badly as you do, but I don't want to spend five years in jail. I did the best I could under the circumstances."

"Why didn't you call me? Maybe I could have helped?"

"There's nothing you could have done."

"Shit, Warren, Stuart is going to be furious."

"We're not lost yet, Maggie. There's still another great opportunity."

"What are you talking about?"

"The play closes this Sunday night. There will be a big cast party afterward. Theresa is sure to get drunk. I'll be there to make sure that she does. When I take her home, I'll get her safety deposit box key. I'll bring it to you at the bank on Monday. You open the box that day, take the coins, and we'll hit the road Monday night."

"Are you sure you can get the key?"

"Positive. Think about it, Maggie. If I had taken the coins last night, they would have known they were missing this morning. We would have had around eight hours to get away. This way we can drive out of here on Monday and not worry about somebody being on our tail. Who knows how long it will be before she notices that the key is gone."

"You may be right."

"Of course I am. It's much better this way. When you have the key, will you be able to go in there and do it? Is there any problem with that?"

"I can do it when the other woman goes to lunch. You have to get the key to me before noon."

"Sure."

"I just have to hope that the branch manager doesn't come hanging around."

"He's the guy who got you the job?"

"Yeah. Oh, shit! I just remembered something. I'm supposed to go out with him Monday night. Some swanky deal with his golf partners. It's a dinner for eight to celebrate some tournament thing. If I'm at work Monday, but not there for our date, it will look funny."

"So, go on your date and I'll be there waiting in the car when you get home. When he drops you off, tell him you feel the flu coming on and might not be in to work for a couple of days."

"That's good, Warren. I'm still pissed at you, but that's very good."

"Just earning my pay. Believe me, Maggie, I would have taken them if I could have. It just wasn't possible. I think it was for the best. This way we'll be back in the States before they even begin to think something is wrong."

"You better get that goddamn key."

"I will. I promise."

"Good. The coins were in that brown envelope, weren't they?"

"Yes. Should be the first thing you see when you open the box. You know what they look like, don't you?"

"Of course I do. I'll see you Monday morning."

"Right."

"Be parked outside my apartment by ten Monday night. The flu may come on a little early."

"Sounds great. See you then."

"Oh, one more thing. Turn in your rental car this weekend. Get a new one for the ride out of here."

"Should I go buy some plane tickets?"

"No. We'll drive up to Wellington and leave from there. We'll take the first plane that goes out of the country."

"See ya Monday," I said as I hung up the phone.

I sat back against the wall and laughed. It was probably a fool's dream to think that I could make this happen exactly as I wanted it to. But why not try? It was so much fun to be in control and have them not even know it. My best bet was that Maggie was just now getting on the phone with Willem and telling him the plan. I had to figure that she and I would never get to Wellington together. That something would happen on the way to separate us. That something would be Willem. She'd go off with the coins and I'd be left to look like a sucker. Or so they thought.

Chapter Twenty-six

On Saturday morning I turned in my rental car and got another one. I took it for a ride south on the Canterbury Plain and then west up into the mountains. I pulled off into a little park where the air was cool and a beautiful stream bubbled down the rocks. There was a family nearby cooking fat sausages over a fire, and the parents sent one of the kids to ask me to join them. I would have preferred to be alone, but I didn't want to be impolite, so I went over and sat down with them. They gave me a stick and a sausage and I stuck it in the fire as I talked with the parents. They told me they were homesteaders, building a house and clearing land a few miles up the road. They were the New Zealand version of real country folk. They had a very cute dark-haired daughter. As I watched the daughter nibble at her sausage, I felt that I had somehow been transported back in time, that I was visiting Maggie's family in the hills of Kentucky and watching her as a child.

"How old is your daughter?" I asked the father.

"Eight," he said. "She's a spitfire. Can't imagine what kind of teenager she's going to be."

We three adults laughed and the little girl gave me a big grin. Her face was dirty, but her perfect teeth were dazzling. I sat and talked with them for a while and tried to answer their many questions about America. After the sausages were gone, the father got out his harmonica and we all sat quietly and listened to him play. When it got on toward three o'clock, I said my good-byes and headed back to Christchurch for that night's show. While I was driving, I tried very hard to think through my plans for the next few days. But all I could see was that girl's dirty face. I wondered what would happen to her. I wondered how her coming beauty would affect her life.

After the show that night, I was restless and couldn't sleep. I got out of my sleeping bag and went down to the kitchen and got a glass of wine. When I got back to my room, I opened my suitcase and did some packing. Just as the wine was starting to make me sleepy, I turned around and saw Edith. She was standing in the doorway wearing her nightgown. She didn't say a word. I looked at her, gave her a helpless smile, and went back to packing. When I looked back a few seconds later, she wasn't there.

I spent Sunday killing time. I walked over to the college campus and strolled through an outdoor art show. Afterward, I had a nice slow lunch at the college cafeteria. I walked back to the apartment, read one of Edith's books for a while, and then fell asleep. When it came time to leave for the play, I was alert and rested. My nerves were a little jumpy, but I felt prepared to face whatever the next forty-eight hours might bring.

There was a strange mood in the air at the theater that night. The play had been a success, and there was a feeling of sadness that it was over. And yet, there was a lot of excitement as well, and once again, many of the people were exchanging presents and cards. We got a closing-night pep talk from Steven, and after it was over, no eyes were dry. I sat on the green room couch with Theresa while Steven gave his speech. I put my arm around her and she inched over a little closer to me. She was sitting there with her key chain in her hand, and I had trouble not staring at it. I had to follow the location of those keys tonight like a bloodhound. When it was time for the play to start, we went to our posts and I stood beside Theresa while we waited for the pre-show music to finish up. I had one more thing I had to do to cover my butt, and I decided that now would be the best time.

"This has been a wonderful experience for me," I said to her. "Being involved in the play, getting to know you and all these people. It's just the kind of thing I was hoping for when I decided to travel."

"I think I'm not going to like what's coming," Theresa said as she looked over at me.

"It's time. I'm sorry, and believe me I have very mixed emotions about it, but I'm flying to Australia tomorrow."

"Tomorrow? Why so soon?"

"I've been in New Zealand for over two months. I originally planned to stay three or four weeks. I liked it so much, I stayed longer than I meant to. My course at the university ended Friday. The play is closing tonight. It's the right time for me to move on."

"I wish it weren't," she said.

"I know. Please, let's not be sad. Let's think about how great this has been for both of us. At least, that's what I've been thinking about. Let's have a really good time tonight. Celebrate the fact that we had this. Not the fact that it's over."

"All right," she said quietly.

I went to my chair and sat down. I was able to look in through the wings and see the actors getting into their places. I sat there thinking I was a better actor than any of them. When the pink stage lights came on, the fairy-tale colors spilled over to where I was sitting. Then the curtain opened and the actors started saying their lines. As they said theirs, I mumbled a few of my own.

"Stay in neutral," I said to myself. "Stay in neutral."

The closing night party was at the home of our leading lady. She lived out in the country, west of the city, so I suggested to Theresa that we drop her car off and drive to the party together. When the play was over, we locked up the theater and then I followed her over to her house. On the way out to the party she wasn't very talkative, so I tried to get things going.

"You probably don't realize it, but you've really helped me," I said to her.

"How?"

"Well, liking me for one thing. Here you are, a smart, busy woman with all these theater friends, and you chose to spend time with me."

"Thomas, I don't have that many friends."

"Why not?"

"Because so many people are phonies and I see right through them. I just can't be bothered with them. You're not like that. I'm smart when it comes to figuring people out. I'm not saying I've figured you out, but you seem on a quest for change, for self-knowledge. I admire that. That kind of personal honesty makes you attractive."

"I think you'd have more friends if you gave them a chance."

"Look, Thomas, we live based on our experiences. My experience leads me to the philosophy that most people are jerks until they prove to me they aren't. I'm just the opposite of my father. He's always smiling and glad to see everybody. To him they are all customers or voters. To me they are mostly assholes. Except for the occasional ray of hope. People like you. I drink because there aren't more people like you."

"I think that's a compliment," I said.

"Of course it is. You're like a rare coin."

"Thanks." I nearly choked.

"Why don't you stay a couple more weeks. I'll put you up at the fanciest hotel in Christchurch. I'll pay for everything. I'll come visit you every day and we'll run around the room naked. We'll have sex on silk sheets."

"Theresa, I already have my plane ticket."

"Yeah, and tonight you told me you were leaving just when the play was beginning so I wouldn't be able to scream and carry on. I see right through you, too."

"Yes, you do. You're very smart about people."

"Yes, I am."

"Sorry."

"You're forgiven because I like you. I'm going to feel very lonely after you've gone."

"Then let's have a good time tonight. I feel like getting a little drunk. I want to celebrate how lucky I was to walk into the theater that first night. I want to celebrate how much more confident I feel."

"I may have a drink or two myself," she said.

Perfect. That was exactly what I wanted to hear. The long ride back from the party was going to be a lucky break for me. I was hoping she'd get very drunk and then pass out on the way home. I'd get the key from her purse, hand her over to Douglas and be on my way. Then this poor little rich girl would finally be out of my life.

As soon as everyone arrived, we gathered around and once again drank a toast to George Bernard Shaw. After that, Steven placed one of the programs on a silver platter and lit it with a match. As it burned, we stood and watched without making a sound. When the program burned itself out and collapsed into a pile of ashes, cheers went up and everyone headed for the bar or the food table. Theresa stopped at the bar and made herself the first screwdriver of the evening. I got a beer, and then we both went onto the back porch, where there was a large table overflowing with food.

I stuck by Theresa's side as much as I could, but I lost track of her a couple of times during the evening. I counted seven screwdrivers in the first hour and a half, but then she and Steven went off to do their dance act and I got into a conversation with our leading lady's husband. He was just learning to play softball and got me into a corner for twenty minutes talking about it. When I found Theresa again, she was sitting on a couch in the living room looking pretty dazed.

"How was the dance?" I asked as I sat down beside her.

"You didn't watch?" she asked drunkenly.

"Sorry, I was being polite. Talking to our host about sports. Did you dance up a storm?"

"Steven did. I just got very dizzy."

"How many of those have you had?" I asked as I pointed at her glass.

"I don't know," she mumbled. "I may be in double figures."

"Ten?" I asked.

"It's all your fault. Flying off to Australia just when I'm getting used to having you around. It's not fair."

"There's still tonight," I suggested.

"I doubt it," she replied. "I think I'm too potted. I won't remember it."

"Want some coffee?" I asked like a good boy.

"No, let's finish me off. Mix me one more of these and then drive me home, wandering Yankee boy."

I went to the bar and mixed her a whopper. She slugged it down and then held onto me as we went to say our good-byes. Several other people were leaving at the same time, and we had to wait in line to shake hands with our hosts. As we stood there, Theresa leaned her head against my arm and closed her eyes.

It was a twenty-mile drive back to Theresa's house. Before

COMPANY OF THIEVES 297

we were halfway there, she was slumped in her seat and making little snoring sounds. Twice I've wanted to take things from this sorry drunk, and both times she has obliged me and fallen asleep. One thing about alcoholics: they are very predictable. I wouldn't even need the assistance of some sleeping pills this time.

We came to a high school when we got near the city, and I pulled into the parking lot. Theresa's purse was on the floor by her feet, and I simply reached over and picked it up. I found the key chain lying on the bottom with a lot of pens and pencils. I pulled it out, removed the key I wanted, and put the purse back by her feet. Theresa snorted and squirmed in the seat as I put the key in my pocket. Her face was scrunched up as if she were in pain. I sat there and stared at the face that was going to make me rich—the face I would never see again after tonight. She was going to be devastated by what I was doing to her, but I really didn't care at all. I was in lovely neutral, as deeply as I had ever been in my life. If it would have worked out for my strategy, I would have opened the door and shoved her out. That wouldn't do, though. That would have been letting my emotions run the show. What I had to do was deliver her home and then disappear over the horizon. One of the worst moments of her life was going to be the next time she reached for that key. I'd be long gone by then, and her pain would not affect me. It didn't affect me now.

When we got to the house, I saw that the lights were out in the back cottage. I almost honked the horn to wake Douglas, but then I thought it would be safer to get Theresa upstairs myself. No need to invite complications.

Getting her out of the car and up onto the porch was a difficult job. She almost fell over as I tried to hold her and unlock the front door at the same time. I half-carried and half-dragged her up the stairs to her room. She was moaning and talking to herself, but none of it made any sense. I flopped her down on her bed, put her purse on the nightstand,

and walked out of the room. When I came down the stairs, the prime minister of New Zealand was standing by the front door holding a briefcase.

"Who the hell are you?" he asked as I froze in my tracks.

"I'm a friend of Theresa's. We were at a party and I drove her home. She needed some help getting up to her bedroom."

"Come here," he said. "Tell me your name."

"I'm Thomas. I work with Theresa at the theater. Was she expecting you?" I asked as I casually walked down the stairs.

I had a great desire to run for the door, but I knew that would be a mistake. But if I stayed and he decided to have me checked out, I would be screwed. I realized the only safe way out of this was to get him to ask me to leave.

"No, this was a last-minute thing," the prime minister answered. "How long have you known Theresa?"

"A little more than a month."

"You're the American, aren't you?"

"That's right. Mr. Prime Minister, I'm kind of glad this has happened. I've really wanted to talk to you about Theresa. About how much she wants to work in the theater. She has an opportunity to go to Australia to be a professional stage manager, and she seems to need your approval to go. If you knew how much that would mean to her . . ."

"I'm afraid you'll have to leave," he said abruptly. "It's been a long day and I have an early-morning appointment."

"Maybe we can talk about this some other time," I said hopefully. "It's really important to her."

"Maybe," he said as he opened his briefcase and pulled out what looked like a small radio. "There's a guy coming out," he said into it. "He's one of my daughter's friends. Just let him leave."

I waved to the two men sitting in the dark car as I pulled out of the driveway. One of them waved back and I gave him a great big smile.

To my surprise, I slept like a baby. When the morning came, I took a long shower and then walked down to The Greek and had a leisurely breakfast. It was around ten when I drove over to the bank to pass off the key. Maggie and her co-worker were behind the counter when I came in. I didn't walk right over to them. Instead, I stopped and pretended to fill out a deposit slip. Soon Maggie was there adding new deposit and withdrawal slips to the stacks in front of me. I reached into my pocket, took the key out, and placed it on the counter. Maggie's hand swiftly swept it over in her direction as I turned and started for the door.

I decided to buy myself a knife. A nice, big, very threatening hunting knife. I stopped at a hardware store and got the knife and a roll of heavy-duty tape. After that, I drove home and finished packing. While I was in my room, Edith came up the stairs, and a few minutes after that, I heard her begin to play the piano. She didn't see me as I made my two trips to the car with my suitcases. When I came back after my second trip, I went and sat in the window seat. She was playing a piece that I recognized but couldn't quite place.

"I've heard that before," I said when she finished.

"It's my piece for the Christmas concert. I think it's the first thing you heard me play."

"Sure. That's when the piano needed tuning."

"That's right," she said as she broke into a big smile. "By the way, I have a girlfriend who's interested in moving in. I told her she could, but I couldn't tell her when."

"Tell her she can move in today," I replied.

"Today? Oh. I saw you packing the other night, but then you were still here so I wasn't sure."

"Actually, this is it. I'm all packed and ready to roll. I just came to sit here one last time. When I think of New Zealand, the first thing that will come to mind is me sitting in this window seat listening to you play."

"Sorry for saying it, but I can't help but feel that New Zealand is better off without you," she said bluntly.

"There's some truth in that," I said as I nodded my head.

"It's certainly been interesting. I do feel something for you. It's not so much love, or like, as a longing to know. You're so damned elusive. I had trouble not reaching out for you. Trying to get a hold."

"You did get a hold."

"Good—though I'm not sure what I had a hold *of.*"

"Yes, you are," I said, pointing at the piano. "It comes out there."

"That's true," she agreed.

"Play something as I leave," I said as I got up to go.

"All right."

I turned around and opened the window so I could hear the music when I got down to the street. She watched me do it and then smiled as I turned around and looked at her. When I kissed her on the cheek, she started playing "Perfume Highway." I could hear the music as I walked down the stairway, and even more so when I got out onto the sidewalk. She was up there pounding away for all she was worth. As I drove down the road, the sound quickly faded away.

The five magic coins were sitting in my pocket, and I wasn't sure that was the best place for them. I found a quiet side street and pulled into a spot under the trees. When I saw that no one was around, I pulled my pants down and securely taped the coins to the inside of my right thigh. I intended to tape the knife to the inside of my other thigh, but decided I didn't have to do that yet.

There was a lot of time to kill and I wanted the remainder of the day to be as restful as possible. I decided to drive out to the Land's End Restaurant, where Theresa and I had escaped the fire. It would be a nice ride, and I could have lunch and walk the pier. The drive out was as nice as I expected it would be. It was a beautiful summer day, and even when I was still several miles from the ocean, I could smell the salt air. It suddenly got rather windy as I came down the hill toward the restaurant. The ocean was a deep blue with thousands of whitecaps popping in and out of existence every few seconds. As I looked down at the pier, I could see the fresh blond wood that had been used to repair the section destroyed by the fire. After I parked the car, I walked out the pier and again stopped and talked to some boys who were fishing. When I finally went into the restaurant for lunch, I felt more relaxed than I had in months.

When I got back to Christchurch, I went to a movie, had a light supper, and then took up my position across and down the street from Maggie's apartment. It was dark by now, and I pulled my pants down and taped the knife to the inside of my left thigh. I arranged the rearview mirror so I could keep an eye on Maggie's front door. I was way early, so I settled in for a long wait. I played the radio and sang along with the songs I knew to help keep myself from dozing off.

Just after ten, a very nice car pulled up outside Maggie's apartment, and she and her banker friend got out and walked up the steps. Maggie looked stunning. She had on a low-cut black dress and her hair was up. She wore a sparkling necklace, and I could see that she had on the bracelet she had picked off in Fiji. I laughed out loud when I saw her reach into her purse, pull out a hanky, and blow her nose. She and the man talked for a few seconds and then Maggie blew her nose again. The man kissed her on the cheek and then walked back down the steps as Maggie unlocked the door and went in. When he pulled away, I waited about a minute, then started the car and drove down the street. I swung around at the next intersection and was sitting in front of Maggie's apartment when she peeked out the door a few minutes later. When she saw me, she closed the door again and I saw the lights go out in her apartment. As she was coming down the steps, I threw her door open and pulled the seat forward. She placed her suitcases on the backseat and then got in beside me.

"Did you get them?" I asked.

"Of course," she said with a smirk.

"Where are they?"

"Don't worry about that," she shouted. "Just go! Let's get the hell out of here!"

I put the car in gear, and as I did that, Maggie reached over and fastened her seat belt. That's when I knew what was going to happen. Goddamn Willem was going to appear on the highway and chase us down. I watched out of the corner of my eye as Maggie adjusted the seat belt to make sure that it was a nice, tight fit.

We drove out of Christchurch and north up the coast. Maggie was saying that we could make the ferry landing that night and catch the first boat to Wellington in the morning. When we got to the Wellington airport, we would take any plane that would get us out of the country. I listened to her but spent a lot of time looking in the rearview mirror. Most of the time the mirror was black. After we got out of the city, the highway north turned into a two-lane country road with very little traffic. There was the occasional town every twenty miles or so, but other than that there was nothing. It was rare even to have a car pass us going the other way.

"Don't drive so fast," Maggie ordered. "We don't want to get pulled over."

After we'd been driving for about an hour, Maggie reached over the backseat and opened one of her suitcases. She pulled out a little white pillow. She leaned it on the window and laid her head against it.

"I'm sleepy," she said as she closed her eyes. "Wake me up if anything happens."

About twenty minutes after that, a car got onto the highway behind us. I watched in the mirror as it got closer. It wasn't long before the car was right on my rear end, flashing its lights and honking its horn.

Maggie opened her eyes at the first honk and turned to look back.

"Somebody wants us to pull over," I said.

"How could anybody—" she started to say.

Just then the other car swung around and pulled up along-side us. I looked over and saw that I didn't know the driver, but the passenger was Willem.

"My God, it's Willem!" Maggie shouted.

"Not now, please, not now," I moaned. "We're so close."

"Ram him!" Maggie screamed. "Ram him!"

She reached over and pushed the steering wheel in the direction of the other car. We hit them a couple of times, and then they backed off and fell in behind us again. They sped up a couple of times and gave us two good shots from the back. When the road straightened out for what looked like a long stretch, they pulled up beside us again. I looked over in time to see Willem take out a gun and start taking shots at our front tire.

"He's got a gun! He's got a gun!" Maggie shouted into my ear.

"I know, I know," I shouted back. "What am I supposed to do?"

"Ram him! Ram him!" Maggie shouted again.

I turned the steering wheel toward the other car and we bounced off them again. When we separated, Willem got off another shot and this time got our front tire. The other car dropped back as I tried to get ours under control. Maggie was screaming and I was shouting for her to hold on. Our car lurched off to the side of the road, and when I tried to jerk it back, the car flipped over on its side. In the moment that we flipped, I raised my elbow and whacked it as hard as I could against the side of Maggie's head. Her head bounced back against the window and hit it so hard that the glass cracked. When the car stopped skidding, Maggie hung there like a rag doll. If it hadn't been for her seat belt, she would have fallen on top of me. Her hand was lying against my cheek, and when I looked at it, the first thing I saw was the diamond bracelet. I pulled the bracelet off and wrapped it around the fingers of my right hand. I grabbed her head and shoved the bracelet up against her cheek with as much force as I could. I then pulled the diamonds down across her cheek, leaving two huge gouges and a lot of blood. I threw the bracelet down just as Willem appeared in front of the car with his gun raised and pointed at me.

"Get out of the car!" he demanded. "Any funny business this time and you're dead meat."

"I can't, you idiot!" I yelled at him. "You have to flip the car back."

The other man appeared next to him as Willem lowered the gun and studied the situation.

"She's cut herself," I shouted. "She's bleeding pretty bad. Flip the car back so we can get her out."

I was trying to avoid Maggie's dripping blood as Willem tucked the gun in his pants and talked to the other man. Then the two of them came over and started rocking the car. On the fifth try, the car bounced back upright and Maggie's head smashed up against the window again. Willem held the gun on me and told me to get out as the other guy came around and got Maggie.

"Shit," Willem muttered.

"It was the rearview mirror," I said to him. "It broke and her head banged up against the broken glass."

Willem pointed the gun up into my face.

"You're a real son of a bitch," he said with a growl. "You knew what she had done to me and—"

"She's bleeding pretty bad," the other man yelled.

"You better get her to a hospital," I said quickly.

"Put her in our car," Willem said to the other guy. "Get her suitcases."

Then he turned around and hit me on the forehead with

the gun. I collapsed to my knees and then he hit me again. I fell down on my face and blacked out.

When I came to, a stranger was wiping the blood off my face with a wet cloth. I opened my eyes and looked up to see a woman looking down at me. A very old man was peering over her shoulder.

"What happened here?" the man asked.

"Had an accident," I mumbled

"Can you stand up?" the woman asked.

I tried and was a little shaky at first, but then I managed to stand without them holding me up. She handed me the cloth and took a step back and looked at me.

"My daughter's in our car. She's going to have a baby very soon. We can't stay with you, but another car will be along soon."

"I'm not that bad," I said as I wiped the blood away from my eyes.

"Can you change that tire?" the old man asked.

"Sure," I said. "I'm all right."

"You're going to have a hell of a scar," he said.

"Sorry we can't stay," the woman whispered as she touched my arm. "It's an emergency. You understand."

"Of course," I replied with a wave of my hand. "Thanks for stopping."

The two of them walked to their car and drove off to the south. The sound of their motor slowly faded away. I leaned up against my car and took a deep breath. My head was killing me. I could tell that the gun barrel had taken two large chunks of skin off my forehead. I put my hand down on my leg and felt the spot where I had taped the coins. Everything seemed to be secured. I pulled my pants down and unwrapped the tape from around the knife and threw the useless thing into the woods. I decided to leave the coins where they were. I pulled my pants back up and went over and sat in the grass along the road.

Where we had ended up was actually an intersection where

a dirt road joined the highway. I sat there and stared at the place where the two roads met and watched the dead leaves blow through. I stared at one of the leaves and watched as it rolled and rolled. I felt as if I had landed at the loneliest intersection in the world. The wind picked up and the leaves really started to swirl around. I sat there, unable to move as I watched them. After a while, a car came by and slowed down.

"You all right, mate?" a voice said from the car.

"Yeah. Just have to change my tire."

"Can you manage it?"

"Sure."

"You cut your head," he said as if I didn't know.

"I'm fine. Thanks for stopping."

"All right, then," he said as the car started on its way again.

I got up and opened the trunk and moved very slowly as I changed the tire. It took me almost an hour to do it. When I was ready to get started, I decided to drive north because I knew they wouldn't follow the plans Maggie and I had made. I drove on for a couple of hours until I came to the landing where the ferry docked. There were no other cars around, so I pulled in to be first in line for the next day. I wanted to sleep very badly. When I reached down to adjust the seat, I found Maggie's bracelet on the floor. I got out of the car, opened the trunk, and put the bracelet in one of my suitcases. Then I got back into the front seat and was soon sound asleep.

Chapter Twenty-seven

My vision was slightly blurred when I woke the next morning. I rubbed my eyes, but that only made it worse. I looked up into the rearview mirror and the first thing I saw was a giraffe sticking out of the top of a truck. I blinked my eyes a few times and then turned around to have a look. There were three cars lined up behind me, and then came the trucks from the same circus that Maggie and I had crossed over with. Like myself, they must have finished up with their tour of South Island. I got out and stretched as I looked back down the line of cars and trucks. There was a ticket office by the dock, so I walked down to buy a ticket for the ferry.

"What happened to your head, mate?" the guy selling the tickets asked.

"Fell last night," I said.

"Looks pretty nasty. I've got a first-aid kit in here. You're welcome to go into the washroom and clean yourself up if you like."

"That would be great," I replied.

He let me in a side door and handed me a box that was full of ointments and bandages. I cleaned my forehead and then put a couple of big Band-Aids over the two cuts. There were also some eye drops in the kit, and after a few drops in each eye, my vision improved a bit. I took three of the aspirins and then returned the first-aid kit to the man at the ticket window. The ferry was pulling in as I walked back to my car. The incoming cars and trucks rolled off the ferry and then our group rolled on. After my car was parked on the bottom deck, I walked up the stairs and went to the café for a couple of cups of coffee. I bought a newspaper and was reading it when the ferry pulled out for Wellington. When I looked around the café, I saw the circus people all sitting together having breakfast. Over in a corner, by herself, sat the woman who had told Maggie's fortune. She was staring at me. When our eyes met, she smiled and then held up the deck of cards that was in her hand. I picked up my coffee and walked over to her table and sat down.

"Fortunes are ten dollars, right?" I asked.

"Not this time," she said as she handed me the cards.

She had me place seven cards on the table, and then she studied them for a few minutes. She then had me do the same thing all over again. After she had studied the second set of cards, she picked up my left hand, rubbed it with her thumb for a long time, and then stared down at my palm. She grunted a few times and then placed my hand down on the table.

"So, you're not so stupid after all," she said as she gave me a sly smile.

"I guess that's a compliment," I said.

"Oh, more than that," she replied. "It is admiration that I am offering to you."

"Really?"

"Oh, yes. I think that you have won the game."

"I have, haven't I."

"You'd better hide yourself."

"I know."

"The cards say someplace cold."

"That's good to know."

"Your lady friend is where?" she asked.

"I don't really know. Probably celebrating with her cohorts."

"You mean that you have won, yet they think they have defeated you?"

"For a while. It won't last long. They'll soon know."

"Do you like these games?"

"It's not so bad really. I was thinking of giving it up, but you never know. It always helps to know how to fool the other guy."

"Your palm says that you will always be taking chances."

"That's interesting," I said seriously.

"Go back to your newspaper," she said to me. "Be careful. Try to remember your sore head as well as the money in your pocket."

"I will," I said as I got up and walked back to my table.

I had a light breakfast and then went for a walk on the deck. It was a very windy day, and once again I found myself surrounded by thousands of whitecaps. I gazed off at them and thought about what the woman from the circus had said. I feared that maybe she was right—that I could never go completely straight. Even if I went on to college, I would make a rather shady student. The manipulation was just too damn much fun.

When we docked, I drove off and found my way to the highway for Auckland. I decided it might be wiser to bypass Wellington and leave from Auckland instead. I could easily be there by that afternoon and probably be on a plane that night.

When I got to the pine-woods country around Taupo, I stopped and had lunch. As I looked out the window of the café, I noticed a post office across the street. I got an idea that brought a smile to my face. When I finished my lunch, I went to the car and got the diamond bracelet. I went into the post office and bought one of those padded brown envelopes and addressed it to Edith. As I was putting the bracelet into the envelope, I noticed a spot of Maggie's blood on the side of one of the diamonds. I went to rub it off on my shirt, but stopped. I stared down at the spot of blood for a second and then licked it off with my tongue. The clerk behind the counter looked at me because I laughed out loud as I dropped the bracelet into the envelope.

As I continued through the pine forests, I remembered the man that Maggie and I had dropped off there. I was even able to come up with his name, Neville. He was probably sleeping down one of these dirt roads, exhausted after another graveyard shift at the sawmill. In a way, Maggie had been right about him. He was still back there because he was afraid to step out in front of life. Afraid of going through a period where he'd have to be really alert and think on his feet. As I thought about that, I realized I was driving down the road with this huge smile on my face. I was feeling like winged victory as I zipped along toward Auckland. Thinking about Neville made me aware of the fact that I had already lapsed from my own place of alertness. My feelings were telling me that it was over, but my brain was trying to give me the message that it wasn't.

I decided to play this out according to the worst-possible-case scenario: that they would figure out that I had the real coins within forty-eight hours. I also had to assume that they would come looking for me right away. I doubted they would catch on that fast, but it seemed wisest to play it as if they would. An image immediately popped into my mind of Stuart sitting at his computer. It also seemed logical that I should plan on them finding out what plane I got on when I left the country. Whether I used my phony passport or my real one, they would be able to tell. I wasn't really at the end of this thing; I was at the beginning of the end.

I ran through a lot of different plans. I still had enough money to do a little creative routing. However, after I bought my plane ticket, things were going to be a little tight in the wallet. The need to cash in one of these coins was going to arise fairly quickly. Sooner or later, Stuart would find out where I had cashed in the coin and that would be another clue for him. Suddenly, it made sense to go back to Los Angeles right away. They were going to look for me around there anyway. Why give them two places on the map to draw a line between? Why give them any more information than necessary? The more I thought about it, the more I liked it. What settled it was when I started to think about where I could cash in the coin. I remembered a place I had seen in Koreatown in Los Angeles. It was on Western Avenue and there was a big sign that said "RARE COINS BOUGHT AND SOLD." I could do my creative routing from Los Angeles and use a phony name for a bus ticket. That sounded right.

I parked the car on the street about half a mile from the Auckland Airport. I threw the keys into the glove compartment, grabbed my bags, and walked away. After shopping around for a while, I settled on a flight to Los Angeles on Singapore Airlines. I had six hours to kill, so I checked my bags and settled in with two newspapers and a magazine. When I had been reading for about fifteen minutes, I looked up, watched all the people walking by, and realized I shouldn't be here. There were shuttle buses into the city, so I got on one and spent the afternoon burning away the hours. Bought myself some new clothes, had a nice meal, and sat in the park watching a guy with a boomerang. I had never seen anybody work one before, and he was amazing. Often he would throw that thing and not even have to move to catch it as it came back. I studied him as I thought through my plan. The plan seemed all right except for one thing: I had no idea where I was going.

About an hour into the flight they started a movie. It was a comedy about a fire chief and his goofy crew. I watched it and did some laughing, which really felt good. After a while, I got distracted by the place the movie had been shot. It was so clear there. It was set in a smallish city in the mountains, and the scenery was beautiful. The story took place in the summer, but I could see the bright-green grass of the ski runs in the background. When the movie was over, I watched the credits very carefully and saw that the producer thanked the government and people of the city of Nelson, British Columbia. Hadn't the fortune teller said something about a cold place? I wondered if Nelson had a college.

There was a lot of sleeping and eating over the next fourteen hours. The man in the seat next to me did a monologue about selling American tools in New Zealand, and I let him rattle on. We landed in Los Angeles at 11:00 A.M. in the middle of a rainstorm. While I was riding the little bus out to the long-term parking lot, I figured out how much it would cost to bail out my car and didn't like the results. If it didn't start, things would get complicated. But if it did, I would try the ticket switch.

The battery was low, and the engine groaned as it tried to turn over. Then it caught and died. I tried it again, and this time I was able to keep it running. I looked back toward the exit booth and saw a man inside eating french fries. From what I could tell, he was more interested in his food than in what was going on outside his window. I crouched down and moved between the cars until I was near the entrance, getting soaked in the process. After a couple of cars had gone through, I hurried over and punched out a ticket. When I drove to the exit, the guy in the booth was licking the ketchup off his fingers. He slid the window open and poked out his shiny hand.

"I just pulled in," I said to him as I handed over the ticket.

"What?" he asked.

"I just got here. I'm going to New Zealand and I've forgotten my passport. I've got to get home quickly."

"Still have to pay the minimum," he said.

"How much is that?"

"Five dollars."

"I've only been here two minutes."

"Sorry, buddy, but I have to account for all these tickets. You know how it is."

"Yeah," I agreed with a smile. "My job is like that."

I gave him the five bucks and drove away. It must be something in my blood or my genes, but that kind of stuff just feels so good. I started getting that huge grin again.

After changing my clothes in the restroom of a Bob's Big Boy Restaurant, I headed down to Koreatown. No sense in wasting time.

When I pulled up in front of the coin shop, I was reminded of good old Bill Swift. I hoped that his Korean equivalent was in there behind the dark-glass windows. It occurred to me to put on my baseball hat because there were bound to be video cameras. I fished through my suitcase for the hat and put it on. I yanked it down as low as I could get it.

There were two men behind the counter when I walked in and I told them I wanted to talk to the boss. One of the men went into an office and came out with a man who walked over and shook my hand. He said his name was Melvin Choi.

"You can call me Mel," he said as we walked back into his office.

He closed the door and offered me a chair. I sat down and he went over to the microwave and pulled out a steaming cup of tea.

"Would you like some tea?" he asked.

"Don't need any caffeine today," I replied with a smile.

"What can I do for you?" he said as he sat down.

"I have in my pocket one of the Old Globe Sovereigns. Are you familiar with these coins?"

"Familiar enough to know that if you have one, it is either a phony or it is stolen. You have made everybody very nervous by coming in here with your hat pulled low. We are all very concerned about what you want."

"You're a smart man, Mel," I said with a small grin. "It is not a phony, but you're right about it being stolen."

"What you are doing makes no sense. It means that you have one of the most valuable coins in the world in your pocket. My friends and I could easily take it away from you and there would be nothing you could do about it."

"True. However, I plan to sell it to you at an extremely low price, and back home I have another just like it. Treat me right on this one and I will consider bringing you the other one."

"Let me see it," Mel said as he put his glasses on.

He studied the coin and then got a magnifying glass and studied it some more. He got a couple of books from the shelves and consulted both of them. After a lot of grunting and nodding he got on the phone and talked to someone in Korean.

"The owner is coming," he said as he hung up the phone. "Before he gets here, tell me what price you are asking."

"Fifty thousand."

Mel just nodded. The owner showed up fifteen minutes later and the two of them did the inspection and book routine all over again. At one point they looked at me and asked if I'd ever been to New Zealand.

"Just got back," I said.

I could tell they liked that answer. After that, there was a lot of talk in Korean. When I heard the owner say Amsterdam, I knew things were going well. After another brief conversation, the owner turned and looked at me.

"Of course you want cash," he said.

"Of course."

"I must go to my safe. I will be back shortly."

"Fine," I replied as I slipped the coin back into my pocket.

Smooth as silk. You can always count on self-interest.

The owner came back fifteen minutes later carrying a paper bag. We went into the office and counted the money, and I handed over the coin. As I walked out the front door, the owner called after me.

"Sixty thousand for number two," he said.

I nodded my head and went out and got into the car. I started driving toward my apartment so I could pick up some things. When I got there, I just kept going. I realized at the last minute that there wasn't anything that I had to have, and to see my roommate would be a mistake. I thought about calling Martha but came to the conclusion that I just had to let her go.

I drove the car down to the seediest part of Hollywood. After parking in front of a bar, I opened all the windows, left the key in the ignition, grabbed my things, and started looking for a taxi. A woman taxi driver picked me up and I told her to take me downtown to the Greyhound station.

When I got there, I found that there was a bus leaving for Salt Lake City in twenty-five minutes. I asked about connections to Canada and was told I could move on to Calgary the next day. I bought a ticket under the name of Clifford Fox. I figured that foxes were smarter than coyotes.

I got onto the Salt Lake City bus and was relieved to find that the seats were very comfortable. As the bus rolled out of the station, I looked out at all the people walking around on the sidewalk. All those strangers. What was I supposed to think or feel about all that humanity?

I'd make my way to Nelson and hide out for the winter. Find a nice place to live, read a lot, maybe learn to ski. If there was any kind of college in Nelson, I'd give it a try. Even if it was just a two-year school. If there wasn't, maybe I'd move on to Vancouver or Calgary in the spring. Plus,

of course, a winter in Nelson meant a town full of vacationing
skiers. Who knew what opportunities that might serve up.
I had made a big score and I should learn to be satisfied,
but the truth was, I loved to fool people. I loved the game.
I doubted that I could ever truly give it up.

Complete Your Collection of
Fern Michaels

__**Dear Emily**   0-8217-5676-1 $6.99US/$8.50CAN

__**Vegas Heat**   0-8217-5758-X $6.99US/$8.50CAN

__**Vegas Rich**   0-8217-5594-3 $6.99US/$8.50CAN

__**Vegas Sunrise**   0-8217-5893-3 $6.99US/$8.50CAN

__**Wish List**   0-8217-5228-6 $6.99US/$8.50CAN

The Wingman Series
By Mack Maloney

__#1 Wingman	0-7860-0310-3	$4.99US/$6.50CAN
__#2 The Circle War	0-7860-0346-4	$4.99US/$6.50CAN
__#3 The Lucifer Crusade	0-7860-0388-X	$4.99US/$6.50CAN
__#4 Thunder in the East	0-7860-0428-2	$4.99US/$6.50CAN
__#5 The Twisted Cross	0-7860-0467-3	$4.99US/$6.50CAN
__#6 The Final Storm	0-7860-0505-X	$4.99US/$6.50CAN
__#7 Freedom Express	0-7860-0548-3	$4.99US/$6.50CAN
__#8 Skyfire	0-7860-0605-6	$4.99US/$6.50CAN
__#9 Return from the Inferno	0-7860-0645-5	$4.99US/$6.50CAN
__#12 Target: Point Zero	0-7860-0299-9	$4.99US/$6.50CAN
__#13 Death Orbit	0-7860-0357-X	$4.99US/$6.50CAN
__#15 Return of the Sky Ghost	0-7860-0510-6	$4.99US/$6.50CAN

Call toll free **1-888-345-BOOK** to order by phone or use this coupon to order by mail.

Name _____

Address _____

City _____ State _____ Zip _____

Please send me the books I have checked above.

I am enclosing	$_____
Plus postage and handling*	$_____
Sales tax (in New York and Tennessee only)	$_____
Total amount enclosed	$_____

*Add $2.50 for the first book and $.50 for each additional book.

Send check or Money order (no cash or CODs) to:

Kensington Publishing Corp., 850 Third Avenue, New York, NY 10022

Prices and Numbers subject to change without notice.

All orders subject to availability.

Check out our website at **www.kensingtonbooks.com**

DO YOU HAVE THE
HOHL COLLECTION?

Romantic Suspense from
Lisa Jackson

__Treasure
   0-8217-6345-8 $5.99US/$6.99CAN

__Twice Kissed
   0-8217-6308-6 $5.99US/$6.99CAN

__Whispers
   0-8217-6377-6 $5.99US/$6.99CAN

__Wishes
   0-8217-6309-1 $5.99US/$6.99CAN